MAGGIE CHRISTENSEN

Summer in Bellbird Bay

Cover and interior design: J D Smith Design
Editing: John Hudspith Editing Services

Dedication

To my wonderful husband and soul mate
without whose support none of this would happen.

Also by Maggie Christensen

Oregon Coast Series
The Sand Dollar
The Dreamcatcher
Madeline House

Sunshine Coast books
A Brahminy Sunrise
Champagne for Breakfast

Sydney Collection
Band of Gold
Broken Threads
Isobel's Promise
A Model Wife

Scottish Collection
The Good Sister
Isobel's Promise
A Single Woman

Granite Springs
The Life She Deserves
The Life She Chooses
The Life She Wants
The Life She Finds
The Life She Imagines
A Granite Springs Christmas
The Life She Creates
The Life She Regrets
The Life She Dreams

A Mother's Story

One

Ailsa McNeil stood in the shower, tears streaming down her cheeks, glad Christmas Day was over. She normally enjoyed the holiday, spending time with her family. It was one of the few times of the year when they all got together – Mum and Dad, Bob and the boys, Pat and Nate, and her sister, Liz. This year they'd been joined by the new man in Liz's life and, for the first time in twenty years, her sister had a smile on her face.

But while she was glad for Liz, pleased her sister was finally moving on as Ailsa had been urging her to do for as long as she could remember, Ailsa's own life seemed to have gone into freefall. It was all to do with Bob. Over the past year, her husband had become a different person from the lively young man she'd met at uni and married as soon as they both graduated. It was difficult to pinpoint exactly when it happened, when the normally cheerful man morphed into the surly loner who now shared her life.

Now the boys were in their twenties and had moved into student accommodation for Nate and a share house for Pat, it was just the two of them. It was the time in their lives when many of their friends were making plans for overseas trips, home renovations or downsizing. But nothing like that was happening in the brick veneer house in the leafy suburb of Farrer. Some people thought the city of Canberra, which was Australia's capital, was a sterile place, a planned city with no sense of community, but Ailsa loved it. It was where she'd grown up, attended university and lived all her married life. She couldn't imagine living anywhere else.

She lifted her face to allow the water to cascade over it, smoothing back her short hair, its original dark brown showing flecks of grey, images of the Christmas lunch replaying over and over in her mind's eye. Why couldn't Bob at least try to be polite to her family? Mum had made such an effort, pulling out all the stops to provide what she deemed to be a traditional Christmas lunch. A Canberra December day was really too hot for the roast turkey and vegetables she liked to serve – had done every year Ailsa could remember – but she'd never change. There was something oddly comforting in the knowledge that, come hell or high water, Sheila Browne would soldier on as she'd always done, recreating the type of Christmas Day more suited to the frosty English climate.

Ailsa had wanted to kick Bob under the table, but wouldn't have been able to reach, so she'd had to make do with glaring at him from the other end while he sat there looking as if he wished he was somewhere else. Thank goodness for Pat and Nate who kept up a running commentary on their life, uni, and the peculiarities of their flatmates.

Sam, Liz's new fellow, had helped too. As a former political correspondent and now editor of the local paper in their town of Granite Springs, he had a wealth of stories to share. Ailsa's mum clearly thought he was a godsend and kept heaping his plate with food till Liz tactfully told her to stop.

The one bright spot of the day was when Ailsa and Liz managed to escape into the yard. To start with, it was as if they were teenagers again sneaking out to complain about the parents, but it became fraught when Liz started to ask about Bob's weird behaviour. Although she managed to parry most of her sister's questions, Ailsa knew Liz wasn't satisfied and would bring the subject up again next time they met.

She was stepping out of the shower when she remembered the Christmas card from Bev Cooper. She and Bev had met on their first week of teacher education studies at Canberra University and had ended up sitting next to each other in their first lecture. It was as simple as that, and they'd become best friends. Bev had never married, always claiming she could never find a man who'd put up with her, but Ailsa thought it was more that she liked her solitary life too much to want to share it. Now settled in Bellbird Bay on Queensland's Sunshine Coast,

Bev had established a garden centre and café which, from what Ailsa could gather from their frequent emails and phone calls, was proving popular.

In her card, Bev invited Ailsa and Bob up after Christmas citing the delights of the small coastal town she called home. Ailsa knew Bob wouldn't be interested in going, and she couldn't imagine spending time with him away from home. But an idea began to take shape. The thought of getting away for the rest of the summer – away from Bob, away from her mother's concerned looks, away from her sister's well-meaning questioning – suddenly sounded incredibly attractive.

Two

'I need some space!'

Ailsa McNeil never thought she'd hear herself say those words. They were what those hippy women in the upmarket gym said, the one she'd attended briefly before deciding a run along the shores of Lake Burley Griffin was more her style.

They were in Bob's study, the room he retreated to more and more these days. Bob swung his chair round to meet her gaze, then dropped his eyes. 'Whatever,' he said, sounding more like one of their sons than her husband of almost twenty-five years.

Ailsa shrugged. 'I thought I'd go to Bellbird Bay for a bit. Bev has invited me to spend the rest of the summer there.' She waited for Bob's reaction, hoping against hope that, for once, he'd show some sign he cared.

There was no response for some time, and she'd almost given up when he said, 'Are you leaving me?'

'No.' At least she didn't think so, but things between them had gone from bad to worse in the past year. Ailsa had almost given up hope of seeing some improvement. She'd grown tired of making excuses to her parents when Bob didn't appear at Sunday lunch, of avoiding her sister's questions. And now Liz was happy in her new relationship, it was becoming even harder to prevaricate.

Christmas had been the final straw.

Bev's invitation seemed like a lifeline. Even so, Ailsa had been hesitant to accept. She wondered what everyone would think. Could she really leave Bob and Canberra for two whole months? What would Bob and the boys do without her? She knew the boys would survive. They were both leading independent lives, even if they did like to come home for a proper meal from time to time, accompanied by the odd bag of laundry.

But how would Bob survive? Ailsa still loved the boy she'd met at university. But he'd changed so much, become engrossed in work, isolating himself, seemingly more concerned with the problems of his students than his own family. And when he was home, he disappeared into his study for hours at a time. He'd even started sleeping in the spare room, claiming he didn't want to disturb her when he wakened during the night.

'Okay,' she said. 'I'll be off tomorrow. You can ring me if you need anything.'

There was no reply.

'Bob, can't you say something? What's wrong with you? You've been acting oddly for months, I've had to make excuses to Mum and Dad, fend off Liz's questions. And now, when I tell you I'm heading to Bellbird Bay for a couple of months, all you can say is *whatever*, then ask if I'm leaving you. It would serve you right if I was.'

Ailsa stared at her husband. His face was almost devoid of colour. Her heart plummeted. 'You're sick. I knew it. Oh, Bob, why couldn't you tell me?' Ailsa immediately felt guilty imagining all sorts of things that could be wrong. *Why had he kept it to himself? Why hadn't he told her?* Worry about a serious illness would explain why he'd been so distant, why he'd shut himself up in this room so often, why he was choosing to sleep alone. *But why hadn't he shared it with her? Surely he knew she'd be there for him, whatever was the matter?*

A red blush suffused Bob's face. 'No Ailsa, I'm not sick, though there's some who might say I was.'

'Then what?'

'You'd better sit down. I have something to tell you.'

Puzzled, her heart thumping madly, Ailsa perched on the edge of the old leather armchair that had seen better days. It had been one of their first purchases when they moved in together and held fond memories of those early days. *Was Bob going to tell her he was sick, dying?* She pressed her lips together firmly, determined to be there for him, whatever the matter was.

Bob said nothing for several moments, then, 'I…' He looked down at his hands which were clenched into fists, then raised his eyes to meet Ailsa's. 'I'm gay.'

For a moment, Ailsa thought he was joking. How could Bob be gay? They'd been married for almost twenty-five years, had two children. She thought she knew him through and through. She stared at him in disbelief. This was the last thing she expected. She didn't know what to say. 'How long have you known?' she asked, her voice shaking.

'I guess I've always known, but I managed to hide it.' He looked down again.

Ailsa's whole life seemed to fall apart. *Why had he married her? Had he ever loved her? Had their entire marriage been a lie?*

Bob seemed to read her mind. 'I love you, Ailsa, you and the boys. This is nothing to do with you. It's just the way I am, have always been. I thought… I hoped… We've had a good marriage… but now…'

'But why now? Have you ?' Had he been seeing someone else – a man – for all those months when she'd been wondering what was wrong?

'I haven't met anyone else, if that's what you're asking. And why now?' He looked up and sheepishly met her eyes. 'I've hidden it for too long. I don't want to get to the end of my life, knowing I've been living a lie.'

'And what about us?'

He sighed, twisting his hands together. 'I've been giving it a lot of thought. It's probably why I've seemed distant, difficult. I know it hasn't been easy for you, why you decided to go to Bellbird Bay to spend time with Bev. Perhaps being on my own in Canberra will help me work out what I want to do.'

Ailsa's stomach did a double flip. *What he wanted to do? What about her? Was Bob going to say what she thought he was?* She couldn't speak.

'I don't think it's fair to you to continue as we are, as we were. I'm happy to move out to let you have the house. I've been looking at apartments to rent and can find something close to the school…' He paused, seeing Ailsa's shocked expression.

How long had Bob been considering this move?

He reached for Ailsa's hand, but his felt unfamiliar in hers. She pulled it away. How could he do this to her, to them? Surely they could find a way forward together for the boys' sake?

Bob read her mind. He knew her so well.

'Pat and Nate are grown up. They don't need us anymore. Pat will be setting up his own home soon with Vee, and Nate... They'll understand.'

Ailsa swallowed. She had to agree. Their sons would probably cope. But would she?

'And we...' Ailsa gazed at the familiar face of the man she'd loved for so many years, the man she'd spent most of her life with, her lovely, gentle, thoughtful husband. The man she'd expected to grow old with. Her eyes filled with tears. She began to sob uncontrollably. 'Is it something I've done?'

'No, my darling. This is nothing to do with you. It's something I've had to come to terms with. I wish I'd had the courage earlier, but... I hope we can stay friends. My feelings for you haven't disappeared, they've just...' Bob's eyes filled with tears, too. 'We need to both be there for the boys, and the grandkids when they come along.'

'You're thinking ahead,' she said, her voice breaking. 'Don't make any decisions about moving out just yet.' She was unsure why she wanted to delay what now appeared to be the inevitable end of their marriage. 'What about the boys?'

'I'll tell them when I've decided what to do.'

'But what about me?' she wailed, unable to contain her anger and grief. 'What about our marriage?'

'I'm sorry. As I said, perhaps your decision to go to Bellbird Bay is timely. Spend time with your friend, think about what you want to do. Then, when we've both had time to think, we can talk this through, decide where we go from here.'

Ailsa couldn't speak. The lump in her throat threatened to choke her. 'That's all you have to say?'

'I'm sorry,' Bob repeated. 'I never wanted to hurt you. I tried to be the person who you wanted me to be. I wanted to be that person. I love you, Ailsa.'

Her breath caught in a strangled gasp. What had just happened? Her marriage, the relationship she'd relied on for years, was gone in a burst of words she had trouble comprehending. Her eyes filled with tears, Ailsa turned away and walked out, closing the door behind her.

*

Ailsa wasn't sure which emotion was uppermost as she went to the bedroom to pack – anger at what she saw as Bob's betrayal, or grief at the end of their marriage. And those feelings were tempered by a sense of relief Bob wasn't terminally ill and it was nothing she'd done. As she stuffed her clothes into her case less carefully than normal, she wondered how the boys would react to their father's news.

She'd told Nate and Pat she was going to Bellbird Bay the previous evening. Their reaction was what she'd expected.

'Wow! Bellbird Bay,' Pat whistled. 'Maybe Vee and I will pop up for a weekend,' he said, referring to his current girlfriend, one in a long line of girls who hung around her handsome older son. But this one seemed to be more serious, and Ailsa had hopes Pat might be thinking of settling down.

Nate only winked cheekily and said, 'Go, Mum. You deserve a break. Serve Dad right.'

Ailsa had flinched. She hadn't been aware her son had noticed the change in Bob's behaviour.

She was interrupted by the ringing of her mobile phone. 'Hi, Liz,' she said, seeing her sister's face on the screen. 'What's up?'

'Just wanted to thank you again for the amazing gift you gave Sam and me. I've always wanted to spend a weekend in Bowral, and Peppers Craigieburn. Wow!' Liz said. 'Sam and I will have a ball. We plan to spend Easter there. But what gives with Bob?' she asked on a more serious note. 'I know I've asked before and you've always been so evasive. But this time… Ailsa, it was as if he was on a different planet.'

Ailsa sat down on the bed with a thump. Liz was right. She'd been asking about Bob's behaviour for at least a year and, so far, Ailsa had managed to avoid giving her a straight answer. Now, she knew she had to come clean – at least in part. She couldn't share Bob's revelation over the phone. 'Things have been a bit difficult lately. I didn't want to unload on you or the folks. Mum's so down on Bob at the best of times.' She took a deep breath. 'I've decided to go to Bellbird Bay to spend a couple of months with Bev Cooper.'

There was a shocked silence at the other end of the phone, then her sister said. 'Are you sure it's wise? Shouldn't you be talking things through or something? What about Pat and Nate?'

'They're old enough to look after themselves. They pretty much do so anyway. I've told them and they're cool with it.' No need to repeat their reactions.

'And Bob?'

'We've talked.' Ailsa's voice broke. 'Oh, Liz! I can't believe…'

'What's the matter? Is he sick? Or having an affair? I can't imagine Bob…'

'No, it's… Sorry, I can't talk about it now.'

'You sound terrible. What can't you tell me? When are you leaving?'

'I plan to leave tomorrow,' Ailsa said, trying to sound normal, while feeling anything but. 'Now Christmas is over I have no reason to stay.' She was glad now she'd elected to do casual teaching since the boys started school. It had provided her with the flexibility she needed at the time, and she had seen no reason to change it. Now it meant she could stay away indefinitely.

'Have you told Mum and Dad?'

'Not yet.' Ailsa sighed. She wasn't looking forward to the conversation she knew she must have with her parents, her mother in particular. Dad would always back her up, but her mum would no doubt manage to blame her for some failing or other. 'I'll call in on my way out of town.'

'Why not spend a night with us on your way, too?'

'Thanks, Liz, but I don't think so.' After twenty years of widowhood, Liz had moved in with Sam and was living on an acreage on the outskirts of Granite Springs. The thought of spending even one night watching their loving bliss was too much to contemplate. Although she was glad her sister had found love again, and thoroughly approved of Sam, Ailsa didn't want their happiness to be in her face.

'Maybe when I get back,' she said to satisfy her sister.

'You *will* be back?'

'Of course.' Had Liz read her mind? Growing up they had always been close, and she and Bob had often double-dated with Liz and her husband when they were in their early twenties. 'I can't just walk away from over twenty years of marriage.' *No matter how attractive the idea sometimes seemed. But what if it's what Bob wanted, if their marriage was really over?*

By the time Ailsa went back downstairs, Bob had come out from the study and was standing in the hallway. 'You've told the boys you're going?' he asked.

'I have. They're okay with it. Pat says he might pop up one weekend.'

'Hmm.'

'It'll be fine, Bob.' Ailsa tried to sound upbeat, to pretend her whole world hadn't collapsed. 'Without me around you'll be able to…' Ailsa's voice faltered at the realisation they'd moved so far apart she really didn't know how he spent his time when he wasn't at work. Was it all his fault, or did she share some of the blame for the distance which had developed between them? Was there something she could have done to prevent this? Did she wish he'd told her sooner, wish they'd never married? She couldn't dismiss the good years they'd had together. They'd been happy, hadn't they? And she couldn't imagine life without Pat and Nate. 'I'm sorry,' she said, biting her lip as a wave of guilt threatened to overwhelm her, though what had she to be guilty about? Bob was the one who'd lied to *her*, lied by omission.

'I am, too. I know recently I may not have been…' He dragged a hand through his hair. 'It's been difficult. Maybe you're doing the right thing… going off like this. It will give you time to…'

Ailsa's mouth fell open. For a moment she wanted to throw her arms around him, tell him she'd made a mistake, she wouldn't go after all, she'd stay, and they could try to work things out together. But his shuttered expression stopped her before she could speak.

'Right,' Ailsa muttered, unable to think of anything else to say. She was glad that by this time tomorrow she'd be far away.

Three

Ailsa gave a sigh of relief as she crossed the Queensland border. It had been a gruelling two days of driving since she left Canberra to head north. Her eyes were red and sore from weeping. She felt as if she'd been crying the whole way, and the conversation with her mother before she left the city hadn't helped.

'I don't know why you want to go all that way on your own,' Sheila Browne said peevishly, 'when your family is all here. Maybe there's a reason Bob…'

'That's enough!' Ailsa's father interrupted his wife as he often did, trying to be the peacemaker. 'I'm sure Ailsa knows what she's doing. Maybe a couple of months apart is what she and Bob need to give them both time to work things out.'

Ailsa had given her dad a grateful look, but his words did nothing to pacify her mother who glared at him. If looks could kill… Her mother hadn't said any more about it at that point, but the expression on her face as they hugged goodbye said more than any words.

Before long Ailsa would be in Bellbird Bay and able to relax for the first time in what seemed like an age. It was years since she'd visited the sleepy coastal town, but her heart rose as she remembered the long stretch of white sand, the wild ocean and the friendly people as if it was yesterday. She could almost feel the sand between her toes and smell the salty aroma of the sea as the car powered up the highway.

As the sign for Bellbird Bay came into view, Ailsa felt the tensions of the past year ease. She was here. Before heading into town, she drove to the headland and stepped out of the car, the breeze whipping strands of hair across her face. She gazed out at the multicoloured ocean, the deep blue and turquoise mingling to produce an artist's delight, the sand seeming to stretch for ever, the boardwalk bordered by a string of small houses. They were former beach shacks, one of which belonged to Bev. It was even more stunning than she remembered. Ailsa closed her eyes and breathed in the fresh sea air.

Last time she was here, the boys had been little, and she and Bob had ventured north to visit her old uni friend who'd bought a rundown seaside shack in a town they'd never heard of on Queensland's Sunshine Coast. Ailsa remembered the long lazy days on the beach, followed by margaritas on a wooden deck watching the sunset when Pat and Nate were sound asleep, having tired themselves out jumping waves and building sandcastles.

Reluctantly, she pulled her eyes away from the view and got back into the car. Bev would be expecting her.

Ailsa couldn't help smiling when she drew up outside the small, white-painted house. It looked exactly the same as she remembered, apart from the fact the front yard was now a riot of colour, azaleas and petunias competing with native plants designed to promote Bev's business. Ailsa was looking forward to visiting *The Pandanus Garden Centre and Café* to see what her friend had achieved.

As soon as the car stopped, the door to the small house was thrown open and a tall wiry figure, her faded blonde hair pulled back into an untidy ponytail and dressed in cut-off jeans and a tee-shirt with the logo, *Life is Good*, came dashing down the path. 'You made it!' Bev barely waited till Ailsa got out of the car before pulling her into a warm hug. 'You must be exhausted.'

Half an hour later, Ailsa was seated with Bev on the deck she remembered, overlooking the boardwalk and the ocean. The house itself had undergone a transformation in the years since her last visit, but the ambiance was still the same. Bev had managed to create a sanctuary here away from the bustle of the city. When she'd returned to her hometown to care for her elderly parents after graduating, no one had thought she'd stay. But here she was, thirty years later, seemingly content with her choice.

'So, what gives?' Bev asked, cradling her cup of herbal tea in both hands.

Ailsa breathed in the aroma of fennel and cardamon and felt herself relax. Even Bev's question failed to have the same effect as Liz's more pointed inquiries. 'I needed to get away. Your invitation was a godsend. It came at exactly the right time.'

Bev's eyebrows raised. 'Husband? Family? Job?'

'All of the above. I can't go into it now.' Ailsa took a sip of tea, hoping her friend would accept this.

'When you're ready. We have lots of time and there's no need to go into detail unless you want to. You said you had two months?'

Ailsa nodded, glad to find Bev didn't push for an explanation. She'd no doubt spill her guts to her old friend, but not yet. Perhaps over a glass of wine one evening when she'd had time to work out her own feelings. But Bev's question proved how perceptive her friend was and how well she could read her, despite the years which had passed since they shared lecture notes and confidences. It wasn't only Bob she was running from, it was her mother's interminable questions, Liz's more well-intentioned ones and the job. It wasn't till Bev mentioned it that Ailsa realised how exhausted she was with the changing pattern of her days in the classroom; working casually, the days and weeks of facing so many different groups of children beginning to take their toll. Many of her colleagues compensated by developing poor eating habits – the junk food in the canteens was tempting – or binging on Netflix on their weekends. Ailsa couldn't bring herself to do either. Perhaps it was time for a complete change. It was a relief to be able to forget about all of it for a few weeks at least.

*

Next morning Ailsa awoke to the delicious aroma of coffee wafting into her bedroom. Still wearing the oversized tee-shirt she slept in, she wandered through to the kitchen, blinking at the bright sunlight streaming in through the window. Bev was sitting at the kitchen table fully dressed, drinking coffee and eating a bowl of fruit and yoghurt.

'Morning. Sleep well?' she asked.

'Amazingly well.' Ailsa couldn't remember when she'd last had such a sound sleep. She normally tossed and turned only to awaken unrefreshed. 'It must be the air here.' She stretched and walked over to the window, gazing out at the beach where several swimmers and walkers were already enjoying the morning.

'I need to be off soon,' Bev said, 'but help yourself to breakfast. There's a key on the hall table. I'll be back around five – or you can pop into the garden centre and join me for lunch.'

'Thanks. I might do that.' The day stretched out enticingly ahead for Ailsa, a day with no demands, no work, no sons to worry about and no husband's moods to consider. It was bliss.

'There's a map of the town beside the key. I'm not sure how much you remember about Bellbird Bay, and it's grown a lot since you were here last. Have a good day.' Bev rose, put her dishes into the dishwasher, gave Ailsa a peck on the cheek and left.

Ailsa heard Bev start up her car and drive off, then there was silence, only broken by the distant sound of the waves through the open window. She made herself a cup of herbal tea, toasted a slice of bread which she spread with a mashed banana and took both out to the deck.

This was heaven, she thought, as she leant back in the wicker chair and looked across at the beach again. The swimmers were emerging from the water, the walkers had been joined by several others, some with dogs which frolicked at the edge of the sea, and a few surfers were paddling out to catch the waves. Canberra and everything and everyone in it seemed so very far away. This was another world.

Four

Breakfast over, Ailsa couldn't resist the pull of the beach. Donning a swimsuit that hadn't seen the light of day, never mind a beach, for years, she slathered on sunscreen. Then, pulling on a large shirt, a wide-brimmed hat and popping a pair of sunglasses on her nose, she picked up a towel, a book and a bottle of water and headed out, slipping her phone and the house key into a shirt pocket.

It was wonderful to feel the sand between her toes, just as she'd imagined. She found a sheltered spot and settled down, putting all thoughts of Bob and home out of her mind, determined to spend the morning relaxing.

But it wasn't as easy as she imagined. Images of her husband kept insinuating themselves between her and the words on the page. *Had she done the right thing coming here? Had Bob ever loved her? He said he did, but could she believe him? And, if not, why had he married her? What was he doing now?* Finally, she put down her book and ran down to the ocean, hoping a swim in the clear blue water would dismiss such unrewarding thoughts.

It was glorious to feel the sun and the water on her skin, to breathe in the smell of the ocean. She lay floating on her back looking up at the sky, her body buoyant, all thoughts of Bob fading into nothingness as nature took hold.

By the time she emerged, her skin tingling from the saltwater and the exertion, it was close to midday. Remembering Bev's suggestion about lunch, Ailsa hurriedly made her way back to the house. After a quick shower, and dressed in a candy-striped sundress, she picked up the map Bev had left, got into her car, and followed the directions on the map till she came to an arched entrance which proclaimed it was *The Pandanus Garden Centre and Café*.

The centre was more impressive than Ailsa expected. She parked the car and walked through the archway to be greeted by an amazing display of trees and plants of all descriptions. The place was abuzz with customers, most of whom were pushing trolleys containing a variety of plants and bags of potting mix. She spotted Bev talking to an elderly couple in the section labelled *Native Plants*. She waved, and Bev gestured towards the far corner which Ailsa could see was where the café was situated.

Ailsa wound her way through the selections of plants to where a sign at a gap in a carefully trimmed plumbago hedge indicated it was the entrance to *The Pandanus Café*. She walked through the deep blue blossom to discover small tables had been artistically placed among a series of low bushes and towering palm trees. In its centre was a large pandanus tree, and in the far corner, the kitchen was neatly hidden from view by a screen of grevillea.

Choosing a table in a shady spot, Ailsa sat down and picked up a menu, delighted to see the choices included a variety of healthy-sounding sandwiches and snacks, plus a mix of blended juices. There was also a mouth-watering selection of cakes. She decided on the courtyard special – an open sandwich with avocado, smoked salmon and tomato on rye bread with a carrot, watermelon and apple juice, and sat back to wait for Bev.

While she was waiting, Ailsa checked her phone. Although making a conscious decision before leaving Canberra to keep communication to a minimum, she couldn't resist the temptation to check both Pat and Nate's Facebook pages to see what they'd been up to. But before she could open Facebook, she saw she had two messages.

She opened the first to read *Sorry you decided not to stop off on your way. Enjoy the break. You deserve it. Liz x*

The second was from Bob.

Sorry. I know it was a shock. Take care. Remember I love you. My love to Bev. Bx

Ailsa winced at this reminder of their conversation and Bob's assurance of his love, but before she could reply, Bev arrived to join her. Ailsa closed her phone. There would be time enough to take care of it later. Bob could wait.

When they had both ordered, Bev insisting it was her treat, Ailsa said, 'This place is impressive, Bev. I hadn't realised how extensive it was.' She gestured to the café and garden centre.

'Not too bad, is it?' Bev grinned with pleasure. 'It's taken a good few years, a lot of work and not a little heartache, but it's all come together pretty well.'

'Pretty well? It's magnificent. You must be proud of what you've achieved.'

Bev glowed.

They had almost finished their meal, chatting about how Bev set up the centre, starting with a small nursery and gradually expanding it over the years till it grew into what it was today, when Bev said, 'There's something I need to tell you. I should have mentioned it before, but I only learned myself a couple of days ago.'

Ailsa looked at her friend warily. She recognised Bev's tone and her embarrassed expression. It was the one she'd always used to hide her guilty feelings. What did she have to feel guilty about now? 'What is it?'

Bev bit her lip. 'I had a call from Martin.'

Martin. Bev hadn't thought of Bev's twin brother for years. Not since… She remembered the evening during their first year at uni. It was before she met Bob, a time when life seemed to be a mad whirl of fun, parties and boys. Martin had appeared one weekend when Ailsa and Bev were throwing a party in Bev's student flat – Ailsa lived at home but managed to spend a lot of her weekends in the tiny apartment close to the university.

Ailsa's legs had gone weak at the sight of this masculine version of Bev – tall, broad-shouldered with the same mane of thick blond hair and startling green eyes.

'Who is this?' he'd asked, as soon as his eyes fell on her. The nineteen-year-old Ailsa had blushed, her legs turning to jelly.

'Ailsa's my friend,' Bev had said. 'Don't you go breaking her heart.'

Ailsa had been immediately drawn to the new arrival. It was as if everyone else at the party ceased to exist. They spent the evening together, his arm around her shoulder as he spun her tales of his life in Sydney which sounded much more glamorous than anything she had experienced in Canberra. Martin was studying Art and Photography at East Sydney Tech, which sounded like a haven for all the arty types in the city. He revealed his dream to become a world-famous photographer travelling to exotic places all over the world as she listened wide-eyed in amazement.

Ailsa couldn't believe he'd chosen to spend the entire evening with her. She was young, she was impressionable. She'd never believed in love at first sight, but that night Ailsa fell in love with this handsome and exciting man who was unlike anyone she'd ever met.

When he asked to walk her home, Ailsa was in seventh heaven, and when he kissed her at the gate of her parents' home, even though their lips barely touched, she shivered with pleasure, an unfamiliar sensation stirring in her gut, disappointed when he pulled away.

'Take care little one,' he said, before sauntering off.

He left Canberra next day and Ailsa didn't see him again. She met Bob soon after, and they became inseparable, memories of Martin Cooper fading but never quite disappearing. From time to time, when she felt low, when life became difficult, she would remember Martin Cooper, that one night, and wonder what if…

Over the years, Bev would sometimes mention Martin and read Ailsa excerpts from his letters and postcards from the various parts of the world his job sent him to. Martin Cooper had achieved his dream. His photographs were in all the glossy travel magazines. He'd won the coveted Atlas prize three years running and was the idol of travel photographers all over the world.

Ailsa had never forgotten that one night when his attention had been solely on her, but she'd known even then Martin wasn't for the likes of her. He belonged in a different world, one which she could never enter.

'Martin?' she asked, her stomach churning. It was as if she was nineteen again.

'He's coming home.'

Five

Martin Cooper stepped off the plane into bright sunshine, glad to be safely back in his hometown of Bellbird Bay. It was ten years since his last visit, then only for a fleeting trip to attend his father's funeral. He hadn't made it for his mother's, being stuck in the middle of the Amazon rainforest at the time.

It was his dream job, photographing the world's secret locations for the glossy travel magazine. But all dreams come to an end, and his had come to a sticky one. He winced at the memory of the confrontation with his editor prior to his leaving New York, at the accusation which had been levelled at him. As if he'd ever need to steal another photographer's shot in an attempt to win the Atlas award one more time.

He knew the photograph was his. He'd almost got himself killed, climbing up the steep cliff to take the damned thing. Then, when it was published, Barry Young, his long-time rival, claimed ownership, making Martin look like a fraud. What incensed Martin most was the fact the editor with whom he'd worked for years, believed he'd do such a thing.

'You have to realise,' Jackson Green said, the inevitable cigarette in one hand, 'Young has powerful friends. He's married to the niece of one of the board members. It's more than my job's worth to contradict him. We're lucky he's chosen not to sue. I'm sorry, we'll have to change the attribution and as for any future work…' He looked regretful.

Martin left the meeting his reputation in tatters, with no option but to accept Jackson's decision. The word would soon get around. No one would believe him. His future, which had seemed so assured before he walked into the room, had now disappeared. No magazine would want to deal with a photographer who'd been accused of breaching copyright, of stealing someone else's work, no matter how successful they were, or how many awards they'd won in the past.

Then his personal life had collapsed too. He sighed remembering the woman he'd met before all this had blown up.

For the first time in his life, he'd allowed himself to get close to someone, to Sofia Romero, the curvy brunette he'd met in Acapulco, the woman he'd thought he was going to spend the rest of his life with. She'd suddenly appeared in his life immediately after his last Atlas award, claiming interest in him and his photographs. That night, he'd been full of his success – and a surfeit of alcohol – and hadn't questioned her interest or fascination with his work – and with him.

Martin should have known better, but he'd been seduced by her beauty, her honeyed words, and a sense time was running out. He'd passed his fiftieth birthday. He didn't want to grow old alone, to die alone. Sofia was only thirty but claimed to love him, be impressed by his achievements, willing to put up with his nomadic lifestyle. He'd even considered settling down in one place, making a home together with her, finally accepting the offers he'd had to organise his photographs into collections for what they called coffee table books, a suggestion he'd often ridiculed as smacking of too much commercialism.

When the scandal emerged, she'd left him, run off with a movie star they'd met on location. As if that would last. But Martin couldn't compete with the burst of publicity their liaison created. It seemed she wasn't the person he'd taken her to be. She was shallow and only wanted to hang onto his coattails, cash in on his fame while it lasted. The movie star could provide a better avenue for the fame and publicity she sought. Martin was history. His reputation was, too. He was only as good as his last shots, and those had been stolen.

Martin didn't intend to take this lying down. He was determined to find out why Young had chosen to frame him like this, to salvage what he could of his reputation.

Before leaving New York, he'd consulted a lawyer, one who worked on contingency fees. Rick Cox claimed he could get Martin over a hundred thousand dollars in compensation, but compensation wasn't what he was after. All he wanted was his reputation to be restored intact. The bad news was that Rick told him the civil suit could take months if not years to come to court.

Angry and depressed, he was back where he started, heading for the town to which he'd never intended to return. At the ripe old age of fifty-two, he was going to have to make a fresh start.

'Martin!' He heard his sister's voice seconds before he saw her waving a hand in the air. She hadn't changed. The twin sister he'd always been able to rely on to get him out of scrapes when they were growing up had come to his rescue again.

'Bev!' He allowed her to enfold him in her embrace, before extricating himself sufficiently to discover she was not alone. Beside his sister stood a tall woman, her short dark hair streaked with grey, who appeared amused at this demonstration of affection. He had a vague recollection of Bev mentioning something about an old uni friend spending the summer with her.

'Hi, Martin.' The voice was strangely familiar and, as he peered closer, he recognised the woman with some embarrassment, recalling they had met. It had been a long time ago, when he'd considered himself God's gift to women. If he remembered correctly, he'd gone to Canberra to visit Bev, probably to borrow money to get him out of some scrape or other. There had been a party going on, and the girl with the long, dark hair and big eyes had fascinated him. He'd monopolised her, loving the way she eagerly ate up his tall tales and his dreams of fame. It had amused him to impress her, and he'd probably exaggerated his life in Sydney and his dreams and goals – he'd done that a lot back then.

'It's…' Damn, he couldn't remember her name.

'Ailsa,' she said.

'Of course. I knew that,' he lied. This was all he needed, a face from his past appearing to haunt him. He wasn't proud of the person he'd been back then, the young man determined to charm every girl he met. And charm them he had – until he discovered the string of one-night stands did nothing to enhance his life or his career. That was one of the reasons he'd hoped he and Sofia could make it. After a life of travelling, of never knowing where he'd be next, he was ready to settle down.

But, even then, he hadn't learnt his lesson. He had finally come to the conclusion he and women were not a good mix and, whatever he decided to do in the future, he'd avoid them like the plague. The trouble was, they did have the habit of popping up in his life. Take now, when all he wanted to do was forget the opposite sex existed, apart from Bev. But he'd never regarded Bev as a woman. She was just Bev, the sister he turned to when his life fell apart.

Martin became aware the two women were staring at him.

'Is something wrong?' Bev asked. 'You seem…' She glanced at her friend who was looking uncomfortable.

Martin merely shrugged.

Bev peered at him as if about to ask more, then said, 'Well, let's get this show on the road. Is this your gear?' She gestured to the two bags lying at his feet, one holding a few clothes, the other his precious cameras, all he'd managed to salvage in in his hurried departure from the United States.

Martin nodded, wishing he hadn't been forced to rely once again on his sister. It was one thing to turn to her for help when he was nineteen, but at fifty-two? Then he saw the concern in her eyes, the green eyes so like his own, and a wave of gratitude swept over him. Who was it who'd said home is the place you return to when you have nowhere else to go? That just about described him right now. But he wished they didn't have company. He'd come home to lick his wounds and he didn't need an audience.

Six

There wasn't much conversation on the drive back from the small, local airport. Ailsa wasn't sure what she'd expected when she met Martin Cooper again, but the weary man with cavernous cheeks and cropped fading blond hair streaked with white, certainly wasn't it. She wished now she hadn't gone to the airport with Bev, but had followed her inclination and stayed home or gone to the beach.

It had been a shock to be greeted by the older version of the man she'd idolised at nineteen and who had become such a legend to his peers. But neither of them was nineteen anymore, and time had taken its toll, with him more than with Bev and her. It was a pity his arrival coincided with her stay with Bev.

One man in Ailsa's life was enough, and she'd come up here to get away from him. But surely Martin wouldn't be staying for long, and she could manage to avoid him? He was Bev's brother after all, nothing to do with her. And her infatuation with him all those years ago had been just that, the foolish fascination of a young girl with someone way out of her league. Thank goodness she'd met Bob and found love with him.

Though look where that had got her. Two children, and nearly twenty-five years later she had fled to this seaside town to figure out if she could find a new future for herself, one without Bob in it. She shivered. She wasn't in a position to criticise Martin Cooper, or whatever had brought him back home after all this time. Bev had mentioned something about things going wrong for him and his needing to regroup but hadn't gone into details. Perhaps she didn't have any.

'Here we are.' Bev pulled up outside the white house. 'You two go inside while I put the car in the garage. I expect you'd like something to eat, Martin?'

Martin only grunted.

Ailsa flinched. This wasn't what she'd come to Bellbird Bay for. She could get plenty of it at home. But she forced a smile and said, 'I'll put the kettle on and see what there is to eat.'

'Thanks.' Bev smiled back and gave an almost imperceptible shrug.

'A strong coffee would be good.' Martin came out of the dark mood he'd been in all the way back and joined Ailsa on the pathway. 'Still slumming it, Bev?' he asked, his lips twisting into a grin.

'You wouldn't say that if you knew what the place next door sold for a few years ago,' Bev said. 'People with more money than sense.' She shook her head. 'See you shortly. You might want to get your bags out of the boot before I drive this in,' she said to Martin.

'Sorry, Bev. Don't know where that came from. Didn't mean to insult you. It's a nice place you have here and I'm glad you're willing to take me in. Otherwise, I'd be stuck in a hotel room somewhere.' Martin hefted his bags out of the boot and followed Ailsa to the door while Bev maneuvered the car into the tiny garage.

'That yours?' he asked, nodding to Ailsa's silver Volkswagen Beetle convertible sitting by the kerbside.

Ailsa's car was her pride and joy. Bought when the boys left home. It was perfect for scooting around Canberra but was no doubt not what Martin was used to. She felt a surge of protective pride, daring him to disparage it.

But what he said was, 'Good little cars.'

She relaxed.

Once inside, Ailsa headed for the kitchen and filled the electric jug. She was trying to work out how to operate Bev's coffee machine – it was a different brand to the one they had in Canberra and she rarely used that one, preferring tea – when she heard Martin drop his bags in the hallway. Then he was standing staring at her, his bulky presence filling Bev's small kitchen.

'Let me.' He edged past her to fill the machine with water then looked around. 'Where does my sister hide the coffee?'

Ailsa pointed to the cupboard, before turning on the jug and taking down three mugs from their hooks. There was something about Martin's presence that made her feel uncomfortable, transformed her into the teenager who'd imagined herself in love with her best friend's brother. Ailsa stifled the emotions which arose unbidden. She wasn't that young girl anymore, hadn't been for years.

She had as much right to be here as he did – more. She'd been invited. Martin had just turned up – like a bad smell.

Martin busied himself with making coffee without speaking. Ailsa couldn't think of anything to say either. The silence was beginning to become strained when, to Ailsa's relief, Bev appeared.

'Ah, tea!' Bev said, seeing the two mugs of peppermint tea Ailsa had prepared. 'And you figured out the machine,' she said to Martin, who turned to face her, a mug of black coffee in his hand. 'I have some banana bread I brought home from the café. We can sit on the deck and have a proper meal later,' she said, picking up her mug.

'Not me,' Martin said. 'If you tell me where to park myself, I'll take this and make myself scarce.'

Bev raised her eyebrows but merely said, 'You're in the room next to the bathroom. Will we see you for dinner? We're planning to…' But the rest of her words were lost as Martin wheeled out of the kitchen and through the hallway. They heard him stop to pick up his bags, then a bedroom door close.

'Well! Sorry, Ailsa. I don't know what's up with Martin. He's not usually like this, though how would I know what he's like?' She pulled on the end of her ponytail. 'I haven't seen him for ten years, not since Dad passed away. But he was always more sociable, perhaps too much so.' She frowned. 'Well, *we* can go out onto the deck to enjoy our tea and banana bread, anyway.'

Once outside, Ailsa could almost forget Martin's boorish behaviour, but the way he'd made her feel, the reminder of what she'd come here to get away from, still rankled. 'I can move out, find a B&B,' she said, taking a sip of tea. 'I can see Martin might want more privacy.'

'No, you've only just got here.' Bev appeared upset. 'I've been looking forward to our spending more time together. Martin…' She sighed. 'I don't expect he'll stay for long. He never does. Bellbird Bay has never been big enough for him, not since he finished school, maybe even before that,' she reflected. 'But I've always been there for him, picked up after him. Not what I expected to do at this age.' She grimaced.

'Do you know…?'

Bev shook her head. 'He hasn't said, but I'll winkle it out of him if he hangs around long enough. It can't be too bad – a photo shoot gone wrong, a woman being too persistent.' She paused and shook her head again. 'Though he's never come back here before, so maybe…' Her forehead creased.

'Are you sure you don't want me to go? It might be easier for you both.' Ailsa didn't know if she wanted to stay here, to have to face Martin every day, be subjected to his moods, to the discomfort she'd experienced in the kitchen. On the other hand, she did want to spend time with Bev.

'No, really. Please stay.' Bev put a hand on Ailsa's arm. 'It'll be fine. I'll talk to him tomorrow, give him today to recover. He's had a long flight, probably jetlagged.'

'Okay, but… if you change your mind…'

'Sure, I'll let you know. Now, since I've taken the day off, why don't we take a walk along the boardwalk, and I can point out some of the new developments since you were last here. You won't recognise the place.'

Ailsa agreed and went to change into her trainers, but she wasn't entirely convinced with Bev's explanation of Martin's behaviour and decided to reserve judgement on her decision to stay. She'd give it a few days, then reconsider.

Seven

Martin closed the bedroom door with a sigh of relief. The presence of the two women was doing his head in. He'd come here to get away from one woman only to be faced with one from his past. Dropping the bag containing his clothes on the floor and placing the one containing his camera equipment carefully in a corner by the window, he downed his coffee and threw himself on the bed.

He wished he hadn't come back. It was just his luck his return had coincided with Bev's reunion with her old uni friend, the one he'd spent an evening in Canberra with before fleeing back to Sydney and his familiar haunts. But what did he know back then? Not a lot, it seemed. Although pretending to himself he'd forgotten her, his sister's pretty, long-haired friend had made more of an impression on him than he cared to admit. It had scared him. He had dreams, a life to live away from Australia. He didn't want to be tied down at the tender age of nineteen. He'd seen it happen to a couple of his mates whose lives had been cut short by involvement with a woman. No, commitment hadn't been for him, not then, not ever, and there was something about this girl that made him want to flee, to get as far away from her as possible.

She was different from the girls he usually hung around with in Sydney, gentler, more vulnerable, unaccustomed to the alcohol swigging, cannabis smoking, arty crowd he mixed with, the women eager to be seen on the arm of the budding travel photographer. He'd left Canberra next morning before he could change his mind, making some excuse or other to Bev.

Now here she was again. He had a vague recollection of Bev telling him she was married. If so, where was the husband? Perhaps he was here too, out and about while the two women picked him up at the airport. He tried to imagine the sort of man Ailsa – yes, that was her name, it tripped off his tongue – would have chosen. Someone boringly conventional, he'd guess, his direct opposite. *Had she been carrying a torch for him all those years?* Then he castigated himself for being egocentric. The woman probably hadn't given him another thought, or if she had it would have been to think what a lucky escape she'd had.

His eyes closed as tiredness and jetlag caught up with him.

*

When Martin awoke, it was dark outside and for a few moments he wondered where he was. Then he remembered, groaned and turned over, closing his eyes again. But the ache in his stomach told him he was hungry, and Bev had mentioned something about food. Reluctantly, he sat up and slid his legs from the bed, rubbing his eyes and forehead in an effort to force himself fully awake. He could hear women's voices coming through the open window and sighed. If he wanted to eat, he'd have to join them.

Rising, he pushed his hands through his cropped hair. His long blond locks had been so messy when he returned from his last shoot in the rainforest, he'd had it all cut off before he had time to think. Now he regretted it, as every time he caught sight of himself in a mirror he felt as if he was looking at a wanted poster. But at least his hair would grow again. It was more than he could hope for with his reputation. There was a faint possibility the news hadn't followed him here. Australia was still an outpost of civilisation despite the Internet and ease of travel. Maybe, just maybe, he could start again here. But did he want to? He was only fifty-two, but some days he felt twice that. Could he really regain all he'd lost, become once again the revered photographer, the icon to travellers all over the world – or was he kidding himself? Had he ever been that person? Right now, he felt he never wanted to hold a camera again.

He sluiced his face with cold water before making his way to the kitchen where Bev and Ailsa were chatting while preparing a meal. The delicious aroma of onions and garlic greeted him, reminding him it was hours since he last ate.

'Something smells good.'

The two women turned.

'You've decided to join us for dinner?' Bev asked, continuing to chop vegetables. Ailsa was stirring a pan on the stove.

'Sorry I rushed off earlier. Jetlag.' Martin realised from Bev's tone an apology was in order. She always had been able to make him feel guilty, even when he wasn't at fault. He brushed a hand across his hair. 'Can I do anything to help?'

'How about you pour us a glass of wine? There's beer in the fridge, too, if you prefer.'

'Thanks.' A cold beer would hit the spot. He'd missed Australian beer on his travels. He set to making himself useful.

It was pleasant, sitting on the deck to eat, looking out into the darkness broken only by the distant lights from a ship on the horizon. Martin listened as the women chatted about things he knew nothing of – books they were reading, movies they'd seen, an exhibition of paintings Ailsa had attended in Canberra. There was, he suddenly realised, no sign or mention of Ailsa's husband.

Bev had taken the empty plates into the kitchen, promising to return with cake for dessert leaving Martin and Ailsa alone. They sat in silence for a few moments. Then, unable to stop himself, Martin said, 'You're married, aren't you? Your husband isn't here?'

There was an awkward silence. Ailsa looked down at her hands. 'He couldn't get away.'

Martin was curious. He had the impression there was more to it, but then Bev returned, so there was no opportunity to ask anything more. She gave them both an enquiring look before setting a strawberry flan on the table along with three plates.

'What do you intend to do while you're here, Martin?' she asked.

Martin pulled on one ear. He hadn't given any thought as to how he might spend his time here, in the town he'd considered a backwater and been so anxious to leave.

'Ailsa's going to come to the garden centre with me tomorrow. Why don't you join us? I'm sure I can find something useful for you to do.' She gazed at him expectantly.

Hell, no! He hadn't come here to potter around his sister's little hobby farm. But what did he intend to do? Lie in bed and feel sorry for himself? He looked out at the darkness of the ocean and remembered how, despite how he'd despised the town, he'd always loved the sea. 'Thanks, but no,' he said. 'I plan to go swimming.'

Eight

There was no sign of Martin when Ailsa joined Bev for breakfast next morning. 'Is your brother still asleep?' she asked, helping herself to a bowl of muesli and slicing a banana over it, followed by a dollop of yoghurt.

'He wasn't in his room when I peeped in. Tea?' Bev held up a ginger and lemon teabag.

'Yes, please. I'm enjoying your variety of herbal teas. I'm usually much less adventurous. Does he normally get up early?' She wasn't sure why she asked, but something was making her curious.

'I wouldn't know what normal is for him these days, or when he's on a photo shoot on one of his excursions into some godforsaken place. But when he was younger, he did like to rise early and go for a swim or a surf.' She looked out the window to where the heads of some early morning swimmers and surfers were visible above the waves. 'He could be out there, but I wish he'd left a note or something. He doesn't have a key and, if he's not back before we leave, I'm not sure what to do.' She frowned. 'It's just like Martin. He never did have much concern for others.'

'I could wait here if you like, come along to join you later.'

'Thanks, but you shouldn't have to. It's just so annoying.'

'Morning, ladies.'

Bev's tirade was interrupted by the arrival of a very wet Martin. A pair of board shorts clung to his hips and thighs and he had a towel over one shoulder. 'Had an early morning swim. You should try it. The water's spectacular and it's glorious to be out there just as the sun's coming up. I'd forgotten what it was like.'

Ailsa swallowed at the sight of Martin's naked chest, averting her eyes from his lower body. He was tanned from clearly spending lots of time in the sun, and he was fit. If his face and hair made him appear older than his years, his body could have been that of a twenty or thirty-year-old. To hide the blush creeping over her cheeks, she picked up her cup and took a gulp, almost choking.

'All right for some,' Bev said, I didn't know where you were, and Ailsa and I will need to go soon. I'll leave you a key if you want to go out again, and there's plenty of food in the fridge.' She looked around distractedly. 'I think...'

'I'll be fine. I'm a big boy now, used to taking care of myself. You don't need to worry about me, sis. And I won't be in your hair for long.' His forehead creased. 'Well, not for too long anyway. I'll have a shower and make myself a decent cup of coffee. You two do what you have to. I won't get in your way.' He strode off, dripping water on the tiled floor as he went.

Ailsa looked up to see Bev grinning.

'Isn't he the limit? He turns up out of the blue, treats the place like a hotel and never a word of thanks. But that's Martin. He's always been able to get away with blue murder, probably always will. And yet, he's my twin brother and I'll always have a soft spot for him.' She sighed. 'I promised my mum, you know, that I'd always be here if he needed me. He didn't come back, had this successful career that took him all over the world, but it was as if she knew it wouldn't last.'

'You mean you think...?'

'No, nothing like that. But it is odd for him to turn up back here in the place he tried so hard to put behind him. Well, no doubt we'll find out soon enough.' She swept up the dirty dishes from the table and carried them over to the dishwasher. 'I did mean what I said about us having to leave soon. The garden centre opens at seven-thirty, and I like to get there a bit earlier to make sure everything is in place.'

'The café?'

'I'm lucky I don't need to worry about it. Cleo takes care of it. I found her four years ago when I was thinking of opening it. She walked in one day looking for work and I discovered she was perfect for the job. She ran her own café down the coast a bit for years before she married then, when her husband died suddenly, she wanted a change and moved to Bellbird Bay with her daughter. You'd have seen her yesterday.'

'The woman with long dark hair?' Ailsa remembered seeing an exotic looking woman flitting around behind the scenes in the café. She looked younger than both Ailsa and Bev and a bit of a hippie.

'That's Cleo. She and her husband lived a pretty much self-sufficient lifestyle and she's a marvellous cook. She makes most of the dishes we offer – except the cakes.' Bev chuckled. 'The cakes are Ruby's province.'

'Ruby?' Clearly Bev had developed a team of loyal helpers, alongside her other staff.

'I'll introduce you. She's a character. No one knows how old Ruby is and no one would dare ask her. She runs the B&B you would probably have booked into last night if I'd let you. She's lived here all her life and she seemed old when we were growing up. She's a bit of an oddity, too. You'll see what I mean when you meet her.'

Ailsa laughed. It was beginning to look as if this trip was going to be more interesting than she'd anticipated.

*

Once at the garden centre, Ailsa saw a different side of her friend. As soon as they entered the small office area, Bev became all business. She donned a bottle-green apron bearing the centre's pandanus tree logo and threw another one at Ailsa.

'You'd better put this on to protect your clothes and show you're not a customer. And take one of those hats too.' She pulled a wide-brimmed straw hat from a pile of similar ones. 'We tend to get busy early, then it tapers off towards lunchtime before picking up again in the afternoon. Since it's school holidays, there are a lot of visitors here. They mostly like to browse, but a surprising number want to buy pots and plants to take home with them. Then there are the seasoned gardeners who want to chat. If you come across any of those you can refer them to me or one of the other staff.'

Ailsa gulped. *What had she let herself in for?*

'Don't worry.' Bev chuckled. 'I'm not expecting you to do a crash course in gardening. We need to keep everything moist so I was hoping you wouldn't mind wielding a hose.'

'I can do that.' Ailsa was relieved. Back home in Canberra, she'd always enjoyed pottering around in the garden, but this place was on a completely different scale from anything she was used to. Even the nursery where she purchased her annual supply of border plants and potting mix paled to insignificance compared to what Bev had created here. She watched as a team of efficient workers streamed in through the gates, donned their uniform aprons and set to work, seemingly knowing exactly what to do.

Ailsa followed Bev's instructions and was soon armed with a hose and moving along the aisles watering plants of every description. It was pleasant here, relaxing to be involved in this mundane task. There was nothing to worry about, no one to take care of or placate. There was just her, the hose and the plants, which didn't answer back. With the sun on her back, she could lose herself in her task, immune to the customers who wandered around her chatting to each other. There was the occasional interruption when a customer asked for assistance, but she directed them to one of the staff members as Bev suggested and went back to her task.

It was a surprise when she heard Bev's voice in her ear.

'Fancy some lunch?'

Ailsa turned off the water and looked up. It couldn't be lunchtime already.

'It's noon. Time for a bite to eat. I think you're about done here.'

Looking around, Ailsa realised she'd come to the end of the last row of plants. And her stomach growled at the mention of food. 'Sounds good.'

After putting the hose away and divesting herself of the apron, Ailsa joined Bev in the café. It was busier today, but they managed to find a spot close to the kitchen.

'Cleo keeps this one for me if she can,' Bev said, as they took their seats at the round, white, wrought iron table. 'I'm going to have the salad of the day. What about you?'

Ailsa looked at the blackboard menu where the day's salad was described as being a mixed leaf salad with mozzarella, mint, peach and prosciutto. 'I'll have that, too. And another of the juices I had yesterday. It was delicious.'

A bright young girl wearing a pair of green shorts topped with a white tee-shirt bearing the pandanus logo took their order. Then the dark-haired woman emerged from the kitchen.

'This is my old friend, Ailsa, Cleo,' Bev said. 'She's spending some time with me and has been helping out this morning.'

'Welcome to Bellbird Bay,' Cleo said. 'I'm sure you'll enjoy your visit. It's a good place to work things out. I'm a newcomer. I've only been here for four years, but the town – and Bev…' she smiled at Bev, '…have taken me to their hearts.'

'Thanks, Cleo. Good to meet you. I had lunch here yesterday, too, and love your food.'

'Thanks.' Cleo smiled, her face lighting up. 'That's what we like to hear, isn't it, Bev? Now I'll leave you to enjoy your lunch and get back to work,' she said, as the young girl appeared with their meals.

'That was delicious.' Ailsa laid down her knife and fork. 'You were right about Cleo's cooking, though I guess there's not too much cooking involved in a salad. It's knowing how to put it together.'

Bev just grinned. 'Now, you have to taste one of Ruby's cakes,' she said. 'Be right back.' She disappeared into the kitchen area to reappear a few minutes later carrying two plates each containing a large slice of decadent-looking cake. 'You have to try this. It's her signature hummingbird cake, the one she calls her bellbird special. She swears the recipe has been passed down in her family for generations, and I wouldn't dare contradict her. I've ordered coffee, too. This is a cake to be eaten with coffee, not tea.'

Raising her eyebrows Ailsa took a fork and cut into her piece of cake. She closed her eyes as she bit into the soft concoction, the combined flavours of coconut, pineapple and banana teasing her taste buds. 'Oh! This is divine.' She opened her eyes again to see their coffee had arrived and took a sip of the cappuccino Bev had ordered.

Bev grinned again. 'Told you so.' Then she became more serious. 'I hope Martin isn't going to make things difficult. This morning…'

Ailsa shook her head, though she couldn't forget her shock at the sight of him that morning. She was fifty-two years old, for God's sake, not the impressionable teenager she'd been when they last met. Her marriage might be all but over, but she and Bob were still married, and she had two grown children. 'Why should he?'

'I know my brother. He may not seem to be a lady killer, but he has a reputation with women. I'd hate to see…'

'Bev!' Ailsa was indignant. 'Listen to yourself. You didn't warn me about him back in Canberra, when I was a vulnerable nineteen-year-old. What do you think he's going to do to me now I'm an ancient fifty-two?'

'Sorry.' Bev had the grace to look apologetic. 'I just don't want to see you hurt. You haven't told me why you're here on your own for the rest of the summer. No…' she held up a hand as Ailsa opened her mouth to speak, '…you don't need to tell me, if you don't want to. But I know there must be something seriously wrong for you to have left your home, your husband and your family to come here. I just don't want my dear twin brother to take advantage of whatever it is you're running from.'

Ailsa blushed. She fiddled with her teaspoon and repositioned her fork on the empty plate. 'I'm not running from anything. Things were a bit difficult with Bob. I'll admit it, and I needed time to myself. But that's all.'

Bev looked sceptical but said nothing.

Ailsa gazed into space as if she could find the answer among the various plants surrounding them. *Why was she here? And why did seeing Martin Cooper again made her feel so uncomfortable?*

Nine

Martin had been relishing his early morning swims for several days. He liked getting up early, before Bev and Ailsa were awake, and running down the steps to the beach. At that time in the morning, there were only the few diehards out and about. A few swimmers like himself, and a number of surfers eager to catch a wave before heading off to work.

He enjoyed it here, the tenor of the place helped banish the thoughts of what had happened in the US, memories of the rejections he'd suffered – from both Sofia and Jackson Green. It only re-emerged in the nightmares which disturbed his sleep, forcing him to awake in a cold sweat as he remembered. In retrospect, he wasn't sure which troubled him most. He was tempted to banish them with alcohol, but he'd tried that before he left the States, and it only left him bleary-eyed next morning and with a ginormous headache. No, it was better to remain clear-headed and try to work through it himself.

He hadn't seen much of Ailsa. She and Bev disappeared each morning and, if Ailsa didn't spend the entire day at the garden centre, she managed to keep out of his way. For his part he had no desire to spend time with her, with any woman, though it did cross his mind to wonder what brought her up here on her own. Surely she'd prefer to spend this post-Christmas period with her family?

But it was none of his business.

After a shower and a breakfast of two boiled eggs and several slices of toast and vegemite – a meal which reminded him of his childhood

– Martin dressed in a pair of khaki shorts and a tee-shirt. Finding a selection of hats on a stand in the hallway, he chose one with a wide brim and set off, deciding to walk along the beach which stretched as far as the eye could see.

He had reached the far end and was on his way back, when he noticed a young surfer performing well and stopped to watch. It was years since he'd handled a surfboard himself. All of a sudden, he was filled with the urge to be out there on the water, to feel the remembered thrill as he caught a wave and rode it into shore. What had happened to his old surfboard? Did Bev have it stashed away somewhere? It wasn't till now that he wondered what she had done with everything from the old house when their mother had died.

Lost in his thoughts, Martin started when a voice said, 'It's Coop, isn't it? What the hell are you doing here? I thought you were too important for the likes of us these days.'

Martin looked up to see a face he recognised from the past. It was older, more lined and had been ravaged by the sun, but Will Rankin didn't look too different from the larrikin who'd beaten him in the Bellbird Bay surf competition several decades ago. He was holding on to a surfboard, and wearing a pair of old board shorts, a Hawaiian shirt open to the waist and his feet were bare. He looked as if he hadn't a care in the world. His faded blond hair was tied back in the same ponytail both had worn in their teens. Martin had a sudden flashback to those days when anything seemed possible.

'Hey, Will. You're still here?' he asked, cursing under his breath. It wasn't that he didn't want to see his old mate, but he had hoped to stay under the radar for a bit longer – maybe even for all the time he was here in Bellbird Bay, however long that might be.

'Never left. When you're on a good thing, I always say.' He chuckled and dropped the surfboard onto the sand. 'Run the local surf school these days. That's my Owen out there.' He pointed to the young man Martin had been watching who was now wading in to shore, his surfboard under his arm. 'But what about you? Big time, photographer, eh?' he grinned.

Martin flinched. Not so big, now. What would he say if he knew – when he knew? Because, no matter what he thought, what he hoped, the word would travel here eventually if it hadn't already. He was kidding himself if he thought it wouldn't.

'We should grab a beer while you're here. It's been a while.' He peered at Martin as if calculating the ravages time had made on him.

'Yeah.' A beer with his old mate was the last thing Martin wanted.

'Have you been to the old surf club since you got back? Wouldn't know it, mate. Was completely redone a few years back. Now it's one of the best on the coast, knocks all the others for dead.'

Martin didn't respond.

'Been out recently?' Will nodded to where the waves were breaking some distance from the shore.

'Not for a while.'

'Can lend you a board if you want.' Will met his eyes.

Martin experienced the familiar tingle of anticipation calling to him. He hadn't realised how much he'd missed it. 'Thanks.'

'Anytime. I'm located at the other end of the beach. You'll see my van parked there most days. And that beer... see you tonight... around seven?'

Martin nodded. It was easier than trying to find an excuse, and what harm could it do? It would get him out of the house, away from the two women he was doing his best to avoid. He didn't trust himself around women after Sofia. Bev was okay. She was his sister. But Ailsa... He took a deep breath. He could get into trouble there if he wasn't careful. And he knew they both had questions about his unexplained arrival.

*

'Going out?' Bev asked, raising an eyebrow, when Martin appeared after dinner in a pair of chinos, the sleeves of his white shirt rolled up to the elbows.

'Surf club. Met an old friend on the beach today. Remember Will Rankin?'

'Will? Of course. He's had a bad run. First his son died, then his wife developed cancer. I think the surf school saved him from falling into a deep depression – that and his other son. He'd be in his late teens, now.'

A surge of guilt swept through Martin. He wasn't the only one whose life hadn't turned out the way he'd planned and his problems were nothing compared to what his old mate had suffered. He'd just assumed Will's life had been a bed of roses here in the safe haven of Bellbird Bay, but misfortune could happen to anyone, anywhere. 'I didn't know.'

'No reason you should. I never mentioned it. You were never interested in Bellbird Bay news. And Will wouldn't have told you. He's pretty tight-lipped about it.'

'When did it happen?'

'It's over five years since Evan died – a surfing accident – and Dee passed away three years ago after battling her cancer for a couple of years. He's been amazing about it. Didn't let his grief get in the way of his life – raises funds for the local hospital and the local surf club. He's become a bit of a legend around here.'

Martin was humbled. He'd taken his old mate at face value, never for a minute imagining what his life had been like. In fact, he'd almost envied Will's apparent laid-back lifestyle compared to the frantic pace of his own. Though all that had come to a sudden halt. He sighed. 'Well, I'll be off, now. See you.'

*

'You made it,' Will greeted Martin as he walked into the surf club and joined him at the bar. 'You'll have a Four X or is your taste more sophisticated these days?'

'That'll be fine.' Martin could almost taste the familiar brew on his tongue as the bartender drew down the measure of the popular Queensland beer. 'I've missed this,' he said, taking his first sip. Then he looked around the club. He could see what Will had meant this morning. The place had undergone a complete overhaul. It scarcely looked like the same club where he and Will had downed their first schooners when they were barely old enough to drink. 'You were right about the club,' he said.

'Not so bad, is it?' Will followed Martin's eyes as they took in the busy sports bar complete with television, the spacious restaurant, and the new deck overlooking the beach. 'We don't do too badly here. Not such a backwater.'

Martin flinched. He recalled what he'd said about his hometown before he left all those years ago, eager to leave Bellbird Bay and everyone in it behind him, first for Sydney, then the world.

'I'm sorry about…' Martin gestured with his beer. 'Bev told me.'

'Thanks.' Will looked down into his glass. 'It was tough and some days…' He looked up again to meet Martin's eyes. 'But life goes on, and I have Owen to think about. He has the makings of the sort of surfer you and I only aspired to. He's already finalling in the national comps and we're hoping…' He gave Martin a speculative look. 'Maybe you can help.'

'Help? Me? As I said, I haven't surfed for years.'

'Not with the surfing.' Will chuckled. 'But you take photos, don't you? I'm running a fundraiser to get the boy to Hawaii, and I need some shots taken to promote it. Meeting you today seemed like fate. I wondered if…'

Martin put his beer down on the bar and held up both hands. 'No, Will, I don't take those types of shots. No people. Landscapes. And I've kind of given it away.' He picked up his beer again and gazed down into the tawny liquid.

'But you could,' Will persisted. 'I presume you have a camera? I was going to use the ones I've taken with my phone but… now you're here… you're a big shot photographer. You could make him look professional.'

Martin took a swill of his beer to give himself time to think. Boy, it tasted good. He licked a drop off his lips. He hadn't come to Bellbird Bay to take shots of a teenage surfer, but what harm could it do? No one need know. Will was an old mate and he'd had a rough time of it losing his son and his wife. He knew what Bev would say, but that wasn't what motivated him to reply, 'Maybe. Let me think about it.'

'Good on you, mate. Owen will be stoked.' Will slapped him on the shoulder. 'And I'll have a surfboard waiting for you tomorrow morning.'

'Wait, I haven't…' But Will seemed to have taken his words as an agreement.

They drank a few more beers, reminisced about some of the scrapes they'd got into growing up and the photos weren't mentioned again. But as he farewelled his friend with promises to meet him at his van early next morning, Martin knew Will thought it was a done deal.

Ten

By the time dinner was over, Ailsa was ready to drop. She'd put in another full day at the garden centre and was in awe of her friend's energy. She'd must have walked miles today. Funny, she thought, how one still talked of walking miles when distance hadn't been measured in miles since she was a child.

'How about a cup of camomile tea?' Bev asked, when Martin had left to meet his friend at the surf club. 'It'll help you sleep.'

Despite having had no trouble sleeping since she arrived here, Ailsa agreed, and the two women took their mugs out to the deck where they could see the moon reflected on the water.

'We should go to the surf club one evening, too,' Bev said. 'They put on a good spread and it's not too noisy if you sit well away from the pokies.'

'Was this guy Martin has gone to meet a good friend of his?' Ailsa didn't know what made her ask about Martin.

'They were inseparable all through high school, both fiercely competitive where surfing was concerned. But Will didn't have Martin's desire to leave town and make his mark on the world. He was never ambitious. He married a local girl and stayed in Bellbird Bay, set up his surf school and was as happy as Larry until Evan died – then Dee got sick, and he lost her too. Now he lives for surfing and his son, Owen. He's a surfer, too. I sometimes wonder if Martin might have been happier if…' She broke off.

'Isn't he happy? Didn't you tell me he was the toast of the shutterbugs – I think that was the word you used?'

'I guess so, but...' Bev gazed out into the darkness only relieved tonight by the moon and a few stars, '...I've always wondered if he was happy. He's moved around so much, never staying long in one place. Sure, he made his name as a photographer, a bunch of money too, I expect. But he's never had anywhere to call home, never been in a permanent relationship.' She chuckled. 'I can't talk. I haven't done too well in the relationship stakes either. Oh, ignore me, I'm just his sister, concerned he's suddenly arrived back in the only place he ever could call home, and I don't know why.'

'I guess we never know what's really going on in our loved one's lives.'

From the sudden silence, Ailsa knew she'd given Bev a lead in.

'Want to talk about it?'

Ailsa took a breath. Was she ready to talk about what had led to her trip north?

'Your husband?' Bev prompted.

'Bob?' Ailsa sighed. She shook her head. She thought back to their last conversation. She wasn't ready to share it with Bev yet, maybe she never would be. 'I had no idea what was bugging him, but he turned into someone I don't know – and didn't want to be around.' It wasn't till she said the words out loud that Ailsa realised how she felt. It was a relief not to have to face Bob's doleful expression each day, to have to put up with his silences, his gloomy face, and to wonder if she had done something to trigger it. At least now she knew what was behind his distant behaviour.

'Have you asked him?'

'Ye...es. Sorry, Bev. I'm not ready to talk about him just yet. But...' she smiled, '...you have no idea what a relief it is to be here where I don't have to put up with his moods.'

'Only to meet my bad-mannered brother.' Bev grinned.

'There is that.' Ailsa laughed. 'But at least I'm not married to him.' As she spoke, she blushed and felt a frisson of something she couldn't identify. Luckily Bev didn't appear to notice in the darkness.

'What do you plan to do tomorrow?' Bev asked. 'You could come to the garden centre with me again, but I didn't invite you up here to get free labour.'

'I know that. I've been enjoying being there. But tomorrow, I think

I might go for a walk. I see the boardwalk seems to go all the way up to the headland where I stopped on my way into town. I'd like to do a bit of exploring, maybe take a couple of sandwiches and make a day of it.' *And keep out of Martin's way.*

'Good plan. If you're going up that way you may run into Ruby. Her place backs onto the path up to the headland. It's an old two-storey house that has been in her family for generations. Far too big for her on her own, of course, which is why she runs it as a B&B. She gets a good lot of holidaymakers all summer, and in the other school holidays too. And in-between there are those retired couples who come here for the peace and quiet. I think she does pretty well. Luckily for me, she loves baking, too.'

'Sounds good.' But Ailsa didn't want to meet anyone. She needed some time to herself, something she hadn't had for years, she realised. There had always been Bob and the boys. Even with Bob the way he'd been acting lately, he was still there in the house, and the boys tended to pop in unannounced from time to time, expecting her to drop everything and accede to their demands. She intended to use this time productively to consider her future, and what her life would be like without Bob.

Eleven

Martin made his way along the beach until he came to a white van parked on the grassy edge of the sand. Its back door lay open to reveal surfboards carefully stacked along each side of the interior. A large sign indicated it was the home of the *Bay Surf School* and that surfboards could be hired here, too. It all looked very makeshift, but even at this time in the morning there was a line of young bloods waiting to hire boards, and groups of parents with young children clearly there for their surf lessons.

Martin hung back, amused as he watched Will deal efficiently with the crowd, till the young guys left carrying their boards, and the parents were busy signing up their children. Then he moved closer to the van. His old mate wasn't as laid back as he appeared. Will had a good business going here – a business with no overheads, much like Martin's own, but with fewer hassles.

'Hey!' Will said. This morning he was wearing a tee-shirt with the logo *Bay Surf School* and the same daggy pair of board shorts as the day before. 'Just in time.' He dragged a board from the van and placed it on the sand at Martin's feet. 'This one should suit you.' He waved away Martin's offer to pay. 'This one's on me, but if you decide to make a habit of it, you can pay the going rate.' He pointed to the sign which not only listed the price of surf lessons, but the hire of boards by the hour or day.

'Sure thing. Thanks a lot.' Martin picked up the board, dropped his towel on the sand and headed into the ocean.

*

Time passed quickly, the pull of the waves bringing back memories of days gone by, days when nothing was more important than the call of the sea and the joy of being out there with his mate. Today Martin was alone, and that was the way he liked it. He could see his old mate teaching a new generation of surfers, his bleached blond hair blowing in the wind.

It was close to midday by the time Martin made his way back up the beach towards the van where Will was standing talking to a young man.

'Thanks, Will,' he said, dropping his board on the sand.

'No worries. Meet Owen,' Will said, gesturing to his companion.

The young man grinned and pushed back the shock of blond hair which branded him as Will's son. He was the boy Martin had watched surfing the day before, the boy whose photo Will wanted him to take. Now he was closer, Martin could see the likeness between the two. Owen looked exactly like Will when they'd battled for honours in the surf and drowned their differences in the surf club later.

'Hello, Owen,' he said. 'Your dad and I are old mates.'

'Hello,' the boy said, suddenly shy. 'Dad says you're going to take photos of me with my board to use in the fundraising for Hawaii.' He stroked his board lovingly.

Martin was about to deny it, to say he still hadn't made up his mind, when he saw the excitement in the boy's eyes and instead found himself saying, 'Sure. I'll arrange a time with your dad.' He looked across at his old friend to see him grinning back at him.

Snookered!

*

Wandering back to Bev's place, Martin reflected how Will had managed to trick him into agreeing. Had he known how difficult it would be for Martin to refuse Owen? Or was it just by chance the boy arrived when he did? Whichever it was, now he was stuck with taking what amounted to happy snaps of the teenager – a far cry from what he was accustomed to.

In a strange way Martin envied his old friend, when he should deride him for staying right here in this dead town where they grew up – for not wanting more out of life. Instead, he envied Will's obvious contentment with his lot in life – his surf school and Owen. While fighting shy of commitment, Martin would have liked to have a son, someone to look up to him in awe, to share his dreams, to follow in his footsteps.

It was stupid, he knew. He could never have led the life he had if he'd been tied down with a wife and child, even a child without the trappings of a wife. But he'd been ready to settle down with Sofia. He shook his head in despair. Life was strange. It had a habit of kicking you in the teeth when you least expected it.

He pushed open the gate and fitted the key into the lock. The house was quiet. He breathed a sigh of relief. The last thing he wanted was to have to make small talk with his sister's friend. He wasn't good at small talk at the best of times. And Ailsa McNeil made him feel uncomfortable. There was something about the woman that… Martin shook his head again. He fixed himself a bacon and egg sandwich, cracked open a can of beer and made his way out to the deck where he fell into one of the wicker chairs and put his feet up on the railing,

This was the life. Martin knew he couldn't stay here for ever. Bellbird Bay would drive him mad, just as it had done all those years ago. But for now, it could provide him with a refuge, a breathing space while he worked out his next move. He'd need to wait till the fuss died down, then see who would still talk to him, if anyone was willing to take a risk on him and print his shots. Would any of the magazine editors who normally greeted his every submission with open arms, be open to his next one, if there was a next one?

He gulped down the last of his beer and his eyes began to close, the sun on his face and the sound of the ocean lulling him to sleep.

Twelve

By the time she reached the headland Ailsa was ready for a break. She dropped onto the grass and opened up the packet of cheese and ham sandwiches she'd stored in her backpack, then took a long swallow from her water bottle. Up here, it was as if she was on top of the world. It was a glorious day, the sun so bright it hurt her eyes, and only a slight breeze, just enough to temper the heat. And she had the place all to herself. Canberra and everyone in it seemed so far away.

She hadn't heard from Bob since that first text which she'd answered briefly. She wondered fleetingly what he was doing with himself then dismissed the thought, refusing to allow thoughts of him and their marriage to intrude and spoil her day.

It was so lovely sitting here in the sun, Ailsa closed her eyes.

'You need to watch the sun. You're turning quite red.'

The voice in her ear brought Ailsa crashing out of a dream in which she and Martin were… She blinked and tried to focus. A thin, elderly woman of indeterminate age, her face lined and brown from too many years in the sun, was peering at her from beneath a wide-brimmed straw hat.

'Who are you?' Ailsa spoke more sharply than she intended, embarrassed at having been caught sleeping in public in what must be the early afternoon. She'd lost track of the time and had no idea how long she'd been lying there.

'Ruby Sullivan. And you must be Beverley Cooper's friend from Canberra. You need to watch the Queensland sun. It's not like what you're used to. You'll burn to a crisp in no time.'

Ailsa pushed herself up. 'I must have dozed off.' So, this was Ruby, the woman Bev told her about, owner of the B&B and baker of the scrumptious cakes. Then she realised what the woman had said. 'How do you know who I am?'

'It's not too difficult. You're a stranger, and not one of those who come to spend their days at the beach. You wouldn't catch many of them coming all the way up here to enjoy the view and have a picnic.' She chuckled. 'And Bev told me you might call in on me when I dropped off my cakes this morning.'

'Oh!'

'I live over there.' Ruby pointed to a high-set white house, its paint showing signs of disrepair, the windows gazing straight out to the ocean. 'Why don't you join me for a cup of tea or a cool drink? You look in need of one. It'll be cooler inside.'

Ailsa uncoiled her legs which had been tucked under her and stood up. She was about to decline Ruby's offer when she realised she was burning up from the sun and her singlet was damp with sweat. She glanced at her now empty water bottle. A cool drink would be most welcome. 'Thanks, it's kind of you,' she said and, gathering up her rubbish and stuffing it into her backpack, she followed the woman to a gate in the shabby white fence which surrounded her house.

Inside the house, Ailsa couldn't help staring around while Ruby organised cool drinks. She was sitting in the kitchen which was clearly the heart of the house, and which didn't appear to have changed in the past fifty years. But it had a cosy feel about it, as if it was welcoming her with its scrubbed wood table and the ladder-backed chairs. In the centre of the table sat a large shallow pottery bowl filled with fruit. An oversized fridge hummed in one corner and a double-sized gas cooktop and oven stood against one wall, at right angles to a deep porcelain sink. The kitchen surfaces were of polished wood and were home to a number of blue and white striped canisters which Ailsa recognised as being similar to a set belonging to her grandmother.

'Here we are.' Ruby handed Ailsa a tall glass, beaded with moisture, and joined her at the table. Ailsa took a welcome sip, the cool liquid slipping easily down her throat, the flavour bringing back memories. 'Is this...?'

'Homemade lemonade. There's not many who take the trouble

these days, but there's nothing like it to quench your thirst on a hot afternoon.'

'Mmm.' Ailsa took another sip. 'It's delicious.'

'Have a piece of cake.' Ruby pushed a plate towards Ailsa. It contained fat slices of a delicious looking sponge cake oozing lemon. 'Lemon delicious. It goes well with the lemonade,' Ruby said with a grin.

With a smile, her stomach telling her it was some time since she'd eaten her sandwiches, Ailsa took a piece. She bit into it, the zesty flavour tantalising her taste buds. 'Wow!' she said. 'When I tasted your hummingbird cake at Bev's café, I thought I'd gone to heaven, but this...'

Ruby smiled smugly. 'As they say, there's plenty more where that came from. My grandmother was a cook in one of the big houses in Brisbane back when folk had servants. She taught me a lot about baking, and I have the recipe book she put together. But I rarely need to consult it these days. I've been making them myself since I could reach up to the kitchen bench and stir a cake mix.'

'Well, I can see why Bev is glad she met you.'

Ruby smiled again.

'You've always lived here?' Ailsa asked, remembering Bev had said something about Ruby living in her family home.

'Apart from a couple of years when I travelled overseas. My family has always lived here. Grandmother was the only one who had to leave to find work. Bellbird Bay was much smaller in her lifetime, more of a fishing village. There wasn't much work for women. Of course, she came back when she married a local man. My grandfather drowned at sea and my grandmother came to live with her parents. My mother and I were both born here in this very house. It's a common tale around here as you'll discover if you stay around.'

'Mmm.' It was all interesting, but Ailsa didn't expect to be in Bellbird Bay long enough to find out more about the history of the town.

'Now, what about you?' Ruby asked, to Ailsa's surprise. 'What brings you to Bellbird Bay? You don't strike me as someone who's just come here for a holiday, to enjoy the beach and the sun. I sense you're troubled about something.' She peered at Ailsa, her eyes seeming to bore right into her, to see into her soul.

Ailsa shifted uncomfortably for a moment, then sensed the concern in the other woman's gaze. It was as if a blanket of well-being started to surround her. 'It's… I…' she began.

'Take your time. No need to tell me anything you don't want to, but I've found it sometimes helps to talk with a stranger. It can be less threatening than a good friend.' She held Ailsa's gaze.

Ailsa put down the glass she was holding, clasped her hands together and, almost without thinking, found herself unburdening herself to this woman she'd only just met. All of her worries about Bob burst out, the anger she'd been harbouring for months, the worry he might be ill, or she might have provoked his strange behaviour, the revelation which had shocked her into anger and an overwhelming sense of grief, even her discomfort at meeting Martin again. When she finished, her relief was enormous. It was as if a huge load had been lifted from her shoulders. 'I'm sorry, I don't know why I'm telling you all this,' she said, embarrassed to have revealed so much of her inner feelings.

'It's okay, my dear.' Ruby put a wrinkled hand on hers. 'People tell me things. Things I never repeat. It helps to talk about what's worrying you, get it all out. Then it may be possible to move on with your life.'

Move on, that's exactly what Ailsa wanted to do. But what was she to move on to? She couldn't contemplate what her life might be like without Bob. 'But…'

'The way will become clear,' Ruby said gently. 'You don't have the answers now. I don't either. I don't know you or your husband – or Bev's brother.' She chuckled. 'It sounds as if he arrived at the wrong time to throw a spanner in the works. But your husband. He sounds troubled, too. Has it occurred to you he may be struggling with his own demons?'

Ailsa stared at Ruby in surprise. Was Bob just as troubled as she was? Was that why he'd been so agreeable to her leaving? Surely not. It didn't bear thinking about. But it made sense. This strange old woman's words made sense.

'Thanks,' she said. 'I should be getting back now. And thanks so much for the lemonade and cake.'

'You're most welcome. Feel free to drop in any time. I'm usually here, and my guests are always out during the day.'

'Thanks,' Ailsa said again.

As she made her way back down from the headland and along the boardwalk, Ruby's words echoed in her ears. Had she been too concerned with her own feelings, with her annoyance at the way Bob was behaving, to work out how he might be feeling, to realise how difficult it must have been to be honest with her. *Could she have been more understanding? Should she have insisted on staying?*

Thirteen

Martin awoke with a start at the sound of footsteps. How long had he been asleep? He dropped his feet from the railing and blinked to see Ailsa on the deck. She looked as embarrassed as he felt. 'Hi, there,' he said, trying to force himself properly awake. That was the damnable thing about falling asleep in the afternoon. It often took ages to become fully awake.

'Hi,' Ailsa said. 'Sorry if I wakened you.'

'No, I wasn't asleep,' he lied. 'Just resting my eyes.' Now he was awake, he took a good look at her. She'd been in the sun, too. Her nose was shining, and her shoulders were turning red. She needed to put cream on them. For a brief moment, he imagined his hands smoothing cream on her skin, over her... He stopped his thoughts before they could take root. That was the old Martin, the one who thought every woman was fair game. 'Looks as if you caught some sun,' he said.

Ailsa followed his eyes squinting down at her shoulders and blushed. 'Yes. I fell asleep up on the headland.' She swung a backpack from her shoulder. 'I met the woman who bakes cakes for Bev's café,' she said. 'Ruby. She's quite a character. She...' Ailsa seemed about to say more but stopped herself. 'I'd best go shower.' She disappeared into the house.

Martin watched her go, contemplating how easy it was to discomfit her. She was a strange one, but he was curious to know what made her tick and why she was here without her family. Bev had said something about her spending the rest of the summer here. That was odd. Maybe

53

he should hang around too, find out a bit more about Ailsa McNeil. But he didn't intend to stay around for too long, only till the heat died down, however long that took.

In the meantime, there was his promise to Will and Owen. Damn his old mate for setting him up. He'd vowed never to hold a camera again but had to admit it would be good to be behind the lens again, regardless how basic the task.

*

Martin carefully unpacked his camera and handled it lovingly. He hadn't anticipated using it again and certainly not so soon. It was an old friend, his best friend, and had seen him through some rough times. 'Sorry old mate,' he murmured to it. He'd spent more time with his camera than with other human beings in the past few years and had become accustomed to talking to it.

He'd arranged to meet Will and his son by the van at around eleven and had chosen the other end of the beach for his swim that morning, wanting to avoid being caught up in a conversation with them earlier. His plan was to turn up, take some shots and disappear again. He'd send Will the photos and leave it there. He hadn't come here to rake up the past. But it had been good to see Will again, to remember the good times in Bellbird Bay.

As he repacked his camera in its special bag, Martin thought back to the previous evening. For once, he hadn't disappeared to his room immediately after dinner but had been prevailed upon to join the two women on the deck with a glass of wine. He wasn't sure why he'd stayed, perhaps to learn more about Ailsa. But if that was the case, he was sadly disappointed. The discussion focussed on Ruby, the woman Ailsa had met on her walk and who baked the delicious cakes Bev brought home from her café.

Boy, could those two women talk! But he was happy to sit back and listen. The only break in the conversation was when Ailsa's phone pinged with a text. She read it, grinned and said, 'It's Pat checking in on me.' The ensuing conversation revealed Pat was her son, not her husband, and he was in university. It figured. But it didn't answer

Martin's question about the husband or why she was here on her own. Martin didn't understand his curiosity.

He drew his thoughts back to the present. It was time to leave. This morning he'd chosen to wear a pair of three-quarter length chinos with a black tee-shirt he'd picked up somewhere. He popped a hat on his head, slid his feet into a pair of thongs, slipped a bottle of water into his back pocket, shrugged his camera bag onto his shoulder and was ready to go.

Ailsa was sitting in the kitchen when he walked through. She looked up from the map she was studying. 'Morning.'

'Morning.' She looked good this morning in a flowery dress, her short, streaked, dark hair falling down over her eyes. He noticed her shoulders were still looking red. 'Staying out of the sun today?'

'Planning to check out the town,' she said, a slight blush creeping into her cheeks, 'maybe find somewhere nice for lunch. Bev says it's changed a lot since I was last here. It must have been over fifteen years ago when the boys were little.'

'Boys? You have more than one?'

'Two. Nate and Pat, the one who's concerned about my welfare. They're both in university in Canberra.'

'Right.' This was more than she'd said to him in the few days he'd been here. He didn't know how to respond. 'I'd best be getting off. Promised to meet Will at eleven.'

'You're taking some photos?' Ailsa pointed to his camera bag.

'A favour for an old mate.' Martin didn't want to get into details. 'See you.' He swung out the door before Ailsa could say anything else, aware of her eyes following him.

He had worked himself into a sweat by the time he reached Will's van and wished that like his mate, he was wearing a singlet. Similar to his tee-shirt of the previous day, Will's proclaimed *Bay Surf School* for the world to see. Owen was dressed only in board shorts and was clearly waiting for him.

'Here he is, Dad,' the young man said as Martin rocked up. 'Told you he'd be here. You owe me.'

Martin flinched. He might resent having been talked into this, but he was a man of his word. 'Did you think I'd weasel out of it?'

Will had the grace to look embarrassed. 'Well, you're a big shot now. I wouldn't blame you if you considered this small beer. Thanks for coming. It means the world to Owen and me.'

Martin winced, his throat squeezing shut. Was this how people saw him? Was this how Ailsa saw him? Was it why she seemed awkward in his presence? Though they hadn't been together very often. He'd managed to keep himself out of her way, out of Bev's way, too. It was only a matter of time before his sister wanted an explanation of his sudden arrival back here in the town he'd been so eager to leave. At eighteen, he couldn't wait to shake the dust of Bellbird Bay off his feet, now at fifty-two, here he was, his tail between his legs, back home again bludging on his sister. It was pathetic. *He* was pathetic

'Let's get this show on the road,' he said to Owen. 'How about I take some shots with you standing there holding your board, then a few of you in the water ready to go.'

'Sure.' After some initial awkwardness, Owen got the hang of it, and by the time Martin had taken several shots of him in various poses, he was behaving as if he'd been doing this all his life.

'You're a natural,' Martin said, packing away his camera again. 'I'll get those to you when I get back,' he said to Will.

'I didn't expect you to take so many,' Will said, clearly impressed. 'How much do I owe you?'

Martin waved Will's offer away. 'Happy to do it for a mate,' he said, not wanting to get into an argument. Will wouldn't be able to afford his usual rates.

'Well, at least let me buy you lunch,' Will said. 'I usually close up about now and head to the surf club for a bite to eat. They do a great burger and chips. Goes down a treat with a schooner of beer. Join us?'

Martin hesitated. But it had been a long time since breakfast, he was hungry, and the thought of a good old-fashioned burger and chips washed down with a cold beer in the airconditioned surf club was appealing. He nodded.

The three of them found seats on the deck from where they could watch groups of surfers heading out or sitting astride their boards waiting for a wave.

'Not like in our day,' Will said, when he came back from placing their orders carrying two beers and a can of Coke. 'Remember how we had the ocean to ourselves?'

'Come off it, Dad,' Owen said. 'You talk as if it was in the dark ages.' He snapped open his Coke, took a drink and wiped his mouth with the back of his hand.

It could have been Will sitting there with him, Martin thought, an ache for what he'd left behind swirling in his gut. They had been good times, before he got itchy feet, before he decided Bellbird Bay was too small to satisfy his dreams.

'Cheers!' Will held up his glass. 'To days gone by. They were good times,' he said, echoing Martin's thoughts.

'Cheers.'

'Dad says you and he competed together,' Owen said, looking from one to the other. 'Who was the best surfer?'

'Well...'

'Martin often won,' Will said, 'but...'

'I didn't stick with it, so your dad ended up becoming the champion.' Martin thought back to the year he'd left. School was over and the surfing season was well underway. It had been tempting to stay, to beat his old mate, but the bright lights of Sydney were calling. College was starting soon, and he'd been offered a photo assignment in the city with one of his idols. So, he'd left Bellbird Bay and never looked back. And he'd never regretted it.

But now, looking out at the wild ocean, the surfers with not a care in the world, his old mate sitting opposite him with a son who clearly thought the world of his dad, Martin wondered whether it had all been worth it.

Fourteen

Ailsa watched Martin leave. He was looking particularly attractive this morning, the black tee-shirt over the three-quarter chinos reminding her of the first time she'd seen him. He'd been wearing a black tee-shirt then, too, appearing impossibly sophisticated to her nineteen-year-old eyes. Now she knew better, but his present outfit showed off his tanned skin and broad shoulders to perfection.

Not that it impressed her today. She was too old to be taken in by the charm that had enslaved her on that fateful evening. And the Martin Cooper who had just left was anything but charming. Bev's brother seemed to have undergone a transplant in the charm department. Just as well. Ailsa had no interest in men, charming or otherwise, and it made things easier all round if he maintained his distance.

Ailsa folded up the street map Bev had left with her, stretched and rose to put her cup into the dishwasher. She'd been sitting there since breakfast and should have known Martin would appear at some stage. She peered down at her shoulders. She'd seen him stare at them and realised they were still red from the sun she'd caught yesterday. Today, she wouldn't make the same mistake. Heading to the bathroom, she slathered on sunscreen before popping on a hat and leaving the house.

Once on the boardwalk, Ailsa chose to walk in the opposite direction from the day before. From her study of the map – and a vague recollection of her previous visit – she knew this was the way to town.

It was a glorious day, and to her surprise, Ailsa met only a few people along the way. She passed the surf club which seemed to be attracting a large crowd of holidaymakers, catching sight of a man who she thought was Martin Cooper with two other guys, then came to the end of the boardwalk where it changed into the esplanade.

This part of Bellbird Bay was much busier. Opposite the beach was a shopping plaza. lined with shops and Ailsa enjoyed window-shopping as she wandered along until she came to one she couldn't resist. Stopping outside the aptly named *Birds of a Feather*, she pushed open the glass door.

Inside, she was confronted by racks of beach clothes for all shapes and sizes in every colour under the sun.

'Can I help you?' A smart woman wearing one of the creations Ailsa had seen displayed in the window appeared as if from nowhere.

'I need something casual to wear, something more…' She gestured to the dress she was wearing which was a bit dressy for the holiday town and too tight to be comfortable in the heat.

'I have just the thing.' The woman walked over to a rail and pulled off a couple of baggy cotton dresses, one in bright pink and one in an equally bright blue, each with a geometric design.

They were loose tent-shaped outfits with wide sleeves, exactly what Ailsa was looking for. She could almost feel the cool breeze blowing through them, and the sleeves would protect her burnt shoulders. 'I'll try them,' she said.

Fifteen minutes later, Ailsa had decided to buy both.

'I'm sure you'll enjoy wearing them. They're perfect for this weather. I'm Greta. Are you here on holiday?'

'Not exactly. I'm visiting an old friend, Bev Cooper.'

Greta's eyes lit up. 'Lovely lady. We went to school together, though not in the same year.'

Taking in Greta's short blonde hair and careful makeup, it was difficult to gauge her age – older than Bev and her, or younger?

'I was a couple of years below,' she chuckled. 'One of the horde of girls who tried to be her friend to hook up with her twin brother. Martin Cooper was a real charmer. Do you know him, too?' Greta didn't wait for an answer but continued, 'Who'd have thought he'd become such a big name?' She popped the dresses into a bag and handed it over. 'There you are. Enjoy wearing them and do drop in again.'

By the time Ailsa made it outside, her ears were ringing. The reference to Martin was interesting. It was as she'd thought. Even at school, Martin had been regarded as a ladies' man. She'd had a lucky escape.

*

After wandering past a pharmacy and perusing the collection of hats displayed on a rack outside, and a patisserie she promised herself she'd visit later, Ailsa came to a bookshop. *Bay Books* looked interesting, and she could never ignore the pull of books.

Once inside, Ailsa sniffed up the familiar aroma, homing in immediately on a shelf displaying a collection of her favourite authors. She'd left Canberra in such a hurry she'd forgotten to pack her Kindle and had already finished the Fiona McIntosh novel Bev had lent her. With several weeks stretching ahead of her, she needed something to read. This was supposed to be time for her to rest, work things out, and so far, all she'd done was to help Bev in the garden centre and go for a long walk. And try to keep out of Martin Cooper's way, she admitted.

Almost immediately, Ailsa found what she was looking for – two books by Anna Jacobs which she hadn't read, one by Marcia Willett and another by Liz Fenwick. She knew these feel-good stories would help put her mind at rest and, hopefully, help her sort out her own life. On the way to the counter, she passed another display which caught her eye. She'd never been attracted to self-help books but one of the titles, *Lost Connections*, made her stop.

The book seemed to be calling out to her. Was this what had happened to Bob and her? Had they lost connection with each other? Some of the other titles, relating to intimacy in marriage and improving communication also made her think. Hurriedly and with some embarrassment, she added a couple to her collection.

The elderly man who wrapped her purchases looked as if he'd walked out of one of the Charles Dickens volumes displayed behind the counter, with his mop of white hair and neatly trimmed beard, but his voice was lively as he bade her goodbye and wished her enjoyment of her choices.

By now, Ailsa was beginning to feel really hungry and was on the lookout for somewhere to eat. She was just about to give up and return to the house when she spied a café ahead. The sign outside *The Bay Café* promised to provide food to die for so, amused, Ailsa took a seat at one of the outdoor tables and picked up a menu.

When she took her first bite of what was promoted as The Bay's daily special, she knew she'd made the right decision. The rye bread spread with herbed hummus and topped with ham and a selection of vegetables including eggplant, lettuce and tomato, was delicious, and the avocado and papaya drink complemented it perfectly. She flicked through one of her new purchases as she ate, before closing it to examine more closely later.

Ailsa had finished eating and was contemplating whether a coffee would round off her meal or spoil the flavours, when her phone pinged. This time it was Nate who wanted her to know he'd been trying to contact his dad without any success. Ailsa frowned as she read the few lines.

I don't want to worry you, but it's not like Dad to be incommunicado. Do you think I should drop round? Apart from that all's well here. Saw Pat last night. He's good. Nx

Damn! A curl of fear uncoiled in her stomach. Nate was right. Bob normally answered his phone, especially if it was one of the boys. But, given his recent behaviour, perhaps it wasn't so odd. Surely he hadn't done anything stupid? Ailsa's stomach lurched. Was this why he was happy for her to leave? So he could…? She couldn't bear to imagine the worst. Bob had been acting oddly, been uncommunicative, reclusive, surly, he'd revealed his sexual orientation, but he wasn't suicidal – or was he? She tried to remember what he'd been like the past few weeks, immediately before and after Christmas. He'd been unhappy, she decided. But unhappy with her or with himself and with life?

Do it, she texted, biting her lip.

On my way. The response came immediately.

'Would you like anything else?' Ailsa looked up to see the waitress peering down at her, a smile on her face.

'No. Yes. Coffee. Cappuccino.' She gazed into space, clutching her phone. Please God Bob was okay. She'd never forgive herself if… She couldn't even think of it. Her fingers tapped the table, willing Nate to hurry.

She had drunk two cups of coffee and imagined the worst when her phone rang. Ailsa picked it up at once. 'Nate?'

'Dad's fine. He was working on something in the shed and was pretty annoyed when I turned up yelling and asking if he was okay. Sorry to worry you, Mum. I just had the feeling something was wrong.'

Ailsa let out a sigh of relief. 'How was he?'

'Much as usual. Just annoyed at being disturbed. He said he'd deliberately left his phone in the house as he didn't want to be bothered by calls. But we went inside, and he made me a cup of coffee. I felt a bit of a fool.'

'Good. Not that you felt a fool, but that all is well. Do you think I should come home?' Ailsa didn't know why she was asking advice from her twenty-one-year-old son. Surely she was old enough to make her own decisions? But Canberra was so far away, and Nate seemed her only link to home.

'Don't be silly, Mum. You deserve this break. Sorry I overreacted. Pat and I will keep an eye on Dad. Make sure he's okay. You enjoy your time up there with Aunt Bev. How is it there? Are you managing to relax?'

Until your call.

'It's good,' she said. 'I've been helping out in the garden centre and doing a bit of exploring. Bellbird Bay has changed since we were here when you and Pat were little. There's more development and more people and it's pretty full of tourists at the moment.'

'And Aunt Bev?'

'She hasn't changed, just older and wiser like us all.' Ailsa decided to say nothing about Martin's arrival. She wasn't sure the boys even knew Bev had a twin brother. There had never been any reason to mention him.

'Okay. Gotta go. Will keep in touch and keep an eye on Dad.' He rang off.

Feeling relieved, Ailsa paid for her meal and crossed the road. For a few moments she stood gazing out at the beach, as if the answer to her future lay in the waves which lapped on the shore. But all she saw were groups of tourists with their inevitable beach tents, while out on the ocean surfers were seeking their next wave, and a couple of jet skies were trying their best to deafen everyone with their noise. It was a normal beach scene. She sighed and turned to walk back to the house.

Nate's words had reassured her, but they didn't solve her problem. *What was she going to do? What did Bob intend to do? Was he serious when he talked of moving out? Was there any future for their marriage or was it really over?*

Once Ailsa was home, she sat in the kitchen for a few moments, her mind going round in circles. She thought about the old woman she'd met the previous day, unable to get her words out of her head. Ruby's remark about Bob struggling with demons had forced her to consider how he must be feeling. Putting her own feelings aside, she picked up her phone and dialled his number.

'Hello?' Bob's voice sounded strange, muted.

'Bob, it's me. I spoke with Nate. Are you all right?'

Bob sighed. 'Why does everyone want to check up on me? I'm fine. I just have a few things to sort through. It's not easy…' His voice trailed off.

'Because we're worried about you. Bob. We love you.'

'I know. I love you too. That doesn't make it any easier. I never intended to hurt you, but I have to do what's right for me.'

'But why now?' she repeated the question she'd asked in Canberra.

There was a long pause, then Bob muttered in a voice so low she could barely hear, 'I couldn't hold on any longer. I'd waited till the boys were settled with their own lives. You, too. You have your teaching, your family. It's my time, Ailsa.'

Ailsa wanted to wail, 'What about me?' but she held back, remembering Ruby's words.

She took a deep breath. 'So that's it, Bob? You want to end twenty-five years of marriage, just like that?'

'I'm sorry, Ailsa, I really am, but I need to find myself, find out who I really am, without…'

'I want to understand, Bob. I really do, but it's so difficult.' She felt an ache in her throat, swallowed back the threatening tears. 'It must be difficult for you, too. I wish there was something I could do.'

'Thanks for trying to understand, Ailsa. I am getting some help. I wish things could be different. I just want you and the boys to be happy, but I can't deny who I am any longer. Perhaps you'll meet someone else one day. I want the best for you, but it can't be with me.'

...it can't be with me.

Those words felt so final, his tone so soft yet resolute.

'Bye then,' was all she could say before she hung up.

The tears came hard, as if they were being squeezed from her heart, any hope she'd held that they could patch things up had been brutally dashed.

Fifteen

Martin sat back from his laptop with a sigh. The shots of Owen were good, but... He checked them again, trying to dismiss the niggle there was something missing. They would do what Will wanted – provide what he'd asked for, the photos he needed for the fundraising. Martin scratched his head. Surfing wasn't about standing on the sand with a surfboard or sitting on it in the shallows. It was about catching a wave, about... movement.

A thrill stirred in his gut, just as it did when he set out on a new photo shoot. What if he could capture the movement of the surfer, the cresting of the wave? He was sure it had been done may times before, but for him it would be a new challenge. Exactly what he needed while he was stuck here in Bellbird Bay.

He sent Will the shots he'd promised, a reply coming through almost immediately.

Thanks a million, mate. Anytime you need a favour, just let me know. Owen's stoked, too. The fundraiser will be held on Friday week at the surf club, entry $50 which includes a beer and burger. Would be great if you could make it. Will.

No chance. Martin closed his laptop and stretched his arms above his head.

It felt good to have a sense of purpose again, but he wanted to delay his research. First, he'd take his camera to the beach and try out a few things. This time he'd make sure he kept well away from Will's surf school. He remembered a wild stretch of beach he and Will used to hitchhike to when they wanted to take more risks. It was along the coast from Bellbird Bay, on the other side of the headland, and just the spot for what he had in mind. He was a bit old to hitchhike. He picked up his phone to call a taxi. If he was going to be here for any length of time, he should hire a car. How long did he intend to stay? It would depend on a variety of things. He'd decide later.

As soon as he stepped out of the taxi and saw the wild ocean filled with surfers, Martin knew he'd made the right decision. This part of the ocean was more open than where Will had his surf school, and a strong wind had blown up providing a swell that sent two-metre waves breaking offshore. He made his way down to the beach and took out his camera.

*

'Want a lift?'

Martin looked up from his phone where he was entering the number of the taxi firm which had dropped him off. A long-haired young guy was stacking a surfboard on the roof of an old rusting panel van, his skin glistening with droplets of seawater. He could have been Martin thirty-four years ago.

'Thanks. I need to get back to Bellbird Bay.'

'No worries. You're not one of those pervs, are you? I saw you with your camera when we were in the water.' He grinned and winked.

'No. I'm a photographer. I usually take shots of exotic locations and thought I'd try something a bit different.'

'Cool. Al.' He held out his hand.

'Martin.' Martin shook it.

'Surf yourself, do you?'

'Used to. Right here, as a matter of fact. Back... probably before you were born.'

'Huh. Well, jump in.' The young man pushed a bundle of clothes, magazines and discarded food wrappers from the passenger seat of the van, hopped into the driver's seat and started the engine. After a few false starts, the van began to move.

'Hey!' Al glanced at Martin. 'Are you the guy who's doing the fundraiser shots for Owen? He said he had some old bloke taking photos, a mate of his dad's.'

'That's me.' Martin grimaced at being called an old bloke. But when he was in is early twenties, he'd considered anyone over twenty-five old, too.

'That what you were doing down there?'

'Sort of.'

Al glanced at him again, a question in his eyes, then he focussed on the road.

'Taking the shots of Owen got me thinking about something I wanted to try. I wanted to check out a few things, the light, the timing – that sort of thing.' He couldn't explain to this young man how the juxtaposition of a wide variety of elements combined to make a good photograph, and surfing photographs were no different.

'You seen what Brian Bielmann and Tim McKenna do? Those guys are fantastic.'

'Right.' Martin made a mental note to check them out. As a newcomer to the field, he couldn't hope to compete, but he always liked a challenge and it would keep him busy.

Al turned on his iPod which was linked to the van's sound system, and for the rest of the trip Martin's ears were subjected to a cacophony of noise. There was no possibility of conversation.

'Thanks,' he said, when they reached the outskirts of town, yelling to make himself heard. 'You can drop me here.'

The van rattled to a halt.

Martin got out, relieved to be away from the noise of Al's music. Here there was just the sound of the ocean and the ping of bellbirds in the trees. It was from this little bird with its grey head and yellow breast the town got its name, back in the days when the area was covered by eucalypt forests. The bird's unique sound – a series of staccato, bell-like notes, followed by a loud "plop" – always reminded him of his childhood. He took a deep breath and started up the boardwalk.

*

It wasn't till he reached the back gate to Bev's place that it occurred to Martin to wonder if Ailsa would be home. Since leaving Al, his head had been filled with images of waves and surfers, and he was eager to check out the photographers the young man had mentioned. He was sure there'd be more of them. Surfing was such a popular sport, not only in Australia, though he'd grown up thinking this was where it all began.

Ailsa had been in the kitchen when he left, but she'd been planning to go out. With a bit of luck, she was still out, and he could sneak into his bedroom undetected and stay there till dinner time.

The house was quiet when he pushed open the door. Breathing a sigh of relief, he grabbed a can of soft drink and a hunk of cheese from the fridge, and an apple from the fruit bowl Bev kept on the kitchen benchtop. Then he headed back to his bedroom and closed the door. Once there, he fired up his laptop and was soon lost in admiration of what fellow photographers had managed to capture. His pulse raced as he anticipated his next step.

Sixteen

Much to Ailsa's relief, Martin had taken to staying out all day. He'd go for an early swim, come back for breakfast then, before her and Bev's day started, head out again with his bag of cameras. It meant she didn't have to try to avoid him. She was still finding it awkward to be in the same room as him. Part of her wished she'd ignored Bev and moved to the B&B, but another part was glad she'd stayed. She enjoyed sharing a glass of wine with her old friend in the evening after dinner, rehashing old times and hearing about Bev's plans for the future of her garden centre.

Ailsa had been here three weeks now and was beginning to feel she could stay for ever. Sitting on Bev's deck, looking out at the ocean was a world away from Canberra and everything it contained. She was picking up her empty mug to take it inside when her phone rang.

'Hi, Liz,' she said, seeing her sister's number on the screen. 'How're things?' Ailsa felt guilty. They hadn't spoken since she left Canberra. She should have called.

'Couldn't be better.'

Ailsa smiled to hear the delight in her sister's voice. She was so glad Liz had found someone after so many years of grieving.

'How are things at Bellbird Bay?'

'Good.' Ailsa chewed on the inside of her cheek. No need to mention Bev's twin brother. 'I've just been enjoying a leisurely coffee on Bev's deck. I wish you could see the view from here. Words won't do it justice.'

'That's why I'm calling. Sam and I have decided to take time off for the Australia Day weekend, and… you'll never guess…'

Ailsa's heart gave a leap. Australia Day was this coming weekend. 'Well, I'm sure you're going to tell me.'

'How would you like a couple of visitors?'

Ailsa didn't answer immediately. She'd love to see Liz here, but where would they sleep? All of the bedrooms in Bev's house were occupied.

Reading her mind, Liz chuckled. 'Don't worry, we're not going to descend on you and your friend. Sam has booked us into a B&B, Friday to Monday. We'll fly up and hire a car. It'll be great to see you and I'm really looking forward to visiting Bellbird Bay. I can't remember the last time I saw the sea and dug my toes into the sand.'

'Oh, it'll be so good to see you.' While Ailsa had been congratulating herself on being so far from Canberra, she had been missing regular contact with her sister. 'How are you going to be able to leave the shop for a whole weekend?' Ailsa knew how much Liz loved the bookshop that had been her whole life after her husband was killed. 'And Marmaduke?' Liz's ginger cat had been her sole companion till she met Sam.

Liz chuckled again. 'You won't believe it, but Sam's daughter-in-law has come to the party. Brooke has been helping me out a bit and offered to mind the store while we're gone. And she and Mitch are going to stay at Sam's…' she hesitated, and Ailsa could picture her blush, '…at our place while we're gone, to look after the animals. Little Abi is thrilled to be able to spend a whole weekend with Marmaduke. She's still hoping to be able to persuade her mum and dad to buy her a cat of her own.'

'Abi, she's Sam's granddaughter, isn't she?'

'Mmm. She's delightful. She's exactly like…' Liz's voice petered away.

Ailsa knew what her sister was thinking. Sam's granddaughter was exactly like the daughter she wished she and her husband had had, but he'd been killed in Afghanistan before they could start a family.

'It'll be lovely to see you,' Ailsa said quickly, hoping to change Liz's mood. 'I'll make a list of things to do, places to see.'

'Not too much, I plan to veg out and catch up with you. We didn't really get a chance to talk much at Christmas.'

'No.' Ailsa was drawn back to the awkwardness of Christmas Day with her mother trying so hard to pretend everything was fine and everyone was happy, her dad bringing out all his hoary old jokes, and Bob acting as if it couldn't be over soon enough. She and Liz had only had those brief minutes outside when she managed to evade her sister's questions. It would be good to be able to spend time with her sister with no family to distract them. Maybe she'd even confide in her. The burden of Bob's confession and its implications for her future had been weighing on her but, apart from the woman she'd met on her walk to the headland, she'd kept it to herself.

After exchanging more details and arranging for Liz and Sam to drop in on their way from the airport, Ailsa hung up with a smile. Liz and Sam were to stay at the B&B run by Ruby Sullivan, the woman who'd befriended her when she fell asleep in the sun, the woman who baked the delicious cakes for Bev's café, the woman who had seemed to see right into Ailsa's head.

When she reached the kitchen with her mug, a notice on the door of the fridge with the photo of the young surfer caught Ailsa's eye. Of course, why hadn't she remembered? Friday, the day Liz was arriving, was the day of the fundraiser at the surf club. Bev had picked up the flier in town and she and Ailsa were planning to attend. It seemed the young man featured on the flier was aiming to participate in some surf championship in Hawaii and the event was being held to raise money for his trip. Ailsa remembered Bev saying he was the son of Martin's old friend, and Martin had reluctantly admitted to taking the photo. It sounded like a fun evening with the promise of a silent auction alongside the usual Friday night meat raffle, and a local group were providing music. Ailsa was sure Liz and Sam would enjoy it, and it would give them a good introduction to Bellbird Bay. Surprisingly, Martin didn't appear keen to attend. When Bev brought up the subject, he'd muttered something about it not being his thing.

Buoyed with the thought of seeing her sister in a few days' time, Ailsa decided to walk up to the headland again. But this time, she'd be more careful and be sure not to fall asleep in the sun. She might even call in on Ruby.

*

The next few days flew past and suddenly it was Friday. Ailsa dressed in one of her new dresses – the pink one – and spent the morning tidying up for Bev. There was no sign of Martin. She hummed to herself as she swept the tile floors and wiped down the kitchen surfaces. She had just finished when she heard a car and, hurrying to throw open the door, saw Liz scrambling out of a blue Hyundai i30 and laughing up at her companion.

'You're here!' She drew her sister into a warm embrace, then turned to shake hands with Sam who gave her a peck on the cheek. 'I'm so glad to see you both.'

'We're glad to be here. The plane was delayed, and we were worried we might not make it.'

Sam chuckled. 'There was no chance of that, Liz. You were just too anxious to get here.'

'He's right. Oh, Ailsa, I want to hear everything.' She tucked her arm in Ailsa's and the two women went inside, followed by Sam.

Once inside, Liz went into raptures over the view and their proximity to the beach. 'Look at it, Sam! Oh, I can't wait to get down there. The water looks so inviting.'

Sam merely smiled, standing behind her with his hands on her shoulders.

They were the picture of happiness.

Ailsa had a pulling sensation in her gut. It was how she and Bob used to be. *What had gone wrong? What had happened to turn them into strangers? Why had he kept his secret for all those years? Why had he chosen now to tell her?* She forced a smile to her face as they turned back to face her. 'I'm sure you're ready for something to eat and drink. Tea? Coffee? Something cold?' She took three mugs from the cupboard.

'Tea for me – preferably herbal – and Sam will have coffee. Right, honey?' Liz looked up at him, her eyes filled with love.

Ailsa flinched. She should have remembered this was how it would be. It was why she hadn't stopped off to visit them on her way here. But it was good to see Liz. She was feeling more relaxed here and she was willing to put up with their loved-up attitude to be able to spend time with her sister. She was even willing to put up with the inevitable questions. Ailsa knew she couldn't fob off Liz for ever.

Sam nodded. 'Black, please. Do you need any help?'

'No, I'm good.' Ailsa filled the electric jug and the coffee maker and turned on both. 'Lemon and ginger tea do?' she asked Liz.

'Perfect. I hope our B&B has a view like this.' She gazed out the window, her eyes feasting on the wide stretch of sand and the white capped waves.

'If you're staying at Ruby Sullivan's, it has. Her place is further up the boardwalk. You can walk to it from here.'

'You've met her?'

'I have.' Ailsa brushed over her meeting with the woman. 'It seems everyone knows Ruby. According to Bev, she's quite a character. Of indeterminate age, she appears to have lived here for ever – and she makes the most delicious cakes.' Ailsa opened a cake tin and slid out a strawberry flan. 'This is one of hers. Bev sells them at the café.'

'Wow!' Liz said as Ailsa cut three large slices. 'Looks like you chose well, sweetheart.' Her eyes met Sam's again.

Ailsa looked away. 'Let's sit on the deck.'

They carried their drinks and cake out to the deck where they had a perfect view of the beach and the ocean.

Ailsa was in the process of explaining about the fundraiser that evening and suggesting they all attend, when she was interrupted by the arrival of the tall blond photographer.

Martin looked stunned to see Ailsa and two others sitting on the deck, but Sam rose, his hand outstretched. 'It's Martin Cooper, isn't it? It's been a long time.'

Seventeen

As he climbed the steps to the back deck, Martin could see Ailsa sitting there with two strangers. He had a vague recollection of Bev or her saying something about her sister coming to visit for the weekend. He hadn't paid much attention, glad they weren't to be staying here. He was about to push past with a nod in their direction when the man stood up, hand outstretched. 'It's Martin Cooper, isn't it? It's been a long time.'

Martin blinked, took a closer look, his hand rising of its own volition to shake the stranger's. But he wasn't a stranger. He and Sam Walker had crossed paths a few times over the years, though not for some time. What the hell was he doing here in Bellbird Bay sitting drinking coffee on Bev's deck?

'Sam Walker,' he said, thinking fast. What was Walker doing these days? It was a long time since they'd both been covering trouble spots in the Middle East, Martin as a freelance photographer, and Sam as a reporter for one of the nationals. Was he still in the loop? Would the word of Martin's alleged offence have reached him?

'This is Bev's brother, Martin,' Ailsa said, interrupting his thoughts. 'Martin, this is my sister, Liz, and… you and Sam know each other?' She looked from one to the other in surprise.

'Yeah, it must have been…' he shrugged his camera bag further up his shoulder and dragged a hand over his hair, '…what? Twenty-five years? What are you up to these days?' In other words – *are you still in the news game, have you heard the latest about me?*

'Oh, gave that away some time back. Now I edit a small-town newspaper in country New South Wales. That's where I met this lovely lady who changed my life.' He nodded towards the curvy auburn-haired woman sitting next to Ailsa.

'Right.' So maybe he didn't know. Martin exhaled.

Sam chuckled. 'What about you? Last I heard you were lost in the wilds of the Amazon or on the Ivory Coast taking impossible shots of places no other photographer dared to reach.'

Martin's gut clenched and a bead of moisture ran down his back.

'You wouldn't catch me taking risks like that,' Sam continued. 'I leave it to the younger guys these days. Happy to stay out of the limelight.'

'Wise man.' Martin repositioned his bag and leant one hand on the back of a chair. 'I grew up here in Bellbird Bay. Came back for a bit of R&R. You know how it is,' he said, hoping that would satisfy Sam.

The other man nodded.

'Well, need to get on. Good to see you again, Sam. No doubt we'll meet again if you're sticking around.'

'Look forward to it. We have a lot of catching up to do.'

Martin left without replying. Catching up with Sam Walker was not on his agenda, though he had to admit it would be good to have a yarn about old times over a beer or two. They had been tough times, never knowing if the next moment would be your last.

Back in his bedroom, Martin unpacked his cameras and fired up his laptop, eager to see the results of his morning's work. This morning, he'd tried different lighting and had been pleased with the effect. Now he had to discover what it looked like on the screen.

But he couldn't get Sam Walker out of his mind. Who'd have imagined the old newshound would turn up here in Bellbird Bay – with the sister of Bev's old friend? They'd both been in their twenties when they'd crossed paths in a war zone, intent on surviving one more day to report on the conflict. They were heady times. A lot of smoking and drinking and living in the present. It seemed like Sam had given it all away, settled down. Hard to do after the rush of excitement danger brought with it. Wasn't he bored? But he had a woman, and hadn't Martin heard something about him being married back in the day? He shook his head.

Martin settled down to studying the shots he'd taken that morning, then to comparing them to those he'd been admiring, He was getting there. He leant back in the chair, almost knocking it over – it wasn't designed for someone his size. If he kept going at this rate, he'd soon be ready for the big time. And, in his mind, that meant covering the championships young Owen was headed to in Hawaii.

He was still sitting there, considering his next move, wondering if he dared venture out into the world of freelance photography again, albeit in a different field, if it was worth the risk, if he still had it, when he heard a gentle knock.

'Come in.'

Bev's face appeared round the edge of the door. 'Since we're going to Will's fundraiser tonight, I'm not planning on cooking dinner. Are you still determined not to go? He was your best mate growing up. You really should make an effort to support him and Owen.'

Damn Bev! She'd always had a way of making him feel guilty and that hadn't changed with time. He'd made up his mind to boycott the event, sure it would be filled with all the people he wanted to avoid, the ones he'd grown up with, who'd want to know what he was doing now, why he was back in Bellbird Bay. But his sister was right. He owed it to Will.

'Maybe…' he began.

'Good. You can ride with Ailsa and me.'

Shit! He hadn't counted on that. 'No, it's okay, I can make my own way.' Martin was glad he had finally hired a car. The little yellow Mini Moke had appealed to him when he saw it sitting outside a local garage sporting a *For Hire* sign. It would be no good in the city or for making long trips, but it was ideal for cruising around Bellbird Bay in the summer, as long as he remembered how hot the metal sides became in the sun. Driving it took years off his age and helped him forget why he was here. 'I may want to leave earlier than you do.'

'Or later.' Bev grinned. 'Okay. We'll see you there. Remember it starts at seven.'

'Right.' Martin sighed. He could see he wasn't going to get out of this. If he didn't turn up, he wouldn't put it past Bev to come back for him. 'I'll be there.'

'Good. Ailsa's sister and her partner are going too. She says he and you are old friends.'

'Not exactly and it was a long time ago.'

'Well, you'll be able to catch up – and you'll know a lot of the guys there. Half of our old year at Bellbird High are still in town, plus those of the teachers who are still alive and kicking.'

Martin groaned inwardly. That's what he was afraid of. But now he'd told Bev he'd be there, he couldn't get out of it.

*

The surf club was bursting at the seams when Martin walked in at seven-thirty. He'd decided if he arrived late, after the event started, he'd be less conspicuous, might even be able to slip in unnoticed. He was wrong. As soon as he reached the top of the stairs, Will caught his eye. It was as if he'd been waiting for him.

'Here's the man who took the amazing photos of Owen,' he said to everyone within earshot, throwing an arm around Martin's shoulders. He sounded as if he'd been drinking since lunchtime.

'Okay, mate. Leave it. Okay?' Embarrassed, Martin slid out of his grasp. 'My sister should be here somewhere,' he said, in an attempt to avoid the crowd surrounding Will and Owen, some of whom he recognised from his schooldays, though most looked as if they'd undergone a face transplant and gained around ten kilos. He and Will seemed to be among the few who had taken care of themselves over the intervening years.

'She's over there.' Will's shoulders drooped, but he gestured towards the door leading out to the deck where Martin could see Bev and Ailsa standing with Liz and Sam. Deciding they were the lesser of two evils – one of the women in the group around Will, who Martin didn't recognise but who appeared to know him, was making eyes at him – he moved towards them, grabbing his complimentary beer on the way.

'Quite a crowd,' he said, when he reached them. He took a sip of beer.

'Will's a popular guy around here,' Bev said. 'As well as running the surf school, he helps out with a number of local charities, and people rallied around him when he lost Evan, then Dee. You can't have forgotten what Bellbird Bay is like.'

'Sounds a bit like Granite Springs,' Liz said, as Sam nodded. 'I was grieving when I arrived there, and the community took me to its heart.'

'I suppose all small towns are similar,' Sam said. 'It's part of their charm.'

And one of the reasons I left. But Martin merely smiled and nodded. The musical group was tuning up, and the chatter was becoming louder. *How long would he have to stay?*

While the group played, the crowd continued to chat loudly around them, and a young man – no doubt one of Owen's mates – approached them selling raffle tickets and pointing them in the direction of the silent auction. Martin bought a ticket to be polite but shook his head about the auction.

'What do you think?' Sam asked Liz, before they and Ailsa wandered off in the direction the young man indicated.

'Glad you came?' Bev asked, when they were alone.

'Not really. It takes me back…'

'You used to enjoy this sort of crush.' Bev grinned.

'Been on my own too long.' Martin gazed around the room. It looked different tonight from when he'd had lunch here with Will and Owen. Now the room was filled with groups of old and young, all dressed to the nines and out to have a good time. He knew what Bev meant. When he was seventeen and eighteen, he'd have revelled in an occasion like this, been the life and soul of the party. He'd changed. He was no longer that man. That's where he and Will differed. It seemed to him that, despite what life had thrown at him, his old friend had managed to retain his sense of fun.

'Some great items at the auction. You should check it out,' Sam said, when the three returned, pushing their way back through the crowd. 'Liz and I bid on a meal at *The Bay Bistro* and Ailsa on a surf lesson.'

A surf lesson? Martin stared at Ailsa, imagining her in a bikini, paddling out into the ocean, then he dragged his eyes away from her, afraid his thoughts would show on his face. What was he thinking? If she was interested in surfing, he could give her a lesson. Screw Will. He must remember to ask Bev about his old surfboard. He'd become so engrossed in photographing the surfers, he'd all but forgotten the joy he'd experienced when he entered the surf again himself.

As if reading his mind, Bev said, 'Martin's old surfboard is in my shed. I couldn't bear to throw it out, too many memories.' She gave Martin a look. 'It's there if you want it, Martin. I should have said earlier.'

'Thanks.'

The music stopped, and Will strode up to the mike, Owen standing hesitantly behind him. 'Welcome everyone. It's great to see so many of you here tonight supporting Owen. As you know, things haven't been easy for us over the past few years and surfing has been what saved us. For me, the school, and for this lad surfing itself. He's managed to surpass what I achieved when I was his age and has qualified for the championships in Hawaii.'

At this there was a loud applause and voices yelling, 'Good on you, Owen.'

'Thanks.' Will grinned and held up his hands for silence. 'Well, I have to tell you we've outdone ourselves and raised more than we need to get him there. So, any extra will be donated to local charities.'

There was another cheer.

'I don't want to take any more of your time now. The results of the meat raffle and the silent auction will be announced at the end of the evening, so there's still time to get your ticket or put in your bids. Remember, it's all for a good cause – several good causes.'

There was laughter.

'So, enjoy the rest of your evening, and thanks again for your support.'

Will and Owen moved away, and the group resumed playing.

'Seems like a genuine guy,' Sam said. 'You and he are mates?' he asked Martin.

'They were inseparable all through school,' Bev said. 'Competed in everything. There was little to choose between them, though I always did think Martin was the best surfer.' She tilted her head to the side and regarded her brother quizzically.

'So, you left, and he stayed?' Sam asked.

'That's about the size of it. I felt there was more to life than spending it on a surfboard.' Martin still did, so why did he feel envious of his old friend? Why did he feel Will had done more with his life here in Bellbird Bay than he had, becoming a famous photographer? It didn't make sense.

Eighteen

Ailsa watched Martin slip away, his tall blond head weaving its way through the crowd till he disappeared. It had been interesting to see him here, to see him greeted warmly by people he'd grown up with, to see his discomfort as they praised him and told him it was good to see him again. But he didn't appear pleased to see *them*. It was as if he didn't want any reminders of his youth, of living in Bellbird Bay, as if he was embarrassed. Ailsa didn't understand.

'This is fun.' Liz's voice brought her back to the present. 'Thanks for bringing us along. Look, they're about to draw the raffle and announce the results of the auction.'

Ailsa glanced towards where the group had stopped playing again, and Will had resumed his position with the mike.

'Here I am again.' He chuckled. 'The evening is almost over, and I hope you've all enjoyed it as much as I have.'

There was a loud applause and some whistles and catcalls.

Will smiled. 'We have to thank *Bay Meats* for their generous donation of the meat tray, and the winner is...' he paused dramatically and closed his eyes as a woman held up a hat containing the raffle tickets. He dipped his hand into the hat and brought it out to hold up a pink ticket. '...pink ticket number forty-six.' He gazed around the room. There was silence, then a yell of delight, and a plump woman with short blonde hair wearing a low-cut dress wobbled up to accept the large tray of meat.

'And now the results of the auction.' Will took a sheet of paper from a man standing beside him and started to read out the items followed by the winning bids and the names of the successful bidders.

Ailsa let her mind wander till she felt someone nudge her. Bev was yelling in her ear. 'It's you, Ailsa. You placed the winning bid for a surf lesson.'

'I did?' Ailsa couldn't believe it. She hadn't expected to win. She didn't even know if she wanted a surf lesson. She'd body surfed on the south coast as a child and teenager but, living in Canberra, had never spent long enough by the beach to consider learning to surf. *Was it too late? Was she too old? It seemed she was about to find out.*

'Ailsa McNeil,' Will said again. 'If the lady's here, can she come to chat with me later so we can arrange a time for her lesson?'

Bev nudged Ailsa again, forcing her to put up her hand. She felt foolish, as if she was back in school. Everyone cheered. Ailsa blushed.

'You'll love it,' Bev said. 'And Will's the best.'

Ailsa swallowed. Well, she supposed there was a first time for everything. She glared at Liz who had encouraged her to put in the bid, telling her it was for a good cause, and she wasn't likely to win.

Her sister grinned and gave her a thumbs-up.

There were two more announcements, then the music started up again and people began to drift off while the bar remained open for the hardened drinkers.

Ailsa and Bev decided it was time to leave but before they did, Bev steered Ailsa towards Will and introduced her to him.

'So, you're the lucky lady,' he said, handing her a card. 'Here's my number. Give me a call and we'll get you set up. I conduct group lessons on the beach every day, but your bid entitles you to a private lesson, so I'll need to book you in.'

'Thanks,' she said, taking his card and stuffing it into her bag.

'Don't forget now,' he called after her. 'Bev and Martin can vouch for me.'

Martin! Ailsa was glad he'd already left. She wasn't sure why, but she didn't want him to hear about her taking a surf lesson. She'd have to ensure she booked a time when he wasn't likely to be on the beach. The thought of him seeing her in a swimsuit was embarrassing. She blushed remembering how he looked when he returned from his morning swim, water beading on his skin, his face gleaming from the exertion. He'd gained muscle since he was nineteen and was seriously hot.

*

Next morning, Ailsa fingered the card bearing the surf school logo and Will's mobile number, then put it back onto the bedside table. Last night had gone well. Liz and Sam had enjoyed themselves, and she'd had fun, too.

She rose and peeked out the window to see another glorious day. Before they parted last night they'd arranged for Liz and Sam to join her and Bev for breakfast. It was doubtful if Martin would join them too, though Sam had said he'd welcome the opportunity to catch up with him for a yarn about the times they were both in the firing line.

As Ailsa expected, and to Sam's disappointment, there was no sign of Martin when Liz and Sam arrived. Breakfast was delicious croissants which Bev had brought back from the café filled with ham and cheese, and washed down with coffee for Sam and peppermint tea for the three women.

'Wow! If this – and the strawberry flan we had yesterday – is a sample, I can't wait to see your café, Bev,' Liz exclaimed, pushing herself back from the table.

'It's nothing to do with me, all thanks to Cleo and Ruby.'

'The same Ruby who runs the B&B?' Sam asked.

'The very one. She's a marvel.'

'Well, it's certainly a very comfortable place to stay,' Liz said.

'You were lucky she had a vacancy. She's normally fully booked.' Bev smiled.

'I think she said there had been a cancellation,' Sam said. 'And I didn't realise it was so close to here. We had a lovely walk down this morning. Almost makes me wish we lived closer to the sea.' He sniffed as if he could smell the sea air.

'Well, I'll show you the rest of Bellbird Bay after breakfast and you can compare it to Granite Springs,' Ailsa chuckled. She was planning to take Liz and Sam to the garden centre today and have lunch in the cafe, but before then, they'd go for a walk together to explore the town.

*

'I saw Bob,' Liz said.

The two women had left Sam to his own devices and were enjoying a coffee in *The Bay Café* across the road from the beach.

Ailsa's stomach clenched. 'Where?'

In Canberra. I was visiting Mum and Dad and had popped over to Belconnen to do some shopping. We bumped into each other at the mall.'

'Did you speak?' Apart a few texts to check how she was, Ailsa hadn't heard from her husband since she'd called him. She winced at the memory.

'A bit. He didn't have much to say, but he did ask how you were.'

'And how did he look?' Despite the lack of communication and his announcement their marriage was at an end, Ailsa still had feelings for Bob. She wanted to know he was really okay. His texts had been brief, the last one saying he was fine and would be in touch.

Liz thought for a few moments then said, 'Haunted is the word. There's something bothering him, Ailsa, something more than the fact you're up here. He's changed. He's not the man he used to be. Something's happened to him.'

Ailsa gripped her cup tightly. This was the nightmare she'd been living with for the past year, the reason she'd left, taken time out. This, and the fact she'd been unable to do anything to help, to get to the bottom of what was troubling him. Now she knew, but was powerless to help him. 'He didn't give you any indication…?' she asked, knowing what the answer would be.

Liz shook her head. 'He was pretty tight-lipped about himself. I asked about the boys, and he was more forthcoming about them. They seem to be managing okay.'

'They are.' Ailsa smiled. She was in touch with both Nate and Pat. They texted her regularly and posted on Facebook and Instagram daily. She was fully *au fait* with their lives, perhaps almost too much so, given some of their posts. 'They're a good pair. Pat's promising to come up for a weekend when he has one free.' She shook her head, wondering if it would ever happen. Her older son seemed to spend his weekends in a never-ending series of social engagements, his relationship with Vee having done nothing to stem them. He showed no signs of settling down. Nate, too, seemed to lead a whirlwind social life. Ailsa comforted herself with the reminder they were young and students. They had the rest of their lives to be sensible.

'You did good there, you and Bob. They're a credit to you.'

'Thanks.' That was one thing she and Bob had got right, Ailsa thought, then chastised herself. They'd got a lot right – a good marriage for over twenty years until… This time away had been intended for her to think things through, to try to work out what the future held. But here she was. She'd been here for over three weeks now and was no further forward in her thinking – or decision making. Would she go back to Canberra at the end of the two months or decide to stay away for good? Now felt like the right time to confide in her sister, despite how fearful she felt at uttering the words aloud.

She took a deep breath and cradled her cup in both hands. 'I have something to tell you, Liz,' she said, unconsciously repeating Bob's words to her.

By the time Ailsa had finished they were both in tears.

'Oh, my dear!' Liz pulled Ailsa into a warm hug. 'What a shock. How do you feel about it?'

'I'm really not sure to be honest. But I'm glad Bob confided in me.'

'Poor Bob,' Liz said. 'All this time…'

'I know.'

'But he says he still loves you?'

'Mmm.'

'And you had no idea?'

'None.' Ailsa shook her head. Since Bob told her he was gay, she'd thought about this so often. He'd always seemed more comfortable with her women friends than their husbands. But a faint memory nagged at the back of Ailsa's mind. It had been when Pat was a toddler, and she was pregnant with Nate. Bob had become friendly with one of the dads at the childcare group Pat attended. It was unusual for him, and at first Ailsa had been pleased to see him take an interest in another of the dads. But somehow the friendship hadn't sat right with her. She'd been glad when Aiden – that had been his name – and his family had moved interstate. They'd never heard from them again. At least, she hadn't. Now she wondered about Aiden. Had there been more to Bob's relationship with him? Had they kept in touch? She'd never know.

'What are you going to do?'

'I don't know.'

'You can always come to us.'

Ailsa shook her head again. 'No, Bob says he'll move out of the house, but I can't imagine staying there on my own. Oh, Liz! I love Canberra. I love our life there. But I feel everything I knew and believed has been thrown into disarray. It's as if I'm living in a nightmare, as if I'll wake up and everything will be as it was. But it won't, will it?'

'No, honey. I can't imagine... Bob's always seemed... How...?'

'I still love him, love the man I married, the man I thought he was. I suppose he still is the same man, but...' Tears filled her eyes again. 'I'm so glad you came up, that I could tell you. It's been hell keeping it to myself.' She didn't count Ruby.

'The boys don't know?'

'Not yet. Bob said he'd tell them when he was ready – whenever that might be. He'd been acting so strangely. At one stage I thought...' Her voice broke. 'I thought he might have been sick or having an affair.'

'Bob wouldn't.'

'No, I realise that now. But I also realise how depressed he's been. I bought these books and he's displayed all the symptoms. I was too stupid to realise it, too focussed on my own feelings.'

'You mustn't blame yourself. You have nothing to reproach yourself with.'

'Thanks, Liz.' Ailsa put her hand on her sister's. 'I feel better now I've told you.'

'And don't forget. We're here for you. Sam and me. And you have a good friend in Bev.'

'I know.' Ailsa sighed. Everyone was being so kind to her. Even Martin Cooper had seemed friendlier last night at the fundraiser. Ailsa wondered what made her think of him. Was she so shallow she'd latch onto the first man she met after her husband's announcement? She thought of Bob expressing the desire for her to be happy, the hope she might find someone else. But she wasn't ready to do that yet, and not with Martin Cooper. No matter how much his presence here might affect her, she couldn't risk the hurt that would inevitably result from getting involved with someone like him.

Nineteen

Martin had headed out to the beach early, intent on avoiding Ailsa's sister and Sam Walker who he'd heard were coming to breakfast. The tension of recent weeks was gradually leaving him as Bellbird Bay worked its magic. Despite the years he'd yearned for his eighteenth birthday so he could leave, his native town held some good memories. Last night had been a surprise. He'd been astounded how many people remembered him, wanted to shake his hand, congratulate him on his achievements. It had been an embarrassment. If they'd known the truth, they'd no doubt have shunned him – or pitied him which would have been worse.

But this morning, the sun was shining, the surf was up, and he felt good. Martin packed his old surfboard into the back of the Mini Moke and set off for the surf beach where he'd been working for the past few days. He'd found his old board in Bev's shed, just as she'd said. It had been stored in its bag and came out as good as new. He felt as if he had a new lease of life as he paddled out alongside the younger surfers.

But, as the sun rose higher in the sky, he realised he'd had enough. Gone were the days when he could stay out there all day waiting to ride in on the next big wave, then do it all again, and again. He made his way up the beach, packed the board back into the Moke, and drove into town, intending to find somewhere to have coffee.

He had parked and was wandering along Main Street, humming to himself when, as he was passing the offices of *The Bellbird Bugle*, a figure came out the door and almost knocked him down.

He had left Bev's early to avoid Sam Walker. *What was he doing here?*

'Martin! This is a stroke of luck,' Sam said. 'I've been chatting to the guys here at *The Bugle*. These small-town papers are pretty much alike, and I wanted to connect with the editor here, but he's out on a story. Maybe we can catch up later. I'm glad to have bumped into you. We didn't get the chance to talk last night. I was about to find somewhere for coffee. Join me?'

Martin couldn't come up with a good excuse on the spur of the moment. And he'd been on the lookout for a café himself. He forced a smile. 'Sure.'

They walked along barely speaking till Sam pointed to a sign which offered coffee, cakes and shakes. *The Greedy Gecko* was situated between a newsagent and a small gallery. 'How about this, or do you have somewhere better to recommend?'

'No, I haven't been back here for years. I'm pretty much a stranger. This looks fine.' The café hadn't existed back when he lived here, but neither had half the town. Since his last visit, the sleepy seaside town had become a tourist mecca.

They found a table, ordered coffee and sat back.

'So,' Sam said. 'How's life been treating you? It's good to see you again. I had no idea Bev Cooper was your sister. Coincidence, huh?'

'Yeah, coincidence.' *A bloody rotten one.* But he was here and should try to be polite, make conversation. After all, he and Sam had shared some hairy moments in a war zone. 'You went into the political scene when you came back, didn't you?' Martin recalled hearing something about how Sam Walker became a big name in Canberra. Hadn't he even hosted a programme on television?

'For my sins.' Sam pushed a hand through his hair. 'It was fine for a bit. I was married back then, you know. But she couldn't hack the travel.' He gazed into space. 'It probably wouldn't have lasted anyway. We were different people. Anyway, I burnt out. Now I've given politics away and edit a local newspaper in Granite Springs. It's a small country town about an hour or so from Canberra,' he said, seeing a puzzled expression on Martin's face. 'We mentioned it last night. That's where I met Liz. She's the best thing that's happened to me. What about you? Still a rolling stone?'

Martin hesitated, the arrival of their coffees giving him time to work out how he was going to reply. He took a sip, then put the cup down and stared into the hot liquid.

'It's a moot point. I guess the word hasn't reached you yet. But I'm *persona non grata* at the moment,' he said, a bitter taste in his mouth as he remembered his last meeting with his editor.

'How so?' Sam picked up his coffee and took a long drink.

Martin looked across the table at the man who'd shared some of his scariest moments. Maybe he'd been wrong about him. Maybe he would understand.

'It's like this,' he said. 'I was shafted by another photographer. He claimed copyright to the last lot of photos I took. No idea how he got access to them. Became *persona non grata* with all the magazines I've been working with. Oh, I know,' he said, seeing Sam about to speak and holding up one hand. 'I've spoken with an attorney, but it could take years to get any kind of result.' He grimaced. 'Made a fool of myself with a woman, too.' He gave a false laugh. 'You'd think I'd have seen it coming, but I was I was well and truly conned. She was only out for what she could get, was quick enough to move on when my career hit the skids and a better prospect appeared on the scene. Bloody Gareth Elliott.' He winced at the memory of the handsome movie star who'd ousted him in Sofia's affections. 'And to think I was considering marrying the woman.' He rubbed a hand over his cropped hair, still unable to believe how he'd been played.

'Rough. Is there anything you can do?'

Martin shook his head again. 'The great Martin Cooper was taken for a fool and screwed up. No one wants my photographs. No one trusts me. I came back here to… to regroup I suppose you might say. I had nowhere else to go. I knew Bev would take me in. But…' he sighed, '…I can't stay here for ever. I need to find a way back, a way to regain something of my self-esteem – and I haven't given up.' He looked up to see an expression of sympathy on Sam's face.

'Sometimes it's best to turn the page, do something completely different. When I…'

Martin held up his hand again. 'I know what you're going to say, but taking photos is what I do. I thought I could give it away, but I was wrong. My camera is part of me, an extension of my arm. I don't know how I could live without it.'

'People are important, too.'

Martin snorted. 'People are what got me into this mess. I can't trust myself with people.'

'What gives with you and Ailsa? Is there a history there?'

'What?' *Where had that come from?* It was as if Sam had stuck a needle into an open wound.

'It's just… I noticed last night… you both seemed to be at pains to avoid each other, and I thought I detected something. Sorry if I've got it wrong.'

'You have, very wrong.' Martin had no intention of replaying his first meeting with Ailsa.

'Sorry. I didn't mean to pry. I'd actually hoped to have the chance to catch up. It's a long time since I had the opportunity to rehash those hectic days. We were both lucky to come out relatively unscathed, though I guess you had the nightmares, too?'

Martin nodded. How could he forget? But he'd managed to put it behind him. 'A lot has happened since then. I guess for you, too.'

'Yeah. But they were good days, the mateship, the danger, then the relief to discover we were still alive. We were a protected species, not like the military. Those poor sods didn't stand a chance.' He shook his head.

'You seem to have got over it. A new life, a new woman.' As he spoke, Martin wondered if it could happen to him, too. Could he start again, find a new life, even a woman who might stick with him, who didn't have another agenda? Unbidden, the image of Ailsa rose up behind his eyes. Had he been too quick to dismiss Sam's comments?

Twenty

All too soon, Ailsa was saying goodbye to her sister, hugging Liz before waving her and Sam off.

'Sorry to see them go?' Bev asked. Being Australia Day, the garden centre didn't open till ten, so she was able to be there to farewell them.

'Yes,' Ailsa sighed. It had been good to see Liz, to talk with her, and she felt better now she'd confided in her sister. But she still didn't know what she intended to do about her future. She knew she had to accept Bob's decision their marriage was finished, but what did that mean for her? What would she do without him, without the security her marriage provided?

'What will you do today?' Bev asked. 'Do you want to help out at the garden centre again?'

'Thanks for the offer, but I'm not sure I was a lot of help. I heard there was going to be some music and a barbecue near the surf club. I thought I might wander down and have a look. And if I'm going to take up this surf lesson, I need to find a more substantial swimsuit, something suitable for surfing – if the shops are open.'

'Sassy will be open. She's across from the surf club and stocks everything anyone would need for swimming, surfing or just sitting on the beach. You'll find what you need there.'

'Thanks.' Ailsa still wasn't sure she really wanted to learn to surf, but Liz had encouraged her, telling her she only lived once and might never have another chance.

She and Bev had a cup of tea together, before Bev headed off, leaving Ailsa alone. As she prepared to leave, she thought about what her sister had whispered to her before she left.

'What gives with you and Martin?' she'd asked.

Ailsa's eyes had widened in surprise. 'Nothing.'

'Well, he likes you.'

'What makes you think that? He avoids me whenever he can.' But the faint memory of his lips on hers all those years ago made her quiver. She had no business feeling like that. She was still married to Bob, even if he didn't want to be married any longer, if their marriage was all but over.

Liz tapped her nose. 'From one who knows. Sam thinks so, too.'

'Sam?' Liz and Sam had been talking about her and Martin, speculating. Despite the warmth of the morning sun, Ailsa shivered.

'He met Martin in town yesterday and they had quite a chat.' Liz chuckled at the expression on Ailsa's face.

Ailsa wondered exactly what Martin and Sam had chatted about. Martin had joined them for dinner last night but there had been no indication the two men had met earlier. Sam hadn't said anything at lunch either. Ailsa hated secrets, especially when it appeared she might have been discussed. She supposed she could ask Martin, but what would she say? She could hardly ask him if he'd told Sam he liked her. No, it was too ridiculous. Liz was teasing her. Despite what Bob wanted, Ailsa wasn't ready to make a new life for herself, not yet.

Deciding to put it out of her mind, she brushed her hair, checked herself in the mirror, smiling at how her new blue dress hung without clinging. She slung her bag across her shoulder, picked up her hat and set off.

*

It seemed everyone had the same idea. As soon as Ailsa reached the end of the boardwalk, she found herself jostled by groups of locals and tourists, all determined to find a good position from which to listen to the music. The air was filled with the aroma of burnt sausages and fried onions from the barbecue manned by members of the local Lions club. As Ailsa settled herself in a vacant spot on the grass, the microphone crackled, reminding her of Friday night, but this time it was the local mayor, not Will, who stood on a dais holding it.

'Welcome to Bellbird Bay Australia Day celebrations. First, I'd like to welcome you on behalf of the traditional owners of the land,' the large, red-faced man said. His open-necked white shirt was already showing signs of perspiration. He wiped his brow. 'Today we are fortunate to have with us our own Bellbird musicians – groups with whom I know you are all familiar – to help us celebrate. Our friends from the Lions club are providing their usual barbecue with all proceeds to go to the Surf Lifesavers, and later in the afternoon our local indigenous dance group will treat us to a display. Now I'll turn over to The Sandgropers to start the proceedings.'

Everyone applauded as three young men and a girl took his place and started to play a well-known country music melody which the girl sang. Ailsa settled down to enjoy the music.

After a while, she began to feel hungry, the smell of cooking tempting her to the barbecue where, after standing in line, she bought a roll filled with sausage and fried onions. Deciding not to push through the crowd to return to her spot, she found a free bench close to the esplanade from where she could still hear the music. She had finished her lunch and was crushing the napkin it had been wrapped in when a shadow came between her and the sun.

'I thought it was you.'

Ailsa screwed up her eyes to see Ruby Sullivan regarding her from under a wide-brimmed straw hat. 'Hello.'

'My recent guests were your sister and her husband, weren't they?' Ruby said, sitting down beside Ailsa on the bench, seemingly ready for a long conversation.

'That's right.' Ailsa fidgeted, wondering how she could leave without appearing rude.

'Lovely couple. You don't look alike.' She peered at Ailsa. 'But sisters often don't. I sensed she'd experienced a deep grief, but has finally turned the corner and found happiness again.'

Ailsa shivered. *How did she know?*

'But you are still troubled. I think you may have a surprise in store – maybe more than one.' She paused, then, 'Did I see Bev's brother back in town? He always had a cheery word for an old woman like me, then he was gone. Left a lot of broken hearts behind him. What a good-looking young man. He and Will Rankin were like two peas in a pod.'

Ailsa let her ramble on. It was like a stream of consciousness. She closed her eyes and stopped listening after a while, content to let the old woman's chatter blend with the music to provide a background to her thoughts.

Suddenly Ruby's words broke into her reflections. 'Have you spoken to your husband again?'

What business was it of hers?

Ailsa rose. 'I'm sorry, I have to go. It's been nice to see you again,' she lied as she rushed off.

Fuming so much she didn't look where she was going, Ailsa tripped on a raised piece of paving and almost fell. Two strong hands gripped her, preventing her from falling. She looked up. Martin Cooper was staring down at her, a wry smile on his face.

Twenty-one

'Steady there.' Martin reached out to catch the woman before he realised who it was. For a moment he enjoyed the touch of her soft skin on his fingers before she pulled away and he saw Ailsa's face suffused with a red stain.

'It's you!' she accused, as if he'd deliberately set out to embrace her. Then she seemed to regain her composure. 'Sorry, and thanks. I should have been looking where I was going.'

'No problem.' Martin didn't know what to say next. They'd barely spoken in all the time he'd been at Bev's, and when they had it had been in the company of other people – except for one occasion. Did she remember their first meeting the way he did? Or was he imagining the frisson between them? Was the awkwardness he sensed merely the result of the intervening years and all that had happened to them? Suddenly he was bursting with the desire to find out.

'You're shaken,' he said, taking her by the arm and feeling her resist his touch. 'Why don't you let me buy you coffee?'

'No... yes... thanks.' Ailsa appeared flustered. She was looking particularly attractive in a loose blue garment clinging to her curves in the soft breeze, reminding him of how she'd felt in his arms only a few moments ago.

Martin glanced around, spying a café not far away. 'How about there?' he said, pointing to the sign, *The Bay Café*. He guided the still trembling Ailsa to a table close to the esplanade and ordered two coffees, one black, one cappuccino which he thought he'd seen her drink at Bev's. The two women seemed to prefer their herbal teas, but he judged this called for coffee – and he had no idea what sort of herbal tea to order, or if they even served them here.

'Better?' Martin asked, when their coffee had been served, and Ailsa had drunk half of hers, her cup clasped in both hands. They hadn't spoken since they arrived.

Ailsa nodded and put down her cup. 'Thanks. I'm not usually so clumsy.'

'Hey, it's okay. We all have shaky moments.' As soon as he spoke, he saw he'd said the wrong thing. 'I mean…' he started, trying to retrieve the situation.

'I wasn't shaky. I was in a hurry to get away from someone, and the sun was in my eyes.'

Martin looked back to where they had come from, but there was no one in sight who might have posed a threat to a woman on her own. He raised one eyebrow.

'Ruby Sullivan.'

Martin chuckled. 'What's old Ruby been up to now?' He knew Ruby, everyone did. She was an institution here in Bellbird Bay with her wonderful cakes and her encyclopaedic knowledge of the town's history. But she could be a bit overwhelming.

'She… she became too inquisitive, asking personal questions about things that were none of her business.'

Ah! Martin guessed Ruby had been interested to know exactly what he wanted to find out. Where was Ailsa's husband and why wasn't he here with her?

'So you left?'

'Yes. I was angry and… I tripped.' She glared at Martin as if it had been his fault.

'Okay. Point taken. Now, how about we discuss something else? How are you finding Bellbird Bay? Is this your first time here?' Martin was surprised he hadn't asked her those questions before, but he'd been intent on avoiding her.

'I have been here once before,' she said, stirring her coffee. 'When the boys were little.' She gazed into space. 'The town's changed a lot. You seem to be well known,' she said, changing the subject. It was as if she didn't want to talk about herself. 'If last night was anything to go by, you're a town hero.'

'Hardly.' But Martin had to admit it might have seemed that way to a stranger. 'I was at school with most of them. They stayed and I left. End of.' He was more interested to hear about her.

'And Will, the guy who arranged the evening. Bev says you two were best mates.'

'It was a long time ago.' Now it was Martin's turn to feel uncomfortable. 'We both surfed. I gave it away when I left.'

'But you've taken it up again. I saw you with a surfboard in your car.' She looked down at the table and blushed.

Damn the woman! She'd been watching him. But she did look pretty when she blushed. 'Not a lot else to do in Bellbird Bay,' he said. Then, remembering what Sam had said about her winning a surf lesson, asked, 'Do *you* surf?' It was an innocent question, but it seemed to disconcert her.

She played with her spoon before replying. 'I've never been on a surfboard but... mine was the winning bid for a lesson with Will Rankin. I don't know...'

'You're not thinking of chickening out? Sorry, I didn't mean to sound rude. Will's the best. You'll love it. There's nothing quite like the feeling of freedom you get out there catching a wave.'

'Hmm.'

Martin could see she wasn't so sure. Why on earth had she bid for the lesson if she didn't want to do it?

'I've done body surfing before, but not for ages and it's not the same. Do you really think I'll enjoy it?'

'Sure.' Martin swallowed as the image of Ailsa on a surfboard flitted behind his eyes. He wanted to try to convey to her just how amazing the feeling was. 'I've been taking shots of the surfers in the bay on the other side of the headland,' he said, pulling out his phone, glad he'd downloaded his most recent shots. 'Look.' He turned the phone towards her.

'Oh!' Ailsa peered intently at the screen as he scrolled through what he believed to be his best shots so far. 'But these are experienced surfers,' she said. 'I could never do that.'

'Not right away, but you'll never know what you can do till you try. Will will start you off gently, on the smaller waves close to where he has his school. He does it every day with people of all ages.' He could see the worry lines gradually disappearing from her forehead.

'So, this is what you've been doing... since you came to Bellbird Bay?'

Martin flinched. He should have been expecting this.

'They're very different to the photos Bev showed me.'

Martin cursed his sister. What had she been doing showing Ailsa the photographs that made his name? And when had she done it? Now, he supposed Ailsa was wondering what had changed to make him photograph surfers. She couldn't know the work that went into selecting the correct lighting, finding the right moment... He pulled his phone back and stuffed it into his pocket.

Seeming to realise she'd offended him in some way, Ailsa said, 'They're very good.'

But it was too late. The damage had been done. How could he ever have imagined they'd have anything to say to each other, that she might understand?

Twenty-two

It was almost a week after the fundraiser before Ailsa screwed up the courage to ring Will Rankin and book her surf lesson. In fact, she'd almost chickened out when he answered the phone and she heard him say, 'Bay Surf School, Will speaking. How can I help you?' It was only the thought of what Bev and Liz would say that had forced her to continue.

Now it was Monday morning, and she was due to meet Will at his van in less than half an hour. Ailsa took a deep breath, glad Martin wasn't there to see her panic. She regretted the incident on Australia Day though he had been too gentlemanly to mention it, plus the way he'd left so suddenly. It must have been something she said, but she had no idea what.

She was wearing a pair of denim shorts and a loose white cotton shirt over the new swimsuit she'd bought at *Sassy's*. Bev had been right about the shop. She'd found the one-piece navy, lycra swimsuit which Sassy assured her was perfect for surfing. It had long sleeves and covered her right up to her neck, but it did cling to her body, showing up every curve and bump. Now, her face and legs slathered in sunscreen, she couldn't delay any longer. Checking she had her towel, phone and wallet in the beach bag she'd bought at *Sassy's* too, she headed out.

Will's van was easy to find. It was surrounded by signs and a large banner announcing *Bay Surf School, Surf lessons and boards for hire*. The adjacent section of the beach was deserted, only a few dark heads visible bobbing among the waves in the distance. Ailsa breathed a sigh of relief. She didn't want witnesses to her awkward first attempts.

'Hi there!' Will, tanned, his long hair tied back in a ponytail, and wearing a pair of multicoloured board shorts and a white tee shirt emblazoned with *Bay Surf School*, greeted her with a smile.

*

To Ailsa's surprise, the lesson was less traumatic than she expected. Will started by showing her how to kneel and stand while they were still on the beach, ensuring she developed some confidence before they went into the water. And, once there, he was beside her to offer support and guidance. *Martin was right*, she thought, the first time she managed to balance on the board without immediately falling off, *this is amazing*.

The hour seemed to pass too quickly, and Ailsa was sorry when Will said, 'That's it for today.'

'What do I do now?' she asked, bewildered. She could see other surfers arriving at the beach, all younger and fitter than she was. She felt a fraud, a fifty-two-year-old woman dressed in a swimsuit which didn't hide the bulges and was more suited to a twenty-year-old. She wanted to hide, but part of her was exhilarated with the rush of excitement she'd experienced.

'I hold group lessons here every day, each hour on the hour,' Will said, smiling. 'Or you can hire a board and do your own thing. You have the basics now, it's just a matter of practice.'

'Right, thanks.' Ailsa dried herself off and slipped her shorts and shirt back on. She'd decide what to do later. But she was beginning to understand why some people got the bug. She was now aware why Martin headed off with his board each morning. Hadn't he said something about another bay, one where the serious surfers went? So, if she came here again, there would be no risk of bumping into him.

Ailsa wasn't sure why it was such an issue. They were living in the same house. But the thought of him seeing her like this brought her out in goosebumps.

'Bye and thanks for the lesson.' She gave Will a wave and headed up from the beach to where she'd left her car, relieved when she closed the car door behind her. She sat there for a few moments without moving, remembering how it had felt, how Will had made it all so easy. Bev and Martin had been right. He was the best, a good teacher and a skilled surfer. Liz had been right, too. It was never too late. She wasn't too old. But most people her age who surfed had been doing it since they were teenagers. Could she take the risk to do it again, to risk being laughed at by those young things to whom it came naturally?

*

Back home at Bev's, Ailsa was still mulling it over, trying to decide whether or not she'd attempt surfing again, as she stood under a cool shower to wash the salt from her body and out of her hair. Feeling refreshed and telling herself there was no need to decide right now, she dressed, grabbed a banana along with a glass of water and took the Marcia Willett book she was reading out to the deck. Her intention was to spend a lazy afternoon there, forgetting about Bob, Martin, and the possibility of a repeat of this morning's surfing.

It was hot there in the sun, and the heat, combined with the morning's exertion, soon led to Ailsa's eyes closing, the book dropping to her lap. She was dreaming of being on the crest of a wave, Martin coming towards her on another surfboard, feeling a sense of panic, when she was rudely awakened by the sound of the house phone ringing.

It took Ailsa a few moments to realise where she was, before she leapt up and hurried inside to answer it, blinking as she left the bright sunlight for the relative dimness of the kitchen.

'Hello.'

'Ailsa, it's Julie.'

For a moment, Ailsa couldn't think who Julie was, then she remembered the waiflike creature who helped out at the garden centre and was Bev's second-in-command. They'd met briefly when Ailsa was there trying to help too, and she'd been surprised how strong the diminutive woman was.

Before she could speak, Julie continued, 'It's Bev. There's been an accident. She's on her way to hospital. I can't leave here, so...'

Ailsa had a sinking sensation in her stomach. She gripped the phone tighter, her hand moist with sweat. 'What happened? How is she?'

'I don't think it's too bad, but she may have broken something. She was in a lot of pain. She was rearranging the hanging plants when the ladder gave way and she fell.'

Ailsa realised she was wasting time. 'I'll go to the hospital right away. Have you contacted Martin?'

'I rang him but there was no answer. I left a message.'

'Right.'

'You'll let me know?'

'Of course.' Ailsa was already pulling off her shorts. She ran to her bedroom to change into her pink dress, splash her face with cold water, add a smear of lipstick and pull a comb through her hair.

Once in the car, Ailsa was glad she knew where the hospital was. It had been a long time ago, but Pat had been stung by a jellyfish when they were here before, and Bob had panicked and insisted they take him to Emergency.

Ailsa pulled into the parking lot of the small hospital – a lowset brick building set among stands of palms and pandanus trees – and hurried to the Emergency entrance. Once inside, there was no sign of Bev. She went to the reception where a pleasant-faced woman was working the desk.

'My friend, Bev Cooper, was brought in recently by ambulance.' Ailsa waited impatiently, drumming her fingers on the desk, while the woman checked on her computer.

She looked up. 'You're not a relative?'

'No, a friend. I'm staying with her at the moment. Can I see her?'

'I'm sorry. She's with the doctor right now. And...' she gave Ailsa a pitying glance, 'I'm afraid...'

'Is Bev here?'

Ailsa turned to see Martin looming behind her. For what must have been the first time, she was glad to see him.

'And you are?' the woman asked.

'I'm Martin Cooper, Bev's brother, her twin brother,' he added, as if their close relationship might give him a stronger claim.

'As I've been telling this lady,' she nodded towards Ailsa, 'the doctor

is with her at the moment, When he has made a diagnosis and a decision as to her treatment, you may see her.' She turned back to her computer.

'Let's sit down.' Martin took Ailsa by the elbow and, too worried to resist, she allowed herself to be led to a row of seats.

'I guess you got a call, too. A woman called Julie left a message on my phone. I came as soon as I could.'

'Julie works at the garden centre. She said Bev had fallen from a ladder.' Ailsa took a deep breath and looked at the man sitting beside her. He must have been surfing and only just out of the water when he received the message. His hair was still wet and dripping onto his shirt, which was half-open and showing his tanned chest. Ailsa shivered, the hair on her arms rising. She averted her eyes and, seeing this, he fastened the buttons.

'Sorry, I didn't take time to… Do you know any more?'

Ailsa shook her head. She was trembling.

To her surprise, Martin took her hand and squeezed it. 'Bev's strong. It can't be too bad. She's a battler.'

'Right.' Ailsa wanted to draw her hand away, but there was something comforting about the warmth from his grasp. She was glad he was here, glad she didn't have to wait for news on her own.

They had only been waiting a few minutes when, 'Mr Cooper?'

Martin released Ailsa's hand and went up to the desk.

Ailsa couldn't hear what was being said but could see Martin nodding, then he turned and gestured to her to join him.

'We can see her now.'

Somehow, Ailsa's hand crept into Martin's again as they made their way through a door and into an area which was sectioned off by curtains. Behind one curtain they found Bev lying on a hospital bed, her usual tanned complexion white with pain.

'Bev!' Ailsa dropped Martin's hand and rushed to her side, Martin following more slowly.

'What have you done to yourself?' he asked, when he reached the bed where Ailsa was now holding Bev's hand.

'I've been a damned fool,' she said, wincing. 'I knew the ladder was on its last legs.' She tried to laugh. 'I should have replaced it ages ago. Instead, it's done for me. The doc says I've broken my right leg and cracked or broken a few ribs and I'm covered in bruises. I've made a right mess of myself. I'm so sorry, Ailsa, and you, too, Martin. They're taking me into surgery later today and looks like I'm going to be laid up for some time.'

'Oh, Bev!' Ailsa squeezed her friend's hand.

'I want you both to do something for me,' Bev said, taking Martin's hand in her free one, and trying to raise herself up. 'Julie can't manage the centre on her own, and she has no idea about the paperwork. I have a good team, but Julie can't supervise them all on her own. I need you two to help out, to keep an eye on things for me. Martin, you can help with the heavy work and Ailsa, you'll be good with the customers and on the admin side. You'll soon get the hang of it, and I'll be back on my feet before you know it.'

'Sure,' Martin said gruffly, as if trying to hide his emotion. 'You need to just concentrate on getting well. Ailsa?'

Ailsa swallowed hard. To be sharing the house with Martin on his own, *and* working with him in the garden centre. How could she cope with spending so much time with him?

'Of course, Bev,' she said. 'Anything to help.'

Twenty-three

'I'm sorry, you have to leave now. It's best you come back in the morning. The surgery may take some time, and Bev won't be up to seeing you tonight. She'll be brighter tomorrow.'

Reluctantly Martin released his twin's hand. It felt strange for Bev to be sick. He'd always been the one who got into scrapes, broke an arm when he fell from his bike, took the skin off his knee when he tumbled out of a tree in their back garden, suffered a black eye when he got into a fight in the playground. And, each time, Bev had been there for him, more important to him than his parents.

Of course, he'd do as she asked, anything, even if it meant working side-by-side with Ailsa. He'd work out how to handle it later. Right now, the important thing was to put Bev's mind at rest. He'd seen the stricken expression on Ailsa's face at Bev's request and suspected his might have mirrored it. Luckily, Bev had been too far gone to notice, at least he hoped she had. It was enough they'd agreed.

'See you at home,' he said to Ailsa when they parted at the hospital entrance.

She was fiddling with her phone. 'What...? Oh, I'm just calling Julie. I promised to let her know about Bev.'

Of course. *Why hadn't he thought of that?* 'Should we...?'

'No.' Ailsa checked her phone. 'The garden centre will be closing up around now. Tomorrow will be soon enough, after we visit with Bev.'

Damn the woman. She was right again. 'Okay.'

He headed to his car, pleased to see Ailsa heading in the opposite direction. At least he had breathing space before he saw her again back at Bev's. And how was that going to be? It would be more difficult to avoid her, and without Bev there to act as a buffer between them, how were they going to manage to be polite to each other, even to carry on a conversation? They hadn't done too well over coffee on Australia Day. But it hadn't been his fault, had it?

The clouds were gathering as Martin slid the Mini Moke into Bev's empty garage. He guessed her vehicle was still at the garden centre. One more thing to take care of. A few drops of rain fell on him as he walked towards the house, the rumble of thunder in the distance forcing him to quicken his steps. He breathed a sigh of relief to find the house empty. He'd beaten Ailsa back. A flash of lightning streaked across the sky as another peal of thunder, louder this time, blasted his eardrums. Then the rain started in earnest. What he needed was a drink and something to eat.

He poured himself a glass of the brandy Bev kept for emergencies – what was this if not an emergency? He was ferreting in the fridge for something to eat when he heard the squeal of tyres, hurried footsteps and the front door opening and closing. Then the bedraggled figure of Ailsa arrived in the kitchen.

'Oh, you're back,' she said in a tone which didn't bode well for any reconciliation. 'I thought I'd get here first, but I had to call Julie. I told her we'd be in tomorrow after we see Bev. She…'

Martin had stopped listening. He couldn't take his eyes off the picture Ailsa made, her hair plastered to her head, the dress clinging in all the right places. He felt himself begin to… 'Want a drink?' he asked, turning back towards the cupboard to take down another glass. 'We've both had a shock.' He wasn't sure if he was referring to Bev's accident or her request they work together. It didn't matter.

'Thanks, but I need to dry off first.'

Martin turned back to face her, seeing a blush suffuse her face as she suddenly realised how she must look.

She stood indecisively for a moment before turning on her heel and disappearing.

That went well. He shivered. The temperature had dropped, and the salad he'd been intending to prepare didn't seem so tempting. He stood sipping his drink and looking out at the wild weather, feeling completely inept. He'd been eating in hotels or snacking on fruit and nuts for so long he'd forgotten how to put a meal together – if he'd ever known. And, to his shame, since he'd been here, he'd relied on Bev to provide the meals. But he couldn't expect Ailsa to feed him.

There was the sound of footsteps. Ailsa was back, wearing a pair of pants and a loose long-sleeved shirt which hid her shape. Had she noticed his body's reaction? Martin handed her the glass of brandy.

'Thanks.' She sipped it cautiously.

'Hungry?'

'Yes. It seems to have been a long time since I ate. You?'

'I was trying to work out what to fix.' It wasn't exactly a lie.

Ailsa looked at the empty benchtop, then at the rain streaming down the window and the wild ocean outside. 'I think something hot is called for. Let me see if Bev has any tinned soup.' She went to the pantry and pulled out a tin of minestrone soup which she emptied into a pot. Then she found the remains of a loaf of sourdough bread and a block of cheese. 'How will this do?'

'How did you do that?' he asked, knowing it would have taken him ages to put even a simple meal like this together.

'Easy.' She smiled. 'I'm used to catering for a husband and two large boys.'

There it was again, the reference to the absent husband, and again he was tempted to ask the question that was bothering him. But now wasn't the time.

At least Martin managed to set the table. It was cosy sitting opposite Ailsa at Bev's kitchen table, the storm howling outside while they were safely inside. The soup was hot and the bread and cheese sustaining. He'd opened a bottle of red wine from Bev's wine rack to accompany their meal and it seemed to have mellowed them both.

'Thanks for this. But I can't expect you to cook for me all the time Bev's laid up.'

'We can take turns.' Ailsa chuckled.

Did she realise how hopeless he was in the kitchen? Maybe he could learn, and there was always takeaway. 'Hmm. About the garden centre...' He decided to approach the elephant in the room.

'We need to help Bev all we can, and if it means working together, I'm sure we can manage it.'

Was there a twinkle in her eyes or was he imagining it? Maybe it was the light shining on them. A sudden flash of lightning lit up the outside yard, followed by a loud bang of thunder which made them both jump.

Ailsa's face turned white. 'Sorry. I've never liked thunder and lightning. When I was a child, I used to hide under the covers when it stormed. Silly, I know.'

'Not at all.' Ailsa's wide eyes reminded him of the first time they'd met, when she'd listened wide-eyed to all his stories of life in the artistic student community in Sydney and his dreams of becoming a famous photographer. What a prat he'd been back then. Was he any better now? He certainly hoped so. But was that how Ailsa still viewed him? If so, no wonder she acted awkward in his company. He couldn't blame her.

'I'll clear these away.' Ailsa picked up their empty bowls and started to carry them to the sink, when there was another deafening crack of thunder. Ailsa shrieked and the bowls fell to the floor and shattered. She stood motionless as if turned to stone. There were beads of moisture on her forehead and her eyes widened in alarm.

Martin was on his feet in an instant and without thinking, he wrapped his arms around her trembling form, his chin on her head. He could smell her unique fragrance of lemon and something... something unidentifiable.

They stood like that for only a moment before she pulled away, her cheeks stained with red blotches.

'Sorry!'

'Sorry!'

They both spoke at once, each embarrassed by the contact.

'I...' Ailsa bent to pick up the pieces of broken china.

'I'll do it. Why don't you turn in. I think the worst of the storm is over.' As he spoke, thunder rumbled off in the distance.

'Thanks.' Ailsa almost ran from the room.

What had he done now? Martin scratched his head. He had acted without thinking – one of his faults. But Ailsa had appeared so upset, it had seemed natural to comfort her. And it had felt so good to have his arms around her, as if he had been waiting all his life for that moment. He could still smell that unique lemony scent. He sighed.

Now he'd probably ruined things between them for good.

Twenty-four

When Ailsa awoke next morning, the sun was shining brightly through a gap in the curtains. The combination of brandy and red wine had meant she slept soundly despite the odd rumble of thunder and the wind and rain still battering at the window.

She rose and peered out. Everything was calm and peaceful. It was as if the storm had never happened. She'd had such a strange dream, of Martin… Ailsa stopped short. Had it been a dream or had Martin really put his arms around her? She shuddered, remembering how her body had leant into his, before she had the presence of mind to pull away. It had been like when she was nineteen, only then he had been the one to pull away. What was she thinking? She wasn't nineteen anymore. She was fifty-two – and still a married woman. *Not for much longer*, a little voice inside reminded her. But she had no business allowing Martin Cooper to put his arms around her, thunderstorm or no thunderstorm. Although she had to admit for the brief second when his strong arms had encircled her, she'd felt… She pulled her mind away from the reminder of how it had felt. She hadn't felt that way in years.

She turned back from the window and made her way to the bathroom, glad to find the house in silence. Martin must still be asleep. A cool shower removed the last vestiges of sleep and, as she inspected herself in the mirror, she could see a new brightness in her eyes. It hadn't been there the day before. She took a deep breath and returned to the bedroom to dress in the capri pants and tee shirt she deemed appropriate for work in the garden centre even though Bev had allocated her to office duties. Not surprising, she thought, given the length of time it had taken her to water the plants on her earlier visits.

'Sleep well?'

Ailsa stopped in surprise to see Martin already seated at the kitchen table with a plate of scrambled eggs and bacon. An enticing aroma of coffee met her nostrils. 'I thought you didn't cook.'

'Only breakfast, I'm afraid. But I'm willing to try my hand at other dishes.' He chuckled at her discomfort. 'There's some leftover eggs in the pan and I can fry more bacon.'

'Thanks, eggs will be fine.' Ailsa walked across the kitchen, aware of his gaze on her. She dropped a slice of bread in the toaster and poured herself a cup of coffee. Her usual herbal tea wouldn't work for her this morning. She was in need of something stronger.

'I called the hospital.'

Ailsa looked up from her plate of scrambled eggs. It was embarrassing to sit here with Martin after last night, but she had no option. *The hospital. Bev.* Why hadn't she thought of calling the hospital instead of beating herself up about how much she'd enjoyed being in Martin Cooper's arms? 'How is she?'

'I got the usual meaningless guff – *as well as can be expected*. But she had a comfortable night and is looking forward to our visit. We should go as soon as...' He gestured to Ailsa's half-eaten breakfast.

'Don't they have visiting hours?'

'It's a small hospital. They're pretty flexible. And...' he grinned, '... Bev and I went to school with Sally, the nurse I spoke to.'

'Given what I saw at the fundraiser, you went to school with half the town.' *Where did that come from?* 'I mean...' she stammered.

'No, you're right.' Martin sighed. 'That's what makes it so hard.' He gazed into space.

Ailsa held her breath. This was the closest Martin had come to offering any sort of explanation of his moodiness, or why he was back here in Bellbird Bay. She waited, but he didn't elaborate. She shovelled up the remains of her toast and scrambled egg and drained her coffee. 'I'll get my bag.'

'Meet you in the car.' Martin pushed back his chair and picked up the dirty plates.

Ten minutes later, a flurried Ailsa joined Martin in the yellow Mini Moke. She'd have preferred to take her car but didn't want to make a fuss.

As if reading her mind, Martin said, 'You'll need to drive Bev's back from the garden centre.'

She nodded. He'd forestalled her again. He was way ahead of her this morning.

At the hospital, he led the way to the ward where Bev was now settled and pushed open the door.

Bev was lying propped up on pillows, looking a lot brighter than she had when they left her the previous day.

'Bev!' Ailsa hurried to her side, followed more slowly by Martin. 'How are you feeling this morning?'

'Sore and slightly embarrassed. I knew the ladder was on its last legs and I shouldn't have climbed up to fix the plants on my own, but I was too impatient to wait till someone was there to steady it – and I've been too busy to replace it. It was all my own fault.'

'Patience never was your strong suit,' Martin said, joining Ailsa at the bedside. 'And now look where it's got you.' But he was smiling gently at his sister. 'What does the doc say?'

'I haven't seen her this morning,' Bev said, trying to sit up straighter, but falling back. 'Ow!'

'I don't think you should be trying to move,' Ailsa said, taking Bev's hand.

At that moment a young woman, her jet-black hair pulled tightly back from her face and wearing blue surgical scrubs entered the room. 'Hello,' she said, looking surprised to see Ailsa and Martin. 'I'm Doctor Hastie, one of the surgical team which operated on Bev last night. I'd like a few words with my patient. If you would leave…' She glanced at Ailsa and Martin.

'Of course.' Ailsa released Bev's hand. 'We'll wait outside,' she said.

Outside the room, Martin paced up and down while Ailsa sent a text to Julie to tell her where they were and confirm they'd be at the garden centre as soon as possible, once they knew what was happening with Bev. Then she took a seat and prepared to wait. From his difficulty in standing still or sitting, it seemed Martin shared his twin's lack of patience.

After what seemed like ages but was in fact only a few minutes, the surgeon emerged. 'You can go back in now, but only for a short time, and please don't tire her.'

'What…?' Ailsa began.

'Bev has suffered from broken ribs and multiple fractures to her right leg. She's not in any danger but will need to take things easy for several weeks. The ribs will heal themselves in time, but she must rest. Her broken leg is a different matter. We've put it in a cast and recommend she keep off it for six to eight weeks. She should be able to go home in a few days as long as there will be someone there to care for her.' She raised her eyebrows at Ailsa and Martin.

'We'll both be there,' Ailsa said without thinking.

'Good.' The surgeon moved off, intent on seeing her next patient.

'She told you?' Bev asked as soon as they walked back in. 'It seems I'm to be stuck like this for longer than I anticipated. Maybe…'

'We'll cope,' Martin said. 'The important thing is for you to get completely well.'

Ailsa nodded her agreement, but it suddenly struck her. Six to eight weeks – longer than she'd intended to stay. How was she going to explain to Bob, to the boys? But she knew how important it was for Bev to remain off her leg if she was to regain full use of it. At least she'd be home soon. But how were she and Martin going to cope with both the garden centre and looking after Bev?

'We'll work something out,' Martin said, when they were back in his car and on their way to the garden centre. 'It can't be too difficult, can it? Neither of us is a complete fool, and minding a garden centre isn't exactly rocket science.'

Ailsa gulped but chose not to reply. Bev would get the best care she could provide, but there was still the garden centre to worry about.

When they parked alongside the white van belonging to Bev, the garden centre logo emblazoned on the side, Martin didn't immediately move. He tapped his fingers on the steering wheel.

Ailsa glanced at him. He couldn't be nervous, could he? She stifled the urge to say something flippant. 'We should find Julie, and see what needs to be done,' she said instead, sliding her legs out of the vehicle.

'Righto.' Martin joined her, jangling the car keys in his hand. 'Where…?' He looked around.

Ailsa almost laughed. It hadn't occurred to her Martin had never been here before. She'd assumed he was familiar with his sister's pride and joy. 'This way,' she said, leading him through the entrance to where Julie was busy dealing with several customers.

Martin hung back while Ailsa donned a green garden centre apron and took over from Julie. This was something she could do and would leave Julie free to work on other things – and to show Martin around. She watched out of the corner of her eye as the other woman led Martin away.

It was almost one o'clock when Julie reappeared. The morning had been busy, the previous night's rain seemingly having encouraged many of the locals to decide to replenish their gardens, along with the usual smattering of tradesmen picking up stocks of mulch and pavers.

'You should take a lunch break,' Julie said. 'I just sent Martin to the café. Why don't you join him?'

'I don't…' Ailsa began. But where else would she have lunch? She'd left in too much of a rush this morning to think of packing anything to eat. Vowing to be more organised in future, she took Julie's advice and headed to the café. She didn't need to actually join Martin there, did she?

But when she reached the café, Ailsa discovered all the tables were full. She could see Martin sitting by himself at the same table where she and Bev had eaten lunch, the one Bev told her was reserved for her. With a sigh of resignation, she walked across to join him.

Twenty-five

Martin raised his eyes to see Ailsa entering the cafe. He smiled to himself as he noticed how she was searching for a vacant table before heading towards the one where he was sitting. He'd had a busy morning, mainly involved in filling bags of mulch from what seemed to be mountains of the stuff, repositioning large ceramic pots, and helping tradies load their trucks. He hadn't realised how much manual labour was involved in Bev's work.

The garden centre itself impressed him. What Martin had imagined was a small nursery catering to the whims of elderly ladies proved to be more, much more. A wave of guilt flooded him. He should have shown more interest in Bev's life, in her garden centre. His sister had established a community resource for all types of garden enthusiasts and was to be congratulated on her achievement. He regretted not coming home before now, belittling her choice to remain in Bellbird Bay. What Bev had achieved here was amazing. He'd underestimated his sister.

Martin was beginning to think he'd underestimated Bellbird Bay, too. No longer the indifferent youngster who couldn't wait to get away, he could now appreciate what the small town had to offer. It was a place a person could come to heal, to discover there was more to life than fame and fortune. He smiled to himself. He was sounding like one of those lifestyle gurus he'd come across on one of his trips.

A chair scraped across the surface of the paved courtyard as Ailsa joined him.

The young waitress who'd served him with the open sandwich of rye bread topped with a variety of vegetables appeared immediately with a menu.

'Hi, Jilly,' Ailsa said, seeming to know the girl. 'I'll have the chicken salad, and a watermelon and carrot juice.' She hadn't looked at the menu.

She'd been here with Bev, Martin remembered. He was the stranger. 'How was your morning?'

'Good. Busy. Yours?'

'Busy, too. This is quite an establishment.'

'Bev has done well for herself. It can't have been easy.'

'No.' And he hadn't helped. When their parents had become sick, it had been Bev who'd given up her life and her dreams to return to take care of them. He hadn't felt guilty at the time, believing his growing career was too important to be interrupted. What a fool he had been, a stupid, ignorant fool. 'I should have come back before now,' he muttered, almost to himself.

'You never came back?' Ailsa asked. 'Not even when your parents died?'

He shook his head, ashamed to admit it. 'I made it back for Dad's funeral but not Mum's. I was always caught up in some godforsaken spot. Transport wasn't always easy.' He tried to excuse himself, but knew it was a lame explanation. 'Anyway, I'm here now, and maybe I can make it up to her in some way.'

Ailsa looked doubtful, but the arrival of her meal prevented her from replying immediately.

Embarrassed at the direction the conversation was taking, Martin finished his lunch. 'I should be getting back,' he said, rising. He could feel Ailsa's eyes on him as he walked away.

*

Ailsa watched Martin leave, wondering if he'd rushed off to avoid saying any more about himself, or if he found her company boring. He certainly wasn't the easiest person to talk to, and he didn't give much away about himself. She couldn't help wondering why he was here now, if he'd found it so difficult to get back when his parents needed him. And those photos he was taking of surfing – did they indicate he was taking his career in a different direction, or was he merely playing around?

While she'd love to know the answers, Ailsa felt it was none of her business. He was only Bev's twin brother who just happened to be here when she was. It was lucky they were both free and able to help Bev out. But once Bev was up and about again, she'd be going home to Canberra and that would be the end of it. She refrained from asking herself the question – the end of what? There was nothing between her and Martin Cooper. He was only the man with whom she was being forced to share a house and work. But she couldn't ignore the quiver of anticipation she experienced in his company, though anticipation of what, she wasn't sure. She was a bundle of contradictions. She still loved Bob, but – and it was a big but – she couldn't ignore the anger she harboured towards him, anger mixed with grief, grief for their marriage and for the man she thought she'd married. Then to meet Martin again, so soon afterwards. It made her head spin.

The afternoon passed in a flash, leaving Ailsa no time to wonder about Martin, fret about Bob, or worry about Bev. She was surprised to discover how busy the garden centre was and developed a renewed admiration for her friend who had built it up and coped with it every day. By the time she and Julie closed up, she was exhausted.

'Oh,' Julie said, as she was leaving. 'I almost forgot. Martin said not to worry about dinner for him, he'll get something to eat at the surf club.' She gave Ailsa a speculative look.

'No need to look at me like that,' Ailsa said. 'You know he's Bev's brother. We're both staying at Bev's. That's all.'

'He's quite a dish for someone his age,' Julie said with a wink.

Where did she get that expression?

Ailsa sighed. 'He's a good-looking man, yes. But I'm married, and even if I wasn't…' She didn't finish the sentence. Ailsa had no idea how she'd feel about Martin if her situation was different, if she didn't feel so distrustful of the male species – and of her own judgment. She hadn't allowed herself to even imagine it. 'See you tomorrow,' she said, before walking away.

To Ailsa's annoyance, Julie's comments about Martin stuck in her mind all the way back to Bev's. It was a relief to find the house empty. Too tired to contemplate cooking, she made a cheese and dill pickle sandwich, poured herself a glass from the bottle of red wine Martin opened the night before, and took both out to the deck.

Once there, with nothing else to occupy her, Ailsa's mind went to Canberra, to Bob and the boys. She hadn't heard from Bob recently but according to Pat, he was okay, if still acting strangely.

'Don't worry about Dad,' he'd said in his last call. 'I think he's enjoying having the house to himself.' But Ailsa couldn't help worrying. She couldn't turn off twenty years of caring for him like you'd turn off a tap. Is that what he'd done? It didn't make sense. Bob had never been one to hold grudges, quite the opposite. It made his present behaviour even more peculiar. He'd said what he had to say. She was the one who should feel slighted, not him.

Sighing, she leant her head back against the chair and closed her eyes. She couldn't rid herself of the feeling something was wrong, seriously wrong. But what?

Deciding to try to ring him – surely Bob was home at this time on a Tuesday night and would answer his phone – she pressed the speed dial. The phone rang three times then, just as Ailsa was expecting to hear voicemail click in, Bob answered.

'Hello?'

'Bob, it's me. I've been trying to reach you. Is everything all right? Are *you* all right?'

'Ailsa?' Bob sounded distracted.

'Yes, it's me.' She waited.

But there was silence then she heard him sigh. 'I'm sorry, Ailsa. I'm not ready to discuss anything more now. I'll call you when I am.' There was a click, He'd rung off. Ailsa stared at the phone in astonishment.

Twenty-six

Martin headed for the surf club, feeling pretty much like a homing pigeon. It was the one familiar place in a town which had changed beyond all recognition from the one he'd grown up in. And even the club had undergone a makeover, though the old fresco on the stairway wall hadn't changed. Martin stopped for a moment to gaze at the image of Ted Crawford, one of the legendary champion surfers about a decade before his time. There hadn't been many like him and, at one time, he'd been Martin's idol, the one he wanted to emulate. He smiled and continued up the stairs.

It was Tuesday, a night which had always been a quiet one in the club. Hopefully that hadn't changed. He wasn't in the mood for company. Reaching the top of the stairs, he gave a sigh of relief to see the place almost empty, only a few diehards leaning against the bar and several others playing the pokies in the far corner.

'A schooner of light, thanks,' he said to the barman, before ordering a burger and chips and taking his beer out to the deserted deck. He took a long swallow of the ice-cold beer and gazed out into the darkness. It was strange to be back where it all began, where the dreams had first started to form in his adolescent mind when he received a camera for Christmas at the tender age of ten. Back then he'd had no idea how successful he'd become. He'd only wanted to get away. And now he was back.

It had been a strange day. First, breakfast with Ailsa McNeil. She was a strange one, too. Martin didn't know what to make of his twin's old friend, the girl who'd attracted him so much it had scared him stupid back in the day. She'd changed, but he had, too. He was no longer the arrogant prick who thought the world owed him a living and women were only there for his entertainment, or he hoped he wasn't, that he'd learnt something over the years. He'd learned the hard way, and maybe it had hardened him, too. He wished... He took another gulp of beer.

He wished things had been different, that he and Ailsa had met at a different time. At nineteen he'd been too young to appreciate her. She'd scared him. More accurately, his own feelings had scared him. He'd spent the past thirty-odd years ensuring those feelings never had the chance to surface again, choosing women who were only interested in him for what they could get from him, to bask in his reflected glory. Until Sofia. And look how that had turned out. It was crazy to think of getting involved with another woman now, especially Ailsa McNeil. But he couldn't put her out of his mind.

Now she was here, thrust into his life again – and it was too late. His career was destroyed, and she was married with two grown sons. What could she see in him now?

Martin was enjoying his meal and was on his second schooner of beer when his solitude was wrecked by the arrival of a large group of women at another table on the deck. They took their seats with lots of chatter and fluttering, shattering the peace he was enjoying. He was in the process of finishing his burger quickly so he could leave, when one of the women caught sight of him.

'It's Martin Cooper!' The loud voice carried across the deck, forcing him to take notice. When he looked up, Martin saw a woman weaving her way unsteadily across the deck in his direction, a glass of champagne in one hand. 'I heard you were back,' she said when she reached his table. 'Remember me? Annabel Wilson – I'm Annabel Todd now, but the Todd part is history.' She gazed at him, her eyes wide with delight.

Behind her, Martin could see the rest of her group watching the proceedings with interest. He flinched. Annabel Wilson, the girl he'd taken to his school formal. It was over thirty years ago, and she still remembered him. He remembered her, too. Back then, she'd been a curvy eighteen-year-old, ready for anything and he'd been happy to oblige. He wasn't the first to take advantage of what she was offering and no doubt not the last. But the blonde bombshell of yesteryear was now a plump and blowsy matron who appeared to be trying to pretend she was still a spring chicken.

'Why don't you join us?' she asked, her uneven gait suggesting this wasn't her first drink of the evening. 'We're celebrating Jackie's divorce.' She waved her glass wildly in the direction of the table she'd left, where four other women were avidly listening to their conversation.

'Sorry, I'm just leaving.' Martin hurriedly swallowed the last mouthful of his burger, before draining his beer and pushing back his chair.

'Don't be a stranger. See you around,' she called.

A burst of laughter from the other women followed him, as the door to the deck closed behind him. He was relieved to reach the relative safely of the club again.

'Getting to you, were they?' the young barman asked with a chuckle, as Martin hurried past, intent on putting as much distance between him and the women as possible. He nodded and kept going, only drawing breath when he was outside.

Annabel Wilson! Martin exhaled. Who'd have imagined she'd still be here in Bellbird Bay and have turned into... that? It wasn't so much the way she looked, but her manner which had sent him scurrying for cover. The come-hither expression in her eyes – despite the difference in age and nationality – had reminded him of that other pair of eyes, of Sofia. And the chortling he'd heard as he made his way out left him in no doubt her companions were just as silly as she was.

'What was it with some women?' he asked himself, as he eased his large frame into the little car he was becoming fond of, without coming up with an answer. He was grateful his sister had escaped such foolishness, even though he sometimes wondered why Bev was still single. She was an attractive woman. Maybe it was in their genes, this inability to make an appropriate choice of partner.

The years sat well on Ailsa too. She and Bev were two of a kind, both strong, attractive, independent women who didn't seem to be fazed by turning fifty. He shook his head in an attempt to dislodge the image of Ailsa sitting opposite him at lunch. He'd behaved like a madman, rushing off like that, but her questions made him twitchy, and he had to get away. Now, he regretted his hurried departure, vowing to be more friendly and polite to her in future. If they were going to be forced to share Bev's house and work together at the garden centre, the least he could do was try to be civil. He didn't need to like the woman.

But that was the trouble. He did... like her, more than like. Ailsa McNeil was getting under his skin like no woman he'd ever met.

Twenty-seven

Ailsa was still clutching her phone and staring into space when the gate from the boardwalk swung open and Martin climbed the steps to the deck.

'What's the matter?' He threw himself down on the seat opposite. 'Is it Bev?'

'No.' Ailsa shook her head. She'd intended to call the hospital after her call to Bob, but his hanging up so abruptly sent everything else out of her mind.

'Want to talk about it?'

She hesitated. She didn't, not with him, but there was no one else around and indignation at Bob's abrupt handling of her call was boiling up in her. 'My husband,' she said.

'He's here?' Martin looked around as if expecting Bob to suddenly appear.

'He's in Canberra.'

'Oh!'

'I'm sorry. I've been less than friendly since you arrived. I've had things on my mind and…' She was suddenly filled with an urge to talk, to share her frustration.

'Looks like you've been drinking,' he said, nodding to the empty wine glass, 'and I've had a couple of beers at the club. Why don't I make us both coffee while you decide what you want to say? I promise I'm a good listener and don't shock easily.'

Ailsa nodded.

As Martin disappeared inside the house, she reflected how easy he made it sound. But maybe it would be easy to speak to him about Bob. The awkwardness she'd felt in his presence was beginning to disappear now they shared their common concern for Bev.

By the time he returned carrying two mugs of coffee, Ailsa had made her decision. Although he was practically a stranger, he was Bev's brother, and they were sharing the house. Like it or not, she would be spending the next days and weeks in his company. Bev wasn't here, and she needed to vent to someone.

'Thanks.' She took the mug he handed to her and wrapped her hands around it before taking a cautious sip. It was good, stronger than she was used to, but the caffeine hit gave her the courage she needed. 'It's like this...' As best she could and making every effort to be non-judgemental, she described the situation with Bob as she saw it.

'Hmm.' Martin took a swig of coffee before replying. 'The poor guy. It must have been hard for him, keeping it to himself for all those years. You never guessed?'

Ailsa's stomach churned. Liz had asked that too. 'How could I? It's not something a woman imagines or expects from her husband. We've been married for close to twenty-five years. I thought he might be sick and didn't want to worry me, but...' Ailsa trembled with anger and disappointment remembering how she'd envisaged their silver wedding anniversary – a family party then perhaps an overseas trip. They'd often talked about going to Europe but never made it. It would have been the perfect opportunity.

'I guess not. But I can empathise with him. I've been pretty good at bottling things up myself over the years, got quite a reputation for it.' He gave a wry grin. 'Has he always been a loner?'

'No, that's just it. He...' Ailsa thought back to when they first met. 'When we met at uni – not long after the party you came to in Canberra,' she blushed and looked down into her coffee, 'Bob wasn't a loner exactly, but didn't have many friends. We clicked right away, and my friends became his. Then, over the years, we made friends with other couples through the boys. So, loner, no.' She tried to picture Bob in a social setting. It was true he'd always tended to be on the outer of groups, preferring to observe rather than be the life and soul of the party. But there was nothing wrong with that, and she'd preferred his more relaxed attitude. It was better than the husbands of some of her friends, many of whom became amorous after a few drinks and had to be warded off.

'Did you think he was having an affair?' he asked, voicing the other possibility which had been worrying her.

'Not really. We've had a good marriage – until recently. Bob's never expressed any interest in other women – or men. We used to joke about it.' She bit her lip remembering how they'd laughed at the antics of several of the couples in their social circle who seemed to change partners regularly.

'But don't they say the wife always knows?'

'So they say, but I never saw or suspected a thing. Bob was aways loyal.' Ailsa certainly hadn't seen any evidence of anyone else in Bob's life, and he'd assured her there wasn't anyone.

'Well, I suspect as you say, he's working through things, and you just need to be patient.'

'Do you think so?'

'Sometimes we men find it hard to speak what's on our mind. I don't know your husband, but it sounds to me as if he has a lot going on.'

It was difficult to read Martin's expression in the darkness, broken only by the light from inside the house. But Ailsa got the impression he was talking about himself, too. What was he hiding? 'Thanks for listening,' she said.

'Any time. And…' He hesitated, then cleared his throat. 'Seems to me we're stuck with this situation. It's not one either of us wanted, but we both care for Bev, so…'

'We should make the best of it,' Ailsa finished for him.

'Right. Friends?' He held out his hand.

'Friends.' Ailsa placed her hand in his large paw which dwarfed hers, his touch providing her with a sense of comfort and… an unexpected flash of something else. It reminded her of how it had felt to have his arms around her.

Abruptly, Martin dropped her hand and, standing up, walked into the house.

Ailsa picked up her empty mug and followed, intending to put it in the dishwasher and head for bed. But once inside the kitchen she found Martin standing there gazing into space. As she reached over to open the dishwasher he turned, his arm brushing against hers.

'Sor...' she began, then the word caught in her throat. They were standing so close she could smell the coffee on his breath, the faint odour of sweat from his skin, see the bristles on his chin his razor had missed that morning. Her stomach churned and her heart leapt as, without any warning, his lips came down to meet hers in a gentle kiss, reminding her of that kiss all those years ago. For an instant Ailsa clung to him, all her good intentions disappearing in a flash as her legs became weak. For an interminable moment, time stood still. Then she remembered. She wasn't nineteen anymore. She was fifty-two. She wasn't free. And her life was in limbo.

Ailsa pulled away. 'No!' A wave of guilt washed over her. *What was she doing?* Her hand went to her mouth as if to erase the touch of his lips. Then, walking as carefully as she could, she made her way to her bedroom, slamming the door behind her. Once there she dropped onto the bed, her head swirling.

She should never have come here. She should have left as soon as Martin arrived. She shouldn't still be here. It was all Bob's fault.

Damn Martin Cooper. *Why did he have to turn up at Bev's? Why did she confide in him? Why did he have to be so damned understanding? Why had he kissed her? And why had she responded the way she had?*

Ailsa knew the answer to the latter. They were two people who were attracted to each other. It was late. They'd shared a confidence. And, yes, she'd enjoyed it. But she wasn't ready for this. She was still reeling from the shock and hurt of Bob's disclosure, and Martin Cooper was... he was Martin Cooper, the man whose own sister labelled a charmer and a player. She closed her eyes determined to put it out of her mind and make sure it didn't happen again.

Twenty-eight

When Ailsa left, Martin headed straight for his bedroom and threw himself down on the bed. What a fool he'd made of himself. How could he have allowed himself to develop feelings for another woman so soon after he'd been betrayed by Sofia? At his age, he should know better than to force his attentions on a woman when they weren't welcome. But he could have sworn that, for a few seconds at least, she'd responded as if...

Ailsa had just been sharing her concern about her husband with him, for Pete's sake. What sort of a prick did that make him? But from what she'd told him, it sounded as if the marriage was over, so maybe there was a chance for him. But he'd have to take things slowly, something he wasn't in the habit of doing.

Unable to think of sleep, Martin opened up his laptop, trying to forget how Ailsa's lips had felt, her body moulding into his, her... He forced himself to critically analyse the portfolio of shots from the previous few days. They were good, but not good enough. Maybe he was wasting his time. Maybe Sam Walker was right, and it was time to try something completely different.

Martin reflected on all he'd learnt from his research and his chats with the young surfers on the open surf beach. The photos in the latest copy of *Surfing Life* lying on his bedside table were amazing. Could he ever hope to reach that standard? Was it all a pipe dream?

Frustrated and realising there was nothing more he could do, he closed the laptop, undressed and slid under the thin sheet. But he doubted he'd get any sleep that night.

*

Ailsa tossed and turned beset with dreams of lying in Martin's arms, of him holding her tight, lips touching lips, then he turned into Bob.... She awakened at dawn, unrefreshed, the sound of bellbirds outside her window welcoming the new day, their unique staccato call harsh to her ears. When she rose and looked in the mirror, the bags under her eyes were testament to her disturbed night. After showering, she patted on a touch of concealer to hide the worst of them, before tentatively adding the rest of her makeup. Who was the makeup for? Her? Or...

She chose a light-coloured lipstick, the lightest pink she had.

Her heart was in her mouth at the prospect of facing Martin this morning with what she thought of as *The Kiss* between them. But the kitchen was empty, a folded piece of paper leaning against a pot of marmalade on the table. She opened it to find a brief message.

Gone surfing. Sorry about last night. Forget it ever happened. It was dumb. I was out of line. See you at the garden centre. M.

Ailsa heaved a sigh of relief, though it would be difficult to forget the sensations Martin's closeness had stirred up. But she was glad he was willing to put it in the past. She wasn't ready to cope with another man in her life right now. She didn't know if she ever would be, if she'd ever be able to risk trusting her emotions again.

She planned a brief visit to the hospital to see Bev before going to work, so settled for a slice of toast and marmalade with a glass of orange juice for breakfast, promising herself she'd get something to eat from the garden centre café during the morning.

At the hospital, Ailsa was pleased to see Bev looking brighter.

'The doc says I can go home in a couple of days,' she said. 'I hope you and Martin are managing to get on okay.' She peered at Ailsa. 'You are, aren't you?'

'Sure.' Ailsa hoped her expression hadn't given her away. She pushed down the memory of the previous evening.

'Good. My brother can be difficult, though...' she frowned, '... he seems to have lost some of his bumptiousness this time around. Maybe something or someone has taken him down a peg. I still don't know what brought him back home. He hasn't said anything to you?'

'Why would he?' Ailsa was surprised at Bev's question, but she had shared her concerns about Bob with him last night. Was it so odd to consider he might have done the same?

'I don't know. I just thought…' Bev paused. 'You fancied him back then, when he came to our party, didn't you? I always thought there was something… He left next morning when he'd planned on staying for a week.'

Ailsa's stomach gave a flip. 'Bev, that was over thirty years ago. Even if…' she swallowed, '…even if I fancied him then, I met Bob, and the rest is history.' She picked at an imaginary piece of lint on her pants, unwilling to meet her friend's eyes.

'I know. I just thought. You and Bob seem to be having problems. Oh, I know…' She held up one hand as Ailsa opened her mouth to reply, '…you haven't spoken about it. You don't need to. The very fact you came up here for two months by yourself tells me all is not well in your marriage. You don't need to go into detail. I'm right, aren't I? And Martin is still an attractive man. No one could blame you if…'

Ailsa swallowed again. Could Bev read her mind? 'Don't be silly.' She gave a laugh which, even to her, sounded false. 'I admit Bob and I are having a few challenges, but we'll sort things out when I get back.'

'And Martin?' Bev persisted.

'I hadn't noticed,' she lied.

'Hmph. Well, I'll be home soon, and I intend to check you two out. I'd have loved it if… but I guess it wasn't meant to be, and now…'

'I'm married, Bev. Don't forget that.' *But not for much longer.*

'No. But… Oh, ignore me. What do I know? I've never felt the need to share my life with anyone.'

Ailsa breathed a sigh of relief when she left Bev and was on her way to the garden centre. Her friend was too darned perceptive. But she couldn't possibly know about their kiss or how Martin's touch turned Ailsa to jelly, could she? Nor could she know the true state of Ailsa's marriage.

Twenty-nine

It felt strange to be driving her own car again, after becoming used to Bev's van, but Ailsa didn't think the garden centre vehicle appropriate for bringing Bev home from hospital.

Martin had gone to the garden centre as usual that morning, promising to return home for lunch to check how Bev was coping. He had readily agreed Ailsa should be the one to collect his sister, knowing the two women would prefer it.

As she drove the short distance to the hospital, Ailsa reflected how she and Martin had managed to put the momentary loss of control behind them and treat each other civilly, almost like the friends they'd vowed to remain. They'd eaten together each evening, discussed their day at the garden centre, visited Bev in hospital – separately and together.

To Ailsa's relief, there had been no mention of *that* moment. Even though the sensation of electricity still crackled between them, they both managed to ignore it. Now Bev was coming home and there would be no opportunity for any recurrence. Ailsa was still congratulating herself on how well things were going when she arrived at the hospital.

When she entered the ward, Bev was already dressed and sitting in a wheelchair ready to leave. 'Hi, Bev,' Ailsa said. 'Have I kept you waiting?'

'Not at all. The nurse got me up and ready, but I'm waiting for all the documentation they seem to need before they let me go. Take a seat and tell me how you and Martin are getting on.'

'Fine. I already said.'

'You did, but I know my brother.' Bev chuckled. 'He can be very charming when he wants to be.'

Charming? That wasn't how Ailsa would describe him, but she remembered the charm he'd projected at their first meeting. It hadn't been charm that had led her to fall into his embrace and return his kiss. She still couldn't believe how she'd succumbed – and how it had kept her awake all night thinking about it. 'He's planning to come home for lunch, so you'll see for yourself. I'm glad you're coming home.' *You don't know how glad.*

'Oh, good. I wish he'd stay around Bellbird Bay. He's been travelling around the world for much too long. It's time he put down some roots.'

Ailsa was saved from replying by the arrival of a nurse with a sheaf of papers which she proceeded to explain to Bev.

'We'll provide you with crutches and you can try to walk a little, but you must remember to rest to allow your ribs to heal. No sneaking off to the garden centre.' She grinned. 'You know I'll hear all about it if you do.'

'That's the trouble with a town this size,' Bev complained when Ailsa was wheeling her out to the car. 'Everyone knows everyone else's business. I heard Martin had dinner at the surf club the other night and almost gate-crashed Jackie Anderson's divorce celebration.'

He did? What night was that?

'Sally told me,' Bev continued. 'She was at school with Jackie and me – and Martin, too. She said an old flame of his was there, too, Annabel Wilson – Todd now. I think she's divorced now too. It's happened a lot in our age group. Sorry, Ailsa, not something you want to hear, is it? But another reason I prefer the single life.'

By this time, they'd reached Ailsa's car so there was no need for her to respond. 'Let's get you out of this,' she said opening the car door and pushing the wheelchair up to it.

'I can manage,' Bev said, determined to be independent, but it took both her and Ailsa to help her into the back seat.

Bev's words stuck in Alisa's head as she returned the wheelchair and picked up the promised crutches. Divorce! Was that where she and Bob were headed? Despite what he'd said, his plans to move out, she couldn't envisage life without him. And how would the boys react? She and Bob had always been there for them. Sure, they were grown men now, but they'd always be her boys. She wiped the tears threatening to spill over. She hated the thought of becoming a statistic.

*

'Hungry?' Ailsa asked when they were back home, and Bev was safely ensconced in a comfortable armchair by the window in the living room.

'Am I ever. But don't go to a lot of trouble. Anything would taste good after the hospital food I've had for the past few days. I swear they try to make it as unpalatable as they can.'

Ailsa chuckled. She'd heard this complaint before – from her father when he was in hospital having his hip replacement – but knew hospitals did the best they could with the number of patients they had to cater for. 'Let me see what I can rustle up,' she said.

Before she could reach the kitchen, there was the now familiar sound of the Mini Moke stopping outside, and Martin appeared in the doorway, a stack of polystyrene containers in his arms.

'Cleo thought you might be missing her cooking,' he said, dropping them onto the coffee table. 'I'm not sure what's there but it looks more than enough for lunch for three.'

'She shouldn't have,' Bev said, levering herself up. But Ailsa could see her eyes light up in anticipation of what Cleo might have sent.

'I'll get some plates,' she said, making for the kitchen.

Martin followed, opening the fridge to extract a container of juice which he poured into three glasses. 'Not quite up to the standard of Cleo's juices, but the best I can do.'

'It'll be fine.' Ailsa took three plates out of the cupboard and a handful of cutlery from a drawer. She followed him back to where Bev was opening the containers, the delicious aromas of chicken curry and Italian seasoning rising from them.

'Wow!' Bev said. 'This will do us for lunch *and* dinner. Give her our thanks, Martin. It's good of her.'

'You're a good boss,' Martin said, 'and it's your café.'

'Yes, but…'

'Anyway, let's eat.' Ailsa handed round the plates and cutlery and added a serving of lasagne to her plate.

*

'What have you done to Martin?' Bev asked, when the meal had been eaten and cleared away, and Martin had left to return to the garden centre.

'What do you mean?'

'He's come out of the glooms he's been in ever since he got back. He's almost a different person. He actually managed to carry on a reasonable conversation.' Bev peered at Ailsa. 'Are you sure you two aren't...?'

'No!' Ailsa spoke more forcibly than she intended. 'I've already told you. There's nothing...' She could feel a blush rise, remembering how there almost had been. But she'd nipped it in the bud. She hadn't come to Bellbird Bay to embroil herself in a new relationship.

'And what about Bob? You still haven't told me what happened there. Don't you think it's time you confessed? What's up?'

'Oh, Bev, it's all too difficult.' Though having already unburdened herself to Martin, it was probably only fair to share her concerns with Bev, too.

By the time Ailsa had finished, Bev was frowning. 'I'm so sorry,' she said. 'And you had no idea?'

Ailsa shook her head. *Why did everyone ask her this?*

'What do you plan to do?'

'I don't know, Bev. I'm hoping...' *What was she hoping – that it would all go away?*

'From what you've told me, it would seem Bob's made up his mind.' There was a note of pity in Bev's voice as she stated the truth Ailsa had been trying to ignore. In her heart of hearts, she'd known her marriage was over. It was only a matter of time before the word divorce was actually mentioned. Ailsa had been deluding herself, pretending the marriage was something that could be fixed, like a broken leg. But deep down, she'd known. Since Bob told her he was gay, that he couldn't live a lie any longer, she'd known. It had taken Bev's words to force her to accept it.

Her fantasy about returning to Canberra to work things out with Bob, was just that, a fantasy. There would be no working things out. Her marriage was really over.

'Sorry,' she said, seeing Ailsa's stunned expression, 'I'm no expert on men as you know. I've never been too successful in that regard. Probably why I'm still single.'

'Maybe I should go back to Canberra. But I don't want to leave you in the lurch.'

'Don't feel you have to stay here for me,' Bev said. 'Martin and I can cope.'

'Really? Your brother is barely house trained.'

They laughed.

'No, I'll stay as long as you need me,' Ailsa said. 'I'm sure Bob will keep till then.'

Ailsa waited till she'd helped Bev into bed and was back in the kitchen before trying to call Bob. She was unsure what she wanted to say to him, perhaps to tell him *she* was ready to discuss their next step. To her frustration, or perhaps relief, the call immediately went to voicemail. She thought for a moment, then called Nate. Her younger son was always more communicative than his brother.

Nate answered immediately and, before she could speak, said, 'Glad you called, Mum. I was about to call you.'

'Is there something wrong?' Ailsa's heart began to beat faster, imagining the worst. 'Has something happened to your dad, Pat...?'

'No, all's well here, but... I know you're not going to like it, but I've decided to take a year out from uni. Thought I'd head up to Bellbird Bay and spend some time with you.'

'Oh!' Ailsa's heart thumped madly. *Had Bob decided to tell the boys? Was Nate upset at the news, too upset to remain in Canberra?* 'Have you spoken to your dad?'

'Course. We had dinner together. I needed to pick up a few things from home.'

So, Bob hadn't said anything yet. 'And? What does he think? You have told him?' Despite a glow of pleasure at the prospect of seeing Nate, Ailsa knew how much store Bob put on both of the boys getting a good education, a good degree.

'He's cool. Well, he didn't actually say much when I told him. He seemed to have other things on his mind.'

Ailsa bit her lip. 'He didn't say anything?'

'No. I was expecting the usual rant. You know how he went on when Pat talked about taking a gap year before uni? But all he said was, "Your mum will like that". It was odd, to say the least. But it means I'll be up there in a couple of days.'

A couple of days? 'How long have you been planning this?'

'I've been thinking about it since Christmas. I didn't say anything till now because... well, I didn't know how you and Dad would react. But with the start of semester getting closer, I knew I had to do something. I'm not sure it's for me, Mum. I'm not like Pat, not like you and Dad. I want to do something different with my life. Maybe I should have been the one to take a year out after school. But it's not too late, and better late than never.'

'And what do you intend to do here in Bellbird Bay?'

'I don't know.'

Ailsa could imagine her son shrugging his shoulders and grinning sheepishly. He'd always been able to get around her with his cheeky grin.

'Maybe I'll learn to surf.'

'Surf?' Ailsa couldn't stifle the image which came to mind of Martin standing on the deck, dropping water onto the surface, his board shorts clinging to his hips. She swallowed.

'I'll look for a job, too, I won't be bludging on you. I've booked into a backpackers.'

'How will you get here? Do you want me to pick you up?'

'I'll ride up on the bike.'

Ailsa shuddered. Against her better judgement, when Bob's father had died, Nate used his inheritance to buy himself a second-hand motorbike, arguing it would get him around Canberra and to his classes on time. She and Bob had never imagined he'd use it for interstate travel. It was a long way from Canberra to Bellbird Bay. 'I don't think...'

'It'll be fine, Mum. Don't worry. I'm not a kid. I can take care of myself.'

When the call finished, Ailsa fumed at her husband. Why didn't he try to reason with Nate? The old Bob would have done. She thought about the books still lying unread on her bedside table. Was Bob clinically depressed? Was that why he hadn't reacted more strongly to her decision to leave, to Nate's decision to drop out of uni? Was his decision to come out affecting his mental health? If so, he should see a doctor. But their local GP was Dave Reid, the father of one of Pat's school friends. They had often socialised with Dave and his wife. Bob would run a mile rather than discuss this sort of thing with him.

Ailsa sighed as she put her phone in her pocket. It was one more thing to add to her worries. But at least there was the pleasure of seeing Nate to look forward to.

Thirty

Ailsa seemed subdued when she appeared at breakfast on Monday morning. Her hair was still mussed from sleep, and Martin thought she looked cute, as if she'd only just woken up.

'I looked in on Bev. She's still asleep,' she said, pouring muesli into a bowl and making herself a cup of fennel and cardamon tea.

How could she and Bev stomach the stuff especially at this time in the morning? Martin couldn't survive without his morning caffeine hit. 'How do you intend to do this?' he asked.

'This? Oh, you mean taking care of Bev and looking after the garden centre? Well, I thought you could go to open up, while I help Bev shower and dress, make sure she has breakfast and so on. Then I can spend the morning there and come back to make Bev's lunch, before doing an afternoon shift.'

'You seem to have thought this through.'

'Someone had to. Sorry, I didn't mean to sound harsh.' Ailsa spooned a generous amount of yoghurt on top of her muesli and sprinkled it with blueberries.

It looked delicious. Martin regarded his own breakfast – three slices of toast slathered with vegemite. Maybe he'd try muesli tomorrow. Then he noticed Ailsa's expression. 'Are you okay? Is something worrying you?'

Ailsa sighed. 'No… yes… It's my husband. Bob.'

'You've spoken with him again?'

'No. But I spoke with my son – Nate, the younger one. I'm worried

about him, too. He's planning to drop out of uni and come up here.'
She bit her lip.

'And that's a bad idea?'

'Of course it is.' Ailsa glared at him. 'But the odd thing is Bob's
reaction, or rather the lack of it. Normally, he'd rant and rave, tell
Nate he was ruining his life, wasting the money we're spending on his
education.'

'But he didn't?'

'No. There's something very wrong with Bob. I think he may be
suffering from depression. Perhaps I should go home.' She frowned.
'But I need to be here for Bev, and now Nate'll be here, expecting
me to... Oh, it's all too hard.' Ailsa folded her arms on the table and
dropped her head onto them.

She looked so vulnerable, the nape of her neck exposed above her
white tee-shirt. Martin resisted the urge to plant a kiss on the inviting
white curve of skin. Instead, he asked, 'When does your son plan to
arrive?'

Ailsa lifted her head. 'Nate said in a couple of days, which would
probably be the day after tomorrow. He plans to get a job here, but I
have no idea what he could do. He's been studying maths and science,
not exactly geared to the sort of casual employment available in
Bellbird Bay.'

Martin wondered what Ailsa's son would be like. He could have
been his if... No, he wouldn't go there. He exhaled. 'I'd better get on
if I have to open up,' he said, pushing back from the table. 'You'll be
fine here?'

'Of course.'

'See you later, then.'

*

Martin was kept busy all morning. One thing about working here was
the lack of time to think, he decided, as he wiped the sweat from his
brow, and loaded yet another stack of bags of potting mix. Since Bev's
accident, his cameras had lain unused in his bedroom waiting for him
to have time to start again. But, somehow, the manual work he was

presently engaged in was strangely satisfying, though he'd never admit it to Bev or Ailsa.

Come lunchtime, he headed to the café as usual. By now he was a familiar figure and, as soon as he sat down, Jilly appeared with a steaming mug of black coffee to take his order. As he bit into the promptly delivered chicken salad roll, Martin mulled over what Ailsa told him at breakfast. Her son was coming to Bellbird Bay. It was strange to think of her with a grown son – two of them. Nate was the younger one. He must be in his early twenties. Martin thought about what he'd been doing at that age, not long after he'd first met Ailsa. But whereas he'd been sure of what he wanted out of life and determined to get it, regardless of who or what he had to run over in the process, it sounded as if Nate McNeil was more of a drifter.

Martin ate quickly, eager to get back to work, but unable to dismiss Ailsa's son from his mind. Would he be a masculine version of his mother or take after his dad and give Martin an insight into what Ailsa's husband looked like?

He hadn't seen Ailsa all morning, so it was a surprise when, halfway through the afternoon, she came to seek him out. He heard her before he saw her, heard his name being called in her now familiar voice – soft with just a hint of bossiness. Martin grinned and stopped what he was doing to greet her.

'What's up?'

'There's a call for you in the office. Can you take it?' She glanced at him. an amused expression flitting across her face.

Martin looked down at himself to see his tee-shirt stained with sweat and dirt from the bags he'd been hauling, and chuckled. Ailsa had never seen him like this. She was as immaculate as usual, the green pandanus apron covering her white tee-shirt, her ankles and feet encased in a pair of smart white trainers – the consummate professional. There was no sign of the worried woman he'd left at breakfast. How he'd love to ruffle her composure, pull her into his arms and plant a kiss on her lips. But this wasn't the time or place. 'Now?'

'Now,' she confirmed. 'A John Baldwin.'

Martin scratched his head. The name meant nothing to him.

'You'd better see what he wants.'

'Sure.' Martin ensured the pile of bags he'd been working on was secure, wiped his hands on his shorts, and followed Ailsa back to the office.

She waited till he went in, then closed the door to give him privacy for his call.

He picked up the phone. 'Martin Cooper here.'

'I'm speaking to Martin Cooper, the travel photographer, right?' The man's voice was curt.

Martin's heart sank. *What was this about? Had the news of his mess reached here?* 'That's me,' he said, his stomach churning.

'My name's John Baldwin. I own a small gallery here in Bellbird Bay. You may have seen it in Corella Way, off the esplanade?'

Martin tried to envisage the gallery. He had a vague recollection of seeing one when he had coffee with Sam at the weirdly named *Greedy Gecko*. He hadn't paid much attention at the time. 'Yes, I have seen it.' *So, maybe it wasn't about what happened in New York.*

'I'm putting together a series of small exhibitions featuring local photographers and... I know it's a bit of a cheek to ask you, but I wondered... would you be willing to contribute some of your work? I'm being somewhat selfish here as I know your participation would greatly increase the interest in our exhibitions. Local lad made good sort of thing.'

Martin was stunned. In all the time he'd been filming, winning prizes for his work, this was the first time he'd been invited to display them in an exhibition. While every vestige of his common sense cautioned him to refuse, his pride in his work, his natural arrogance, overcame his scruples. 'Sounds interesting,' he said. 'I'd like to know more about what you have in mind.'

Thirty-one

The roar of a motorbike broke the peace of the late afternoon, prompting Ailsa to run to the front door. There, standing beside the bike removing his helmet, was her beloved son. 'Nate!' she yelled, running towards him and wrapping her arms around his tall lanky figure. 'It's so good to see you.'

'Mum, steady on.' Nate disentangled himself and hung his helmet on the bike's handlebar. 'It's been a long trip. I could murder a beer.'

'Of course. Come on inside and meet Bev. Do you remember her? You were only little when we were last here.' She led Nate inside and out to the deck where Bev was seated in a cane chair, her foot up on a low stool, her crutches lying beside her.

'So this is Nate?' Bev said, when they appeared in the doorway. 'Excuse my not getting up.' She gestured to her crutches. 'You've grown a lot since we last met. Not a cheeky little boy any longer.'

'Not so little but still cheeky,' Ailsa said with a grin. 'I'll get you a beer, Nate. Bev?'

'Not for me, but a cup of tea would be good.'

'Done.' Ailsa disappeared into the kitchen from where she could hear Bev and Nate chatting out on the deck. She was thrilled to see Nate. It was as if a light had gone on inside her. Not till her ungainly son had stepped off his bike, had she realised how much she missed him, missed him and Pat... and Bob. She wiped away an incipient tear. Although she loved being here, Canberra was home. It was where her family was. It would be so good to have Nate close by, for a time at least.

'How long will you be here?' Ailsa asked Nate, who was lounging against the railing, a beer in one hand, his other gripping the wooden rail, looking as if he belonged. He'd shed the leather jacket he'd worn for travelling and was wearing an old grey tee-shirt that had seen better days. His jeans were travel-stained and his dark, curly hair was dishevelled. He looked not unlike Bob had when they first met. A twinge of sadness pierced her. They'd been so happy then.

'Dunno.' Nate turned to look out at the ocean glistening in the sun. 'It's a damned sight better than Canberra. If I can find some work, I may just decide to stay.'

'But, Nate, your studies…'

'Mum, don't preach. *You* came up here to get away from things.'

'Yes, but…'

'Maybe you both needed time out,' suggested Bev with a smile.

'Mmm.' Ailsa flinched. Bev's words were too close to what she'd told Bob before she left Canberra, before he dropped his bombshell.

'Bellbird Bay is a good spot to regroup,' Bev said, nodding. 'It has healing qualities. Wouldn't you agree, Ailsa?'

Ailsa wasn't so sure healing was the right word. Since coming here she'd experienced so many different emotions. Some days she wasn't sure how she felt. 'What sort of work do you think you might do?' she asked Nate to avoid responding to Bev.

'Dunno,' Nate said again. 'But I did a bartending course before I left Canberra. Got my Responsible Serving of Alcohol accreditation so I can work in a bar.' He grinned. 'Not completely useless, Mum. I'm willing to try my hand at anything. But first…' he glanced out at the ocean again, '…I want to get some of that. Can I learn to surf here?'

'Course you can. Your mum took a lesson.'

'Mum?' Nate stared at Ailsa in astonishment.

She blushed. 'Why shouldn't I?' Bev's accident had come soon after her lesson and Ailsa hadn't followed it up, but she intended to, as soon as she could.

'Where did you get it? Maybe I can…'

It was Bev who replied. 'Will Rankin runs the surf school down on the beach. He's there every day. I believe you can just front up. No booking required.'

'Great,' Nate said with a grin. He drained his beer. 'Thanks, Ma.

Guess I should go and check in at the backpackers before they give my bed away.'

'You'll come back for dinner?'

'Try to stop me.' He gave Ailsa a peck on the cheek, picked up his jacket and was off, the front door banging closed behind him before Ailsa could move.

'He's a nice kid,' Bev said, as they heard the bike start up and roar off.

'Not such a kid, as I keep forgetting. They are both grown up now, have minds of their own and don't pay much attention to what Bob and I say any longer.' Ailsa's mind went back to her husband. *What was he doing? How was he spending his time?* She couldn't help worrying about him, but the longer she was here in Bellbird Bay, the more remote Canberra and Bob seemed.

*

By the time Nate returned, showered and dressed in a pair of khaki chinos and a blue chambray shirt, Martin was home from the garden centre and wearing an almost identical outfit. Looking at the pair of them standing on the deck, each holding a bottle of beer and leaning against the rail while Ailsa and Bev sat with glasses of chilled chardonnay, was like looking at Martin with a younger version of Bob.

Ailsa swallowed as the comparison hit her. But really, Nate was more like Martin than his father in personality. The wild streak in her son was missing in Bob. Perhaps it was Bob's gentle nature that had first attracted her. After Martin, whose stories of his wild student life in Sydney had both fascinated and repelled her, Bob's more down-to-earth attitude to life was refreshing. He wasn't the man's man Martin Cooper clearly was, preferring to sit around discussing books and movies and happy to spend their evenings alone together. He'd never been addicted to sports the way many of her friends' husbands were either, nor had he spent hours in the pub with his mates. He had been the perfect companion, perfect until…

Martin, however, was a different kettle of fish. Ailsa couldn't imagine him being content to sit around discussing literature. He'd been a bit of a hellraiser when he was young according to what she'd gleaned from Bev's carefully worded comments, and he and Will had been the bad boys of Bellbird Bay in their day.

Ailsa shivered.

Nate, having worked out who Martin was, was bombarding him with questions about his travels, to which Martin was managing to remain self-effacing while providing Nate with colourful descriptions of his forays into the unknown.

'What's next for you?' Nate asked, when they appeared to have covered most of Martin's adventures.

'Who knows?' Martin spread his hands wide. 'Maybe I'll try something completely different. I've been experimenting with surfing shots, and I've been invited to contribute to a local exhibition of photographs.'

'You have?' Bev asked. 'You didn't say.'

'Only recently. I still have to find out more about it and decide if and what to offer the guy.'

'The call you had the other day?' Ailsa guessed. She'd wondered who the caller was. It was unusual for Martin – for any of them – to receive personal calls at the garden centre.

'Yeah. This guy – John Baldwin – owns a local gallery.'

'*The Bay Gallery*,' Bev said. 'It has a good reputation. John set it up a few years ago and it's gone from strength to strength.'

'Why is everything around here called *The Bay* something or other?' Nate asked. 'I've only been here a few hours and I've ridden past *The Bay Café*, *The Bay Bistro*... I don't know what else, and I'm staying at *The Bay Backpackers*.' He shook his head with a grin.

'I guess it's because to call things after Bellbird Bay would be too longwinded. But you're right, it is a bit unimaginative,' Bev said, 'and if you take a surf lesson, it'll be from *The Bay Surf School*.' She chuckled.

'Thinking of taking up surfing?' Martin asked. 'You couldn't do better than Will Rankin. Your mum took a lesson there.' His eyes met Ailsa's in unspoken understanding.

She blushed. 'He's very good, Nate,' she said. 'Martin surfs, too.'

Nate looked at Martin, his eyes filled with admiration. 'Wow, but you grew up here, didn't you? I wish... Why did we never come back for holidays, Mum?'

'I don't know. Your dad...' Ailsa tried to remember why their first foray to Bellbird Bay had never been repeated. Bob had thought the trip too long when they lived so close to the south coast of New South Wales. The boys could have surfed there, but neither she nor Bob had been surfers. Then they had started going camping further inland where Bob could pursue his love of fishing, before the boys decided their parents were boring and started going off with their mates. 'You can learn now,' she said.

'It'll be rad.' Nate turned to look out to the ocean again. 'I can't wait.'

'How is it at the backpackers?' Ailsa asked, sorry there wasn't room for Nate at Bev's. It would have been lovely to have him under the same roof. But she supposed he valued his independence now he'd been living away from home for over a year. 'Can you...?'

'I have some money put by, Mum, if that's what you were going to ask.' Nate flushed. 'Gran and Grandpa gave me a cheque for Christmas, and I've saved some of my allowance. I know you and dad won't continue it now I've dropped out.'

'Did your dad say so?'

'He didn't have to. I remember the conditions the pair of you set me when I started my degree.' He grinned. 'I'm not stupid. This is my decision. The fact you're up here only reinforced it, I'd have taken a year off anyway. I'm not sure if I'm in the right course. I need time to find out. And... anyway, I'm here now.'

Ailsa was about to ask him how spending a year by the beach was going to help him decide about his uni course when she bit her tongue. Hadn't she decided to do the same thing? Hadn't she come up here to help her make a decision about her future? She flinched. 'Let's eat,' she said.

*

Once they'd eaten and Nate had been easily persuaded by Martin to check out the surf club, Ailsa and Bev settled down on the deck with their usual glass of wine.

'He's a nice boy,' Bev said. 'He takes after your husband in looks.'

'Both boys do, in looks anyway. But they're both much more sociable than Bob ever was. I was always the one to make new friends, except for...' She remembered that one instance when Bob had seemed to make friends with Aiden... Green was his name. 'Anyway, he's really changed now. I can't believe he didn't raise the roof when Nate told him he was taking a year out. Bob's always set such store on both boys getting a good education. He even insisted we pay their fees to avoid them racking up student debt. Something must really be wrong. I'm worried about him Bev.'

'Maybe he's like you – needs this time to sort himself out.'

'I'm not doing too well on that front, am I?' Ailsa said ruefully. 'All I've done is help you out, take long walks and...' She stopped herself in time from saying, *moon over your brother.*

'Maybe helping out and taking walks is giving you time to think, to work out what needs to be done.'

'You mean if I'm going to stay married to Bob?' Ailsa gasped. It was the first time she'd said out loud what had been going around and around in her head since she left Canberra.

'So, I was right.' Bev took a sip of wine. 'You have been thinking about Bob? Have you reached any conclusion?'

Ailsa shook her head. She picked up her glass, but didn't immediately take a drink. 'We've been married a long time, Bev. I do still love Bob. And there are the boys to think of. It's just all too hard.'

'Ailsa, I know it's difficult. But from a rational viewpoint, you have to take a stance, take action, move forward and do what's best for you.'

Ailsa sighed. Bev was right. She was only delaying the inevitable.

'Are you sure your dallying has nothing to do with my brother?'

Ailsa couldn't stop herself from gasping again. 'Of course not.' She took a gulp of wine, almost choking. She wasn't at all sure. Meeting Martin Cooper again had aroused all sorts of feelings and emotions she'd considered dead for good.

Thirty-two

'Wow, this is some place.' Nate gazed around the surf club in admiration.

'Try a Queensland beer?' Martin asked, pointing to the Four X sign on the bar.

'Why not? Thanks for suggesting this. It was good to see Mum again, but... she and Dad...' Nate gestured with his hands.

'She cares for you. It's what mums do.'

'Yeah, but... Thanks,' he said as their beers were served. He took a swig, wiping his mouth with the back of his hand. 'So, this is Queensland beer.'

'Here on holiday?' the barman asked with a grin.

'Not really, I plan to stay for a while if I can find work.'

'Any experience with bar work? There might be an opening here – casual hours,' he said, leaning on the bar.

'Really?' Nate grinned at Martin. 'Glad you brought me here.' He turned back to the barman. 'Who do I talk to?'

'Come back when we open tomorrow at ten and talk to the manager. Bring along your CV. You can vouch for him?' he asked Martin, who nodded, amused at this turn of events.

'Gee, thanks, Martin,' Nate said again when they were seated out on the deck, the sound of the surf in their ears. 'They know you here?'

'For my sins.' Martin had invited Nate for a beer intending to try to find out more about Ailsa. He'd heard her side of her marriage, her worries about her husband, and was eager to get her son's take on it. He hadn't expected to be called on to vouch for the boy he'd only just

146

met. But he was happy to do what he could for Ailsa's son. With a mother like Ailsa, the boy couldn't be bad, could he?

'Yeah, Mum said you grew up here. When did you leave?'

'As soon as I could.' Martin took a swig of beer. What else had Ailsa told her son about him?

'Why? I mean to have all of this…' Nate gestured to the beach and ocean below the deck. Even at this time of night, there were still a few surfers out there, and a couple of people walking their dogs on the beach, intent on making the most of the last vestiges of daylight.

'I guess I felt about Bellbird Bay the way you feel about Canberra. I had ambitions to do and see more than Bellbird Bay, wanted to spread my wings and make my name as a photographer.'

'And you did.' Nate rolled his glass between his hands. 'You're spot on as to how I feel about Canberra. The place was beginning to stifle me. Mum and Dad love it. Even Pat seems content there. But me? I hate the place. It's such a planned city. I want…' He took a sip of beer. 'I don't really know what I want. That's where you and I differ. You had a goal. I… when Mum said she was coming up here for the summer, it seemed like a good idea to come too, to get away.' He glanced up at Martin as if wondering how much to tell him, to trust him.

'Away from?'

'Everything. At uni, I got in with a crowd who… To be honest, they weren't the best. What my folks would call a bad influence. Don't get me wrong. I didn't get into the hard stuff, but…'

'Drugs?' Martin guessed, remembering his own student days.

Nate nodded, avoiding eye contact. 'But no longer. I got a real scare one night when me and a mate were fooling around on campus on the bike. The damned thing fell on me. We only just escaped being caught. If we had, the uni bods would have called the police. It was a lucky escape, lucky I wasn't too badly injured – and lucky the bike survived. That was one of the reasons. And I wanted to see this place. I can barely remember when we came here on holiday.'

'Your mum seems to like it here.'

'Yeah. She's more relaxed. For the past year it's as if she's been on edge all the time. And Dad hasn't helped. He's… Sorry, you don't want to know all this. Tell me about Bellbird Bay.'

Martin did want to know but couldn't think of a reason to continue talking about Ailsa without revealing his interest in her. But he understood Nate's desire to avoid talking about his parents. He spent the next hour spinning tales of the good times he'd had in Bellbird Bay, times when he and Will were local surfing heroes, and life was all about the sun, the sea and the surf.

*

His mind still filled with Ailsa and her son, Martin left the garden centre early next day and after showering and changing, made his way to the gallery to meet John Baldwin. Surprised he hadn't taken much notice when he and Sam went to the next-door café, he was impressed by the gold lettering *The Bay Gallery* above the door, and the window in which there was a display of two prints each depicting a local beach scene. He pushed open the door to see a tall, slim, silver-haired man who appeared to be in his early sixties, a pair of old-fashioned half-moon spectacles perched on his nose.

'Martin Cooper,' the man said, coming forward to greet him. 'You probably don't remember me, but I recall you and Will Rankin back when you were both vying for surfing honours.'

Another one! Everyone in this town seemed to remember him in his youth. 'Hello, John,' Martin said, taking the man's outstretched hand.

'Just a moment.' John Baldwin went to lock the door and turn the sign to *Closed*. 'I normally close up at this time. We can go through the back to be more private, but first, you might care to check out the current exhibition. I'll make us a coffee while you do. How do you take it?'

'Black, thanks.' Martin walked slowly around the small gallery examining the collection of paintings on display They all appeared to be the work of two local artists, one who was responsible for the beach scenes he'd seen in the window, the other who produced excellent watercolours of native plants. They were impressive, as good as any to be found in the larger city galleries which boasted the work of well-known artists.

'What do you think?'

Martin turned from where he'd been admiring a particularly well-executed depiction of a surfer in the barrel of a wave, to see the gallery owner standing watching him, arms folded, wearing an inscrutable expression. 'They're good, very good.'

'Not what you expected?' John Baldwin smiled.

'You got me. No, I'd expected something more…'

'More amateurish perhaps?'

Martin smiled sheepishly.

'You'd be surprised at the talent we have in the town. Some are native sons and daughters who have returned – a bit like yourself. Others have never left or have moved here to retire and found time to pursue a talent which has lain dormant for years. Bellbird Bay is now home to a large number of creative souls – artists and writers.'

Martin felt suitably rebuked. Maybe he'd underestimated the town, allowed his younger prejudices to colour his opinions. He followed the other man through into a tiny office now filled with the aroma of coffee.

'Now,' John said, when he'd poured them both mugs of the brew. 'Here's what I have in mind. The current exhibition finishes in two weeks' time. I plan to take a break and when I heard you were in town, I thought it a good idea to see if you'd agree to a showing of a selection of your photographs when I return, say in around four to six weeks' time? I'm assuming you own copyright or could gain permission to display them?' He steepled his fingers and raised his eyebrows.

Martin hesitated before replying. Being a freelance photographer, he had always retained copyright to his work. He fought to stifle the memory of Barry Young's claim which threatened to overturn his right to his most recent shots. 'I own copyright. I was interested in a couple of the paintings you have on display – the surf scenes.'

'Oh, yes?' John peered over his half-moon glasses.

'I've been doing a bit of that myself lately – photos of course. I wondered if they might be of interest along with some of my earlier work. I'd welcome your professional opinion.'

'Mmm.' John sounded doubtful.

Martin took out his phone and scrolled to the shots he considered to be his best to date.

'These are your most recent work?' John asked, after scrolling through them and peering at them for several minutes. 'They're good, unusual. You've caught the feeling of freedom. Takes me back. I wasn't always stuck in this gallery, you know.'

Martin exhaled. Almost everyone in Bellbird Bay had been a surfer at one time or another. It was as natural to them as breathing. He waited.

'I'd be happy to take these.' He thought for a few moments. 'But I would like your travel shots too. Those are the ones you're famous for, the ones which would attract attention. I can see how an exhibit of local scenes would work well, but I'm keen to show some of your more well-known pieces. How do you feel about that?'

'Sounds good.' If this guy thought his surfing shots were worth exhibiting perhaps there was a future for him in this new field. Though, he reminded himself, John Baldwin was a small-town gallery owner, nothing like the magazine editors he'd have to convince of their commercial viability. He tried to suppress the stir in his gut at the prospect of the news of his Young's claim emerging when his most famous shots were on exhibition, even if it were held here in Bellbird Bay.

Thirty-three

Ailsa grimaced when she saw her mother's number on the screen. She'd been slack, putting off calling her. 'Hi, Mum,' she said, dropping into a chair and mouthing, 'Grandma,' to Nate who had developed the habit of dropping in between shifts.

In addition to doing casual bar work at the surf club, Nate was helping out at the surf school, hiring out boards for Will Rankin. He and the older man had bonded during his first lesson, and when Will had mentioned his son was no longer able to hire out the boards due to his training schedule, Nate had offered to step in. It was an ideal situation for him, and Nate was thrilled to have found himself two jobs within a few days of his arrival on the coast.

'You're still staying with your friend?'

'Yes, Mum.' Ailsa's fingers pleated the hem of her shirt as she tried to stem her impatience.

'Hmmm. I saw Bob the other day. The poor man looked ill. I don't know how you could leave him and go gallivanting off like that.'

Ailsa let her mind wander as her mother ranted on. Her mother hadn't had a good word to say about her son-in-law for months. Now, because Ailsa had chosen to spend a couple of months in Bellbird Bay, he'd become *the poor man*. It was so like Sheila Browne to change her tune this way. Now, whatever was wrong was going to be all Ailsa's fault. What would her homophobic mother say when she learned the truth? Maybe she need never know.

'In my day...' her mother continued.

'Mum, Bev had an accident. I'm helping out here, that's all.'

'And there's no one else can do it? I heard she had a brother who's staying there too, in the same house. And Pat tells me young Nate's joined you, quite a group of *helpers*.' Her voice emphasised her final word as if they were all engaged in some illicit activity. Ailsa almost laughed. But she did experience a sense of guilt at the mention of Martin.

Deciding to ignore the reference to Bev's twin, she said, 'Nate's working, Mum. He's actually working two jobs, and it's lovely to have him here. It's not unusual for students to take time out. It'll give Nate time to work out what he really wants to do.' Ailsa grimaced at Nate who grinned and made a rude sign.

'And you? What do you need time to do?'

'Mum! I've already said…' Ailsa was losing patience with her mother. Sheila would never change, but at least when she was in Canberra her father was there to mediate. On the phone, it was only Sheila and her inescapable complaining and disapproval. She looked across at Nate who was gesturing for her to wind up the conversation. 'Sorry, Mum. I have to go. Talk again soon.' She hung up before Sheila could reply.

'Gran going on again?' Nate asked, opening the fridge. 'Is there any more of the cake we had last night?'

Ailsa walked across to take out the leftover lemon sponge cake she'd brought home from the café the previous day. Now Bev was recovering, she was managing to do most of the paperwork for the garden centre from home, so Ailsa was only going in to help for part of each day. It meant she was able to practice her surfing, much to Nate's amusement. He had taken to the sport like a duck to water and, while tolerant of his mother's efforts, Ailsa knew he despaired of her ever becoming a skilful surfer. She didn't care. It was enough she enjoyed the sensation of riding a wave into the shore. Martin had been right about that. And besides, it helped keep her fit, maybe she'd even lose a few kilos.

*

Ailsa had just sat back down after serving Nate a slice of lemon sponge when the door opened, and Martin burst in a big grin on his face.

'It went well?' Nate asked.

Ailsa was puzzled. *What went well? How had Nate and Martin managed to develop a friendship in such a short time? And... why did it annoy her?*

Martin must have seen her bewilderment. 'I had a meeting with the owner of the local gallery who's interested in exhibiting my work. Looks like it's going to go ahead. Why don't we all go to the club for lunch to celebrate?' He looked at Nate and Ailsa and at Bev who had just hobbled into the room.

She was managing her crutches better but still found them awkward. 'Congratulations,' she said. 'But I'm not ready for outings like that, but you two go.' She gestured to Ailsa and Nate with one crutch.

'Not me, either,' Nate said with a mouthful of lemon sponge. 'I just dropped by to grab a bite. I'll be at the club, but will be working. I start my shift in thirty minutes.'

'Ailsa?' Martin asked.

Ailsa looked at Bev, but her friend was smiling encouragement. There was no help to be had from that quarter. She couldn't think of an excuse other than the fact she didn't want to be alone with Martin. Each time they had been alone, something had happened to disturb her. But they'd agreed to be friends and friends could eat lunch together, couldn't they? 'Okay,' she said, 'I just need to...' She hurried out, went into her bedroom, closed the door, and leant against it breathing heavily.

Telling herself she was being ridiculous, Ailsa peered at herself in the mirror, seeing her bright eyes and heightened colour. It was only lunch at the surf club in the middle of the day. Martin had invited everyone. It wasn't his fault Bev and Nate had cried off, leaving Ailsa to be his only lunch companion. He probably felt as awkward about it as she did. And what could happen in broad daylight in the no doubt crowded club? But the memory of their kiss had never left her, the sensation of his lips on hers, his firm muscular body pressed against her, the way it made her feel. Ailsa trembled. Damn the man. Damn Bev. And Damn Nate for having to work.

As Ailsa expected, the club was packed with locals and tourists alike, all intent on enjoying one of the last days of their summer break. Seeing Nate behind the bar sent a jolt of pride through her and removed some of her apprehension. His wide grin helped calm the butterflies which were whizzing around in her stomach.

'Wine?' Martin asked.

'Thanks.'

'Chardonnay, Mum?' Nate knew her taste.

Ailsa nodded.

'I'll have a beer,' Martin said.

They ordered their meals and, taking their drinks outside, managed to find a free table close to railing on the beach side of the deck.

'Cheers,' Martin said raising his glass.

'Cheers, and congratulations on your exhibition.' Surely this was a safe topic of conversation?

'Thanks. I'm pleased to have it set up. John's planning a series of exhibitions. Mine will be the first.' Martin twirled his glass before taking a swig, then asked, 'Was there something bothering you when I walked into Bev's? You seemed... I don't know... pre-occupied. Distressed even.'

'No, I was... I'd been on the phone to my mother.'

'Oh! It was a difficult call?'

'Always.' Ailsa was about to expand on how difficult her mother could be before realising it might be insensitive. Both Martin's parents were dead. She had no idea what sort of relationship he'd had with them.

'It's okay. I wasn't close to my parents.' He rubbed a hand over his hair. 'I guess they were part of the reason I felt stifled in Bellbird Bay, had to get away, before it was too late.'

'Too late?' Ailsa was intrigued.

'Before Bellbird Bay sucked me in and I ended up like Will Rankin. Though,' he sighed, 'he doesn't seem to have done too bad for himself. He appears to be content with his life.' His eyes took on the faraway look Ailsa had seen there before. She wondered what caused it.

'He does seem happy with his lot,' she agreed. 'And Nate enjoys working with him. It's a lucky break for him.'

'He seems like a good kid.'

'He is. Both of them are. They...' Ailsa broke off, unsure how much to reveal. 'I think they've found things difficult this last little while, when Bob and I... It's affected each of them in different ways. Pat has kept up a hectic social life but I'm sure he'll settle down soon. He and Vee – his girlfriend. Nate...' she glanced inside the club to where Nate was serving drinks. 'He seems happier here. I think he got into some bad company in Canberra. This is a good break for him.'

'You're probably right.'

Ailsa gave Martin a wary glance. *What had Nate told him?*

'I mean,' he said, shifting uncomfortably in his seat. 'You must remember what it was like to be a student, the temptations, the...' He reddened as if remembering how they'd first met. 'No, you probably don't. I guess it was different for you.'

Ailsa wanted to ask what he meant, then recalled how she'd been enthralled by his talk of the wild parties and the drug scene in Sydney, how her own student experience had seemed so tame in comparison. 'Has Nate been involved in drugs?' she asked.

'Nothing to worry about. He had the sense to get out and come here. He's a sensible lad. You and your husband have done well. It can't be easy being parents these days.'

'No.' Ailsa relaxed. Again, she glanced into the club where Nate was pouring drinks and chatting to a couple of people who were obviously tourists, her pride in her son resurfacing. If only she could sort out her own life as easily as he appeared to have sorted his.

After a delicious serving of calamari and chips and a glass of chardonnay, Ailsa was feeling more relaxed. Martin was proving to be an interesting companion, regaling her with tales of his travels to the more inaccessible parts of the world.

In a gap in their conversation, the chatter of the other patrons almost drowning out the music from inside the club, Ailsa risked asking what she'd been dying to know since Martin arrived on the scene. She leaned forward. 'Why are you here? From what you've said, you love travelling around the world, hate being in one spot.'

'Ah!' Martin picked up his glass and took a swig of beer, then gazed out towards the ocean before turning back to face Ailsa again. 'It's a long story.'

'We have all afternoon.'

Martin said nothing.

'You know my story. There must be a reason why *you* decided to come back to Bellbird Bay after all this time.'

'Don't they say home is where you go when there's nowhere else to go?' he asked with a wry grin. 'Bev is the closest thing to home I have. I'm a sad case, Ailsa, to put it in a nutshell. A broken relationship and a failed career. I made a couple of mistakes. I chose the wrong woman and was caught up in a scam. End of story. I'm not sure if I have a career left. This shindig at *The Bay Gallery* may be my swansong – or it may resurrect my career. It's a bit of a lottery.'

'What do you mean?'

'If I'm to go into details, I think I need another of these.' He held up his now empty glass. 'You?'

Ailsa nodded. They'd walked down to the club so another glass wouldn't do any harm – and she was already feeling mellow from the effects of the wine. As she watched Martin walk away and into the club proper, a burst of music blasting through the open door, she wondered if she'd opened a can of worms. Was the normally taciturn Martin Cooper really going to open up to her, reveal the reason for his sudden appearance in Bellbird Bay?

'Here you are.' Martin set the glass of wine down on the table and took a gulp from his own glass before sitting down. 'You want to know the details?' he asked. 'Well, here goes.'

Minutes later, Ailsa was regarding her companion with sympathy. What a blow it must have been to have his work stolen then to discover how shallow his partner was. But surely it wasn't the complete disaster he made it out to be. Can't...' she began.

Martin held up a hand. 'No more questions. Now we know about each other, perhaps we can agree to put it behind us, let the past be the past and move on.' He smiled warmly. It was as if, by relating his reasons for being here, he'd shed what had been weighing him down.

Ailsa smiled back, a tiny bud of hope unfurling where before there had been distrust. Martin had suffered too, albeit in a different way from her. Maybe they could find a way forward together.

Thirty-four

Three weeks had passed since Martin's first meeting with John Baldwin, and they had been filled with activity for Martin as he prepared his photographs for exhibition. First, he had to decide which of the many in his massive collection to provide for the event. Then, in discussion with John, he discovered there were other decisions to be made. Should he frame his photos and which type of frame would work best? Should he edition them? Editioning wasn't something Martin had ever considered, not being commercially minded. He'd been satisfied to have his work featured in the exclusive travel magazines and the fame and kudos it brought.

But having his work included in an exhibition meant there would be buyers eager to purchase an original Martin Cooper, and John's advice was to offer each photograph as a limited edition. Doing so, he told Martin, would make the work more valuable, recommending editions of twenty. It would mean more work. Martin had to ensure each buyer knew the number in the edition they were receiving. He would need to keep records to make sure only the number in the edition were sold. He would also need to make sure all were printed exactly the same because buyers wouldn't be happy if the image they received wasn't exactly the same as the one they saw in the exhibition. John recommended a local printer he'd used for years who knew the importance of exact duplication where editions were concerned. It was all so much more complicated than Martin had envisaged when he originally agreed to the exhibition. He'd imagined printing out a few of his favourite shots and sticking them up on the gallery wall for the length of the exhibition. This was more, much more.

He was sitting at his laptop which he'd taken out onto the deck, frowning at the screen and beginning to wonder if it was worth the effort, when he sensed someone behind him and smelled the now familiar fragrance of Ailsa's perfume. He turned abruptly.

'Something the matter?' Ailsa leant closer to see the screen. She was wearing a loose shirt over a pair of knee-length shorts. Her hair was mussed by the light breeze, and her skin was showing a light tan from her time in the sun. It was all he could do to stop himself from taking her in his arms.

'It's this damned exhibition.' Martin drew a hand through his hair which was beginning to grow a little and feel more like it usually did. 'I didn't expect to have to do so much preparation. And now, John wants me to provide editions of each piece on display.'

'Editions?' Ailsa wrinkled her nose and took a seat beside him. 'Does that mean you have to have several copies of each photograph? I've seen it with Ken Duncan's work. He's a famous photographer from New South Wales. His photographs are hugely popular and highly sought after.'

'I know his work. It's amazing, But I've always felt it was... too commercial for me. It's a business for him. I'm not... I don't... My mind doesn't work that way. I've always been satisfied with magazine coverage.' He shrugged.

'Maybe you need to change the way you think about your work.' She peered over Martin's shoulder to where he had arranged ten of his South American pieces alongside four of his more recent shots. 'These are good. I love the comparison between the dense forests of the Amazon and the freshness of your shots in Bellbird Bay. Are those the ones you've selected for the exhibition?'

'Maybe.' Martin closed off the computer. 'It's doing my head in. I'm no businessman. I can point a camera but all this keeping records stuff is too hard.'

'It shouldn't be too difficult. Surely it's only a matter of finding a reliable printer and ensuring there are only the required number of each photo sold? I could...' She stopped, obviously embarrassed.

'Go on. You could...?' He raised one eyebrow.

'I could help set up a spreadsheet.' She blushed. 'But I'm sure you don't need my help.'

'Would you really?' Martin gazed at Ailsa in amazement. Since their conversation over lunch at the surf club, things had improved between them, but her offer was unexpected. 'It would be an enormous help. John recommended a printer to use, someone he's known for years. But the recording part of it is what's bugging me. I do understand spreadsheets and all that stuff but… I'm more comfortable with my camera.'

'I'd be happy to.' She looked at the screen again. 'I guess you need to give each of them a name, then I can set it all up. It won't take long. Have you contacted the printer?'

'Yesterday.' But preparing for the exhibition wasn't the only thing bugging him. Somehow, the agent who'd been pursuing him for years had got wind of the exhibition and had emailed Martin, once again begging him to reconsider his decision about publishing his work in books of photographs, citing other photographers who'd enjoyed great success with this.

'What is it? Is there something else?' Ailsa's forehead creased making him want to smooth away the frown lines. He imagined how her skin would feel under his fingers, remembering again the night when their lips had met.

'Martin?'

Martin came back to earth with a thud. 'Oh… nothing you need to worry about.'

'Tell me.'

Martin sighed. He'd come to know Ailsa well enough by now to know she wouldn't be satisfied till she got to the bottom of it. 'I had an email from this agent.'

'An agent?'

'Ed Holstein. He's in New York.' As he spoke, it occurred to him Ed probably knew all about the copyright dispute. And he was still willing to work with him? 'He's been after me for years to publish one of those coffee table books with a collection of my photos. Now, somehow or other – I blame John Baldwin and his relentless quest for publicity – he's heard about the exhibition and sees it as a *wonderful opportunity*.' He grimaced. The whole idea of commercialising his work was an anathema to him.

'It sounds like a good idea.' Ailsa's face lit up. 'Those sorts of books make excellent gifts.'

'It's not the type of photographer I am – or was. Who knows what I am now?'

'Still no news from the magazine?'

'I'm not sure what news there could be. I haven't submitted anything since the Barry Young debacle. Jackson was dubious they'd take any more.'

'What about your surfing shots? They're really good.'

'But not good enough. There are guys out there who've been doing it for years, big names in the field already.'

'John Baldwin thinks they're good enough to exhibit. Perhaps you're being too hard on yourself. And what's wrong with a bit of commercialism?' she asked harking back to Martin's earlier comment.

He decided to ignore her, but it gave him food for thought. Maybe he was being too precious. His work was good. This exhibition would promote it to a wider audience. And he did need to find a way of supplementing his income.

'You could be right,' Martin said, smiling at Ailsa, delighted to see her eyes light up at his agreement.

Thirty-five

Nate had become something of a fixture in Bellbird Bay. He had settled into the small community well, enjoying both his jobs and making friends in the surfing community. His social life was such that Ailsa rarely saw him.

Bev was gradually improving, too, and, while still not completely mobile, was talking about going back to the garden centre, even if she was unable to take such an active role as she was accustomed to. Meantime, Martin was happy to continue there in a casual capacity.

Ailsa felt she was caught in a bubble of indecision. Working together on preparation for his exhibition, had brought her and Martin closer. Sharing their reasons for coming to Bellbird Bay had created a bond between them, and the awkwardness and discomfort she'd felt in his presence was gradually disappearing to be replaced by a sense of respect and even something warmer she was afraid to explore.

But now Bev was recovering, there was nothing to keep her here.

Ailsa was worried about Bob. He sounded so depressed every time she heard from him, and he was still determined their marriage was over. It made sense for her to pack her bags and return home, so why was she so reluctant to do so? She should go home to Canberra, face her husband, take the necessary steps to end their marriage, and make decisions about her own future.

The prospect made her shudder.

Tired of racking her brains for a solution, when she returned from spending a few hours at the garden centre, she walked up to the headland. She hoped the wide vista of ocean and the sea breeze would help her clarify her thoughts – or perhaps that Ruby would appear with her usual gratuitous advice. This time, she'd welcome it.

The view was as stunning as ever, but the breeze only served to tangle her hair. There was no answer here, and no sign of Ruby. With the sense her time in Bellbird Bay was almost over, Ailsa slowly made her way back down the boardwalk.

'Nice walk?' Bev rose from where she'd been sitting on one of her wicker chairs on the deck and reached for the stick which now replaced her crutches. 'I'll soon be able to join you. You can't imagine how much I long to be mobile again. I've been stuck here for too long.'

'It was okay. I wanted time to think, to work things out.'

'You plan to go back to Canberra.' It wasn't a question.

'I can't stay here for ever, Bev. Bellbird Bay is a lovely spot. I love being here. With you.' *And Martin.* She shivered at how much his company had come to mean to her. 'But my home's in Canberra. There are things there I need to sort out.'

'I understand. But once you've done that. You intend to stay?'

Ailsa hesitated. She'd been asking herself the same question and hadn't come up with an answer. 'My home's there,' she repeated, '... and Bob... and the boys.' But even as she spoke, she remembered Nate was here in Bellbird Bay and in his short time here, had managed to make himself at home. 'Oh, Bev. I don't know what I want to do.' She gazed out at the ocean she'd come to love, remembered the feel of the sand between her toes, the exhilaration of surfing in on a wave, her growing friendship with Martin, and shook her head. This wasn't real life. She'd only intended to stay for two months. With the prospect of living on one salary, she needed to get back to work, even to explore the possibility of a full-time position with all it entailed. She couldn't turn her life upside down for... for what? For a whim? For the prospect of spending the rest of her life in this paradise?

All of a sudden it seemed a very attractive proposition.

'At least stay till Martin's exhibition,' Bev said.

'Okay.' It was easy to agree to this and would delay her decision for another two weeks at least. Maybe by then she'd have a better idea of what she wanted from the rest of her life. She was only fifty-two, after all. It wasn't too late to make a fresh start. Though, some days, her head felt so heavy she thought it was going to burst.

Unbidden, Ruby Sullivan's words popped into her head. What was it the odd woman had said? Something about surprises? She'd had enough of those in the past little while to last a lifetime. All she wanted now was a peaceful life, one with no surprises, no worries and no responsibilities.

'Good, now why don't you pour us both a glass of wine before Martin gets back and forget all those worries trying to spoil your time here.'

Chuckling at how Bev could read her so well, Ailsa went into the kitchen and opened the fridge.

*

Ailsa was still at breakfast next morning when her phone rang. Seeing her sister's number, she rose from the table. 'Excuse me,' she said to Bev and Martin who were enjoying tea and coffee respectively and discussing Martin's forthcoming exhibition. She smiled, hearing Bev give her brother the history of the gallery which, while only open for a few years, had gained quite a following in Bellbird Bay.

'Hi, Liz, what's up?' she said, once she was out on the deck, the door firmly closed on the others in the kitchen.

'Not a lot. You still enjoying life up there?'

'Yes,' Ailsa replied and waited. She knew her sister. Liz hadn't called merely to find out how she was enjoying being in Bellbird Bay.

'I had an irate call from Mum. She wanted to know why you were still there and why Nate was there, too. I didn't know about Nate, so I was at a loss what to tell her. I did say your friend had an accident and you were helping her out.'

'Nate's decided to take a year out. He's found himself a couple of part-time jobs here and is learning to surf. He's happier than I've seen him for ages. And he and Martin...' She bit her lip. Damn, she hadn't wanted to mention him. 'They've become friends,' she finished, her voice dropping off as she watched Martin through the window. He had just risen from the table. This morning, he was wearing his black tee-shirt again and the way it stretched across his muscled chest made her heart beat faster. She averted her eyes, gazing out across the beach instead.

'When are you going to tell Mum about you and Bob? She's going to find out, and it's better if it comes from you.'

'I hear you, but there's nothing to find out yet. And he still hasn't told the boys. They need to know first. Then I can work out what to tell Mum and Dad.'

'Dad won't be a problem. But Mum…'

'I know.' Ailsa wasn't looking forward to having the conversation with her mother in which she told Sheila she and Bob were splitting up.

'And Martin?'

Ailsa should have known Liz wouldn't let it go. 'We're becoming friends, too.' She crossed her fingers, hoping her sister would be satisfied.

'Hmm. He seemed like a nice guy. Maybe…'

Ailsa blushed, glad Liz couldn't see her. Since lunch at the surf club when she and Martin had been there alone, relations between them had improved. And now she was helping him prepare for his exhibition she could almost say they were friends. But there was no need for her sister to know that. She was sure to put two and two together and make at least five. The fact was, they'd talked together on numerous occasions, often over breakfast and dinner, when Bev was still asleep or resting, each time revealing more about themselves.

Martin wasn't the arrogant man Ailsa had believed him to be. It was a face he put on to protect what she now realised was the vulnerable man underneath, the man who'd been hurt by a woman he thought loved him and had his career swept from under him. She hoped this exhibition would go part of the way to his recovery. But what influence could an exhibition in a small gallery in Bellbird Bay have in repairing his reputation?

'Finished your call?' The door to the kitchen slid open and Martin's head appeared in the gap.

'My sister.' She waved the phone in the air before slipping it back into the pocket of the knee-length denim shorts she'd chosen to wear today, aware her face was still red. She pushed a stray lock of hair from her eyes.

'I don't have to be at the garden centre till later today. Fancy a walk along the beach?'

Ailsa's tongue stuck to the roof of her mouth. She was too surprised to reply. While they had chatted comfortably at the kitchen table, this invitation was a first.

Taking her silence for agreement, Martin continued. 'I'll wait here while you get your hat.'

'Sure.' Ailsa stepped through the open door to find Bev smiling complacently.

'It's about time you two spent some time together,' she said with a grin, 'only thirty-three years too late.'

Ailsa grimaced but couldn't stifle a quiver of excitement as she picked up her hat, poked her tongue out at Bev and joined Martin on the deck.

*

It was a glorious day to be on the beach, deserted at this time of day, apart from one woman walking her dog. There were surfers to be seen in the distance, but they tended to avoid this stretch of beach preferring the section closer to the surf club where Will Rankin parked his van, the more experienced ones heading to the other side of the headland.

They strolled along in silence for a time, Ailsa's eyes downcast watching the prints her feet made on the wet sand and the mysterious patterns created by the tiny sand crabs. She was so busy staring down at the sand, she barely heard when Martin spoke to her. 'Sorry?'

'I said "A penny for them". You seemed engrossed in something or other.'

'Oh,' Ailsa was embarrassed to be caught out daydreaming. 'I wasn't really thinking of anything – other than how clever those little creatures are.' She pointed to one particularly elaborate pattern with her toe. Then she raised her eyes to meet his, surprised to find him gazing at her with a look of...

'Do I have something on my face?' she asked.

'A few grains of sand sticking to your sunscreen.' Martin reached over to brush them away.

Ailsa's heart pounded so loudly in her ears she was sure he must hear it. The touch of his fingers on her cheek was so gentle, so tender.

For some reason she wanted to weep. Apart from Martin's kiss, it had been so long since anyone had touched her like this. The boys' hugs were far from gentle and took place less and less frequently these days, and it was months since Bob had shown her any signs of affection.

'What's the matter?' Martin placed one finger under her chin and turned her face up to his.

'Nothing.' Ailsa shook her head. 'It's just...' She put her hand on his, marvelling at how his skin felt against hers. She couldn't believe she was standing here on a deserted beach with Martin Cooper and...

'Ailsa?' There was a question in his voice.

She looked into his eyes. These were the green eyes, the memory of which had kept the nineteen-year-old Ailsa awake for nights, and they were looking at her with longing, begging her to agree to...

'We can't...'

'Why not? Don't pretend you're immune to the attraction between us.'

Ailsa felt his breath on her cheek, his lips drew nearer. It was broad daylight, but they were alone, the only sound the lapping of the waves and the raucous calls of the seabirds. The woman with the dog had disappeared into the distance.

'There's no one to see us.'

Ailsa felt something shift deep inside. She thought of Bev smiling at her as she left, Liz's pointed comments, Bob saying their marriage was over, that she might find someone else, and let herself sink into Martin's embrace.

Thirty-six

Martin couldn't believe it. He'd finally kissed Ailsa again – and in broad daylight. He hummed to himself as he drove to the garden centre, gutted he couldn't spend the whole day with her.

Once at work, he had little time to ponder over what had occurred on the beach. It seemed as if the entire population of Bellbird Bay had decided this was the weekend to revamp their gardens, and he was kept busy loading bags of potting mix and mulch and replacing those which had been sold. It wasn't till he took a break for lunch that he was able to reflect on Ailsa and what the embrace meant for their relationship.

Martin took a welcome gulp of coffee and tried to come to terms with what had happened to him. He'd come here to recharge, to lick his wounds, determined not to get involved with another woman, and to sort out his photographic career.

In terms of his career, the exhibition John Baldwin was arranging might do the trick, though Martin had his doubts. But meeting Ailsa McNeil again – she'd been Ailsa Browne back then – had not been on the cards. It had been a shock to discover the old friend who was visiting Bev was the girl he'd run from all those years ago. Despite his attempts to ignore her, to stay away from temptation, it had been no use. The woman had managed to worm her way into his life and into his heart.

He admitted to himself he had feelings for Ailsa, feelings which were deeper than he'd ever experienced before, feelings that made what he'd had with Sofia fade into insignificance. Compared to Ailsa, Sofia was a pampered and painted doll. Now, he didn't know what he'd seen in the younger woman. He'd been flattered to think the young, glamorous woman might be interested in him and had been sucked in, even considering marriage. He now realised how fortunate he'd been that she found a more attractive mark. He'd had a lucky escape, even if it had taken the potential loss of his career to precipitate it.

But how could he know if this was the real thing, or if he was deluding himself yet again? Ailsa might be apart from her husband and, according to her, their marriage was over, but what if she only saw Martin as a distraction from an unhappy marriage, what if…? He shook his head as his lunch appeared.

'Something the matter?'

Martin glanced up to see the café owner about to place the triple decker sandwich he'd ordered on the table. He blinked. It was unusual for the dark-haired woman to appear outside the kitchen. He shook his head again. 'No, Cleo, nothing your delicious food won't cure.'

She stood looking at him for a few moments, her forehead creased, then turned away, leaving him to wonder if she could read his mind. He almost called her back, but realised how futile it would be. There was no way he could confide in her. But he, who normally kept his thoughts and emotions close to his chest, felt the need to confide in someone.

*

'So, there you have it, Will.' Martin took a swig of beer and leant back, balancing his chair on two legs, unwilling to meet his friend's eyes. Will was the only person Martin could think of who'd be willing to listen to him, who might not think him a fool, who might even offer advice. He had been married, after all. And in days gone by, he had been the one to whom Martin had confided his youthful crushes – and scores.

'You're asking me for advice on your love life?' Will sounded amused.

Martin glanced around to check no one was listening. But the occupants of nearby tables were engrossed in conversations of their own and the groups at the bar weren't within earshot. Nate, the only one who might take an interest in their discussion, was busy at the other end of the bar.

'I guess I am.' Martin finally looked Will in the eye. 'I've not had a good run with women. They've always come easy and… Hell, Will, I've reached fifty-two and I've never felt like this before. It's driving me mad.'

'I'm not sure I'm the best person to offer advice. Dee and I got together soon after you left and I've never looked at another woman since, never wanted to, even though it gets a tad lonely at times. Your life has been a lot more complicated than mine ever was. But I agree that Ailsa McNeil seems a good sort.'

Good sort? 'She's not… I don't… She's different to the other women I've known. I guess that's why I didn't hang around to get to know her better when I was nineteen. But I hope I've learned since then, learned what a real woman is like, learned to appreciate one when I meet her.'

'Sounds like you've been hanging around with all the wrong women,' Will chuckled. 'Though many men would envy you for the life you've led, there's nothing like the love of a good woman.' His eyes clouded over, making Martin feel guilty for sharing his problems with this man who'd lost the love of his life.

'I just need to know how to…' He cleared his throat. What a fool, to be asking advice on a woman at the ripe old age of fifty-two. 'Sorry, I should never have brought it up. Forget I mentioned it.'

'No worries, mate.' Will raised his glass. 'It's forgotten. Now what's this I'm hearing about an exhibition? Old Baldwin's pulling out all the stops on this one.'

The remainder of the evening was spent in sinking several more beers, and with Martin expressing his doubts about how well the exhibition would be received.

But when they finally left the club, Will's parting words weren't about the success or otherwise of the photographic exhibition. Clapping Martin on the shoulder, he said, 'My advice, for what it's worth, mate, is to let the woman know how you feel. She's not a mind reader, and she may well be just as uncertain about all this as you are. Good luck!'

Martin gazed after his friend who was swinging his way down the street, before heading in the opposite direction. It wasn't the advice he'd wanted to hear, but of course it made sense. Now, he just had to find the opportunity to be alone with Ailsa again.

Thirty-seven

'What gives with you and Dad?' Nate asked. 'Pat says he called in at home, and Dad seems to be packing up all his books and things.' He leant back against the railing on the deck.

Ailsa put down her book and looked at her son. His skin had tanned from spending time on the beach and his dark hair was showing signs of becoming bleached by the sun. He had lost the appearance of a student who lived in the city and looked every inch the beach bum he was fast becoming. Her stomach quivered. He might be Bob's son, but he was reminding her more and more of Martin.

What should she say? Bob had insisted he wanted to tell the boys himself when he was ready. But when would that be? Meantime, it must be obvious to both Pat and Nate that things were not well between their parents. The fact she was still here in Bellbird Bay while Bob remained in Canberra spoke volumes.

'You and Dad?' he repeated. 'I thought you were solid. I know he's been a bit grumpy recently. But that's Dad.' He shrugged. 'Is there someone else? I've seen how Martin looks at you. Are you...?' He reddened, obviously embarrassed at the idea his mother might have any sexual feelings.

'No! Neither of us is involved with anyone else. It's something we discussed before I left. Your dad... He'll speak to you himself.' But Ailsa knew it wasn't completely true. The more time she and Martin spent together, the more she liked him. And although their kiss on the beach hadn't been repeated, a warm glow suffused her each time she was in Martin's company.

'Sounds very mysterious, Mum. Dad's not sick, is he?' He paused. 'No, you wouldn't leave him if he was. So what is it?'

Ailsa wished Nate hadn't started this conversation. Bob should be here. They should be telling Nate together. 'I can't say, not yet. Your dad will speak to you. But, I… we… we've decided it might be better if we live apart.'

'Apart? You mean I'm from a broken home?' Nate tried to grin, but Ailsa could see her son was battling to keep a smile on his face.

'No… yes… Oh, sweetheart. It's nothing to do with you or Pat. Your dad and I have been together for a long time, and now the two of you are making your own lives, we're going to do the same.'

Nate's eyes widened. 'But…' He suddenly looked like the little boy who had dropped his lollipop in the sand and knew it would never taste good again.

'It'll be fine, Nate. You'll see.' Ailsa laid a comforting hand on her son's arm, wishing someone would do the same to her. She wasn't at all sure everything would be fine when she returned to Canberra. Where would she live if they had to sell their house, the house which had been her home since the boys were tiny? What would their friends say? And how would she explain things to her mother?

'Hmph.' Nate pushed himself off the railing and went inside.

Ailsa heard the fridge door open and close and the snap of a can of beer opening. She sighed. She hadn't handled that well. Not for the for the first time she cursed Bob for wanting to wait before he told the boys. He should have realised they'd work out something was wrong. The thought which had niggled at the back of her mind, resurfaced to taunt her. Bob said he loved her, always had. But could she believe him? What if their entire marriage had been a sham? What if…? But she wouldn't go there. They'd had a good marriage, many happy years, especially when the boys were little. She had to believe Bob when he said he loved her, otherwise she wouldn't be able to go on.

Maybe the sooner she went back to Canberra the better. She could talk with Bob, encourage him to speak with the boys, and set things in motion. She shivered at the thought of unpacking their life together. Another thought thrust itself into her now crowded mind. Martin. They were only just beginning to become close. What would it mean to their developing relationship if she was to leave Bellbird Bay, return to Canberra?

Ailsa stifled the thought as soon as it emerged. Martin Cooper was a drifter. He didn't stay in one place for long. He was unlikely to remain in Bellbird Bay once his reputation was restored. But she couldn't help wishing it could be different, that she could be given a second chance with him. When they were together it seemed as if he cared, more than cared, as if they might even have a future together. But at times like this, she was beset with doubts. All her old sense of insecurity returned. Why would a celebrated photographer like Martin Cooper be interested in her? How could she ever hope to retain his interest? And was she really ready for another relationship when she still had to finalise the end of her marriage to Bob?

Those thoughts were all still whirling around in Ailsa's head, and she had come to no resolution when Martin walked onto the deck and threw himself down onto a chair.

'You're looking very serious,' he said. 'Has something happened?'

'Nate.' Ailsa nodded towards the kitchen where Nate was polishing off his second can of beer. 'He's been asking about Bob and me.'

'Oh! He knows you and your husband have split?'

'He does now.'

'I saw him in the club earlier. He must have come straight here when he finished.'

'He often does. I think he's becoming a bit bored with the backpackers.'

'If he intends to stay, he might want to look for something more permanent.'

A shaft of worry shot through Ailsa. When she returned to Canberra, she'd be so far from Nate. But if she stayed here, Pat – and Bob – would be in Canberra. It seemed that now, no matter what her decision, she'd be apart from one of her boys. She wanted them both to be happy but selfishly, she wanted them to be close to her, too. 'Do you think so?' she asked.

'What about you? Will you decide to stay here?' Martin's lips curled up in the way to which she'd become accustomed, making her want him to kiss her, to lose herself in his embrace, to still all the worries besetting her.

Ailsa hesitated.

'You know I have feelings for you, Ailsa. I've come to care for you more than I imagined I could care for anyone. I know I'm a bad bet, you're still married, your home's in Canberra, but...'

Ailsa's throat tightened. What was Martin trying to say? She wasn't ready for this.

Thirty-eight

The day of Martin's exhibition finally arrived, and the house was buzzing with excitement. Although he pretended to be blasé about it, Ailsa could tell Martin was nervous. It was a big deal. John Baldwin had pulled out all the stops, managing to get national coverage for the event and even inviting the hosts of a popular regional breakfast show to a viewing that morning.

'Don't know what John did in a past life, but it seems he has contacts in the media and was able to pull in a few favours,' Martin said over breakfast. 'I didn't expect all this hoo-ha.'

'He's a good man and is determined the exhibition will be a success,' Bev said. 'You have to trust him.'

'Hmm.'

Both Martin and Bev were planning to attend the session with the television crew, while Ailsa promised to take Bev's place at the garden centre. Bev had only dispensed with her stick a few days earlier and was enjoying her renewed freedom of movement.

'You should go, Mum,' Nate said, when they all had dinner together the previous evening. 'It would really raise my cred to have you appear on television.' But Ailsa had only laughed. The last thing she wanted was to make an appearance on breakfast television. She was pretty sure Martin felt the same way, but didn't have the heart to refuse John who was putting so much effort into making the evening a success.

While the exhibition of the famous travel photographer's work was a coup for the local gallery, it was bringing tourists to the town, too. Despite the tourist season being at an end, all the hotels and the caravan park were fully booked.

'What does it feel like to be a celebrity?' Ailsa had asked, when they were enjoying a glass of wine on the deck after dinner the previous evening. Bev had retired early, and Nate had gone to meet some mates.

'Scary. I never expected this sort of adulation. It was enough to know my work was published, people enjoyed looking at it, they could sit in their armchair and imagine they were travelling through the Amazon jungle or lying on a beach on a tropical island. This…' he waved his glass in the air, sending drops of wine in all directions, '…is why I refused to agree to producing coffee table books of my photographs. After tonight… Hell, I may have to hibernate at the South Pole.'

Ailsa knew he wasn't altogether joking. Now she'd come to understand Martin better, she knew he wasn't the arrogant self-centred man she'd first thought him.

Now the day had arrived, and Martin was a bag of nerves.

'You'll be fine,' Bev said, in an attempt to calm him. 'Maybe we can get a plug in for the garden centre,' she joked. 'I hear the production crew plan to stay all weekend to take in a few of the local sights.'

'Yeah,' Martin replied. 'Will's all set to give them free board hire, and lessons to any who aren't surfers, and young Owen is champing at the bit at the thought of his surfing exploits being on television. They're welcome to it.'

'Did you talk with Sam?' Ailsa asked. 'He was a TV presenter for years. He'd know what…'

'Yeah. He was a lot of help,' Martin said. 'Told me to look at the camera, try not to make a fool of myself and be grateful it was a camera not a gun in my face.'

'Hmm. Good advice. Liz is sorry they won't be here.' Ailsa frowned, remembering her sister's latest phone call. She'd sounded worried about their dad but told Ailsa it was nothing, only a slight chill he'd developed.

'There'll be plenty of others,' Martin said. 'According to John, half the town will be there plus a swag of tourists all eager to meet me. Wish it was over and done with. I'm used to being behind the camera, not the focus.'

'We should get going,' Bev said, looking at her watch. 'Don't want to keep your public waiting.' She chuckled.

'And I need to get moving, too,' Ailsa said. 'Julie will be wondering what's happened to me.'

'She knows it's a big day for us,' Bev replied. 'I told her not to expect you till later. We'll see you for lunch and fill you in then.'

'Great. You both look wonderful.'

For once, Bev was wearing a dress – a lemon linen one in a simple shirt style which flattered her and showed off her tan to perfection. Martin had dressed for the occasion in his khaki chinos and a blue chambray shirt with short sleeves.

Ailsa's heart had leapt when he walked into the kitchen, his skin glowing and his hair still damp from the shower. She wanted to hug him, to feel his body close to hers. Instead, she had only smiled and wished him good morning. It was weird how her feelings shifted from this ache to be close to him, to wanting to flee to Canberra away from temptation. She wished she knew what she wanted.

*

The morning had gone well. When Bev and Martin met with Ailsa for lunch, they were full of exhilaration about the interview and how the host of the breakfast show had praised Martin's work, referring to his photographs in travel magazines and his Atlas awards.

'He was amazing,' Bev said, 'Martin, too.' She nudged her brother. 'Go on, say something.'

Martin sighed. 'It was a reminder of how it used to be, when it was my work, not me on display. I'm still not sure about all this publicity, but I suppose...' He looked so vulnerable Ailsa wanted to hug him again.

'Looking forward to tonight?' she asked instead.

'Not really. I'll be glad when it's over and I can relax. Though with all this edition stuff and Ed Holstein's persistent demands, I wonder if I'll ever be able to relax again.'

'What you need is a manager,' Bev said.

'I don't think so.'

'Well, no need to worry about that now. Let's get tonight over with first,' Ailsa said.

Martin threw her a grateful look. 'Thanks.'

Leaving Bev at the garden centre, Ailsa and Martin drove home together. Once in the house, he took her in his arms. 'I've been wanting to do this all morning,' he said, burying his face in her hair. 'I'm so glad you're here. I don't think I could make it through without you. I don't know what possessed me to agree to this farce. I'm not one of those people who thrive on publicity. I prefer to let my work do it for me. When tonight's over, let's go away somewhere together, just you and me, somewhere nobody knows us.'

'Martin!' Ailsa pulled away from his embrace. Attractive as his proposition sounded, she couldn't just up-sticks and leave. There was Nate to consider, and Bob and Pat in Canberra, and her parents who weren't getting any younger. She remembered Liz's recent comment about their dad. Ailsa still had her life and marriage to sort out before she could contemplate going anywhere with Martin or anyone else. She'd agreed to stay until his exhibition, but then…

*

The gallery was crowded with people when Ailsa pushed her way through the door to be greeted by a waiter carrying a tray of glasses. She accepted a flute of champagne and weaved her way through the throng to where she could see Martin and Bev talking to a smiling, silver-haired man with half-moon spectacles. She assumed this was John Baldwin.

Before she could reach them, Ailsa found herself enveloped in a warm hug.

'Mum, isn't this amazing?' Nate asked, waving his glass in the air and gesturing to the crowd. 'I knew Martin was famous but this… There are reporters and critics here from Brisbane, Sydney and Melbourne and… I even heard a few American accents. This Baldwin guy is amazing.'

Ailsa flinched. American? This was what Martin had been afraid of – afraid the scandal in New York would follow him here, would ruin the exhibition. But, as far as she could see, everyone had smiles on their faces. Perhaps his worry had been needless.

She patted Nate on the shoulder. 'Thanks, Nate, I just need to...' But she could have saved her breath, Nate was already moving away, having seen someone he knew.

Ailsa pressed on, finally managing to reach the spot where Bev and Martin were standing. She hugged them both, a frisson of desire shooting through her at the touch of Martin's hands on her shoulders.

'This is John Baldwin, Ailsa. The man I have to blame for this bash. John, this is Ailsa McNeil, a friend of mine and Bev's.'

Ailsa was glad to see Martin looking happier than he had at lunchtime. She shook John's hand. 'This is an amazing evening,' she said. 'You've worked hard to get a response like this.'

'It was easy, given Martin's reputation. All I had to do was capitalise on it – and encourage him to accept the need to become more commercial. People are thrilled to be able to buy a genuine Martin Cooper photograph. I'm beginning to wonder if we've under-priced them, given the number we've sold already.'

Ailsa glanced around to see red stickers on many of the exhibits. 'Well done, both of you,' she said, to see Martin looking embarrassed.

'Now, I need to take this young man across to meet some of the reporters,' John said. 'Some of them have come a long way to meet him and view his work.' He took Martin by the elbow and led him off.

'Well,' Bev said, when she and Ailsa were alone. 'I never expected such a turnout. There are a lot of locals, but most of these people are strangers. Martin was right about John. He has a huge number of contacts, and I think they must all be here tonight.'

'Nate said there were some American accents,' Ailsa said, glancing around again. 'I hope...'

'Don't worry. Martin has already checked them out. His old editor isn't here, nor is that Young guy. No reason why he would be. I've told him to try to put it in the past and try to forget it happened. But I guess it's not so easy.'

Ailsa nodded, knowing how badly it had affected Martin, causing him to doubt his ability to rise above it. Over the past few weeks, since their first walk on the beach together, they'd fallen into the habit of walking there together on a regular basis. Almost every evening they waited till Bev had gone to bed before heading out across the boardwalk and down the steps to the beach.

Once there, they would run hand-in-hand to the edge of the water, feeling like children released from school, and wander along, only the moon and the stars piercing the darkness. It was so romantic, and they did kiss again. But most of the time they talked. They talked about Martin's adventures on his travels, Ailsa's life in Canberra and her worry that Bob had never loved her. By now they knew all about each other's past lives, but the one thing they didn't talk about was the future. It was as if they were caught in a bubble which would burst if they let themselves think of a possible future together.

'Let's check out the display. They look different now they're all framed.' Bev linked her arm in Ailsa's, and they made their way around the room. Sure enough, the photos they were accustomed to seeing on a computer screen, looked quite different now they were framed, signed, and displayed on the walls of the gallery, each boasting a sticker indicating their edition number. Ailsa felt a small thrill at the knowledge she'd helped in some way, being responsible for setting up the spreadsheets to record each one.

There was a sudden screech, then John Baldwin's voice came over the microphone calling for attention. The chatter quietened, and he welcomed everyone and introduced Martin, describing him as being a native son who'd made good, and listing his career and awards. Martin stood beside him, looking down at his feet.

Then it was his turn.

'Thank you all for coming along tonight,' he said, his face split by a wide smile, 'and thanks to John for offering me this opportunity. This is a first for me. I'm more accustomed to hiding behind the lens of my camera.' There was a roar of laughter. 'Anyway, I hope you enjoy the evening and thanks to those of you who have already made a purchase. John tells me many of the surfing shots taken right here in Bellbird Bay have already been snapped up. Thank you, I'm very grateful.' He stopped and there was a round of applause before the chatter started up again.

'He didn't do too badly,' Bev said. 'I knew he could do it, but he was terrified he'd dry up in the middle. He's not used to public speaking.'

'He did very well.' Ailsa wanted to congratulate him, but he'd already moved from the spot where he'd been standing. 'Where did he get to? I must tell him.'

'There he is.' Bev pointed across the room to where Martin was surrounded by a group of well-dressed people. They were mostly women, and Ailsa glanced across to see a curvaceous brunette wearing a dress which left nothing to the imagination, gazing lovingly up at Martin, one hand possessively on his arm.

Thirty-nine

Where the heck had she come from?

Martin had been trying to shake off the embarrassment of old friends who wanted to congratulate him on the success of the evening, so he could join Ailsa for the champagne he'd promised. Suddenly he became aware of someone standing next to him, of a heady scent he thought he'd never smell again, of a hand on his arm, and there, staring up at him, her brown eyes as calculating as ever, was Sofia Romero.

'Martin, darling,' the familiar voice whispered in his ear, the southern accent more cloying than he remembered. He was engulfed in her scent.

'What are you doing here?' he asked, suddenly oblivious of the group around him who were staring at the woman in surprise. They gradually moved away, leaving him alone with her.

'That's no way to welcome me,' she said, smiling coyly up at him, the expression in her eyes one which had, in the past, made him want to drag her to the nearest bedroom.

'What are you doing here?' he repeated, his eyes scanning the room to see if Ailsa was watching. This blast from the past was the last thing he needed, tonight of all nights. He'd hoped that tonight perhaps after a few glasses of champagne, their evening walk along the beach might lead to something more than the fleeting kisses they'd already exchanged.

Sofia pouted. 'I've come to see you, to tell you I'm sorry. I made a mistake. I know now Barry Young lied about those photos. I love you, Martin. I was wrong to leave the way I did. I…'

'I guess Gareth ditched you. I could have told you he would. He never stuck with a woman for long. But it was a lucky break for me. It showed me...' He rubbed a hand over his head, his eyes again scanning the room. Was that Ailsa talking with John? He didn't want her to catch him with Sofia who was now attempting to wind her arms around him. What would Ailsa think? 'How did you find me?' he asked suddenly.

'It wasn't easy. When your editor didn't know where you were, I contacted Ed Holstein. He didn't want to tell me but after a few drinks, and...' She winked. '...he revealed you were having an exhibition in the small coastal town in Australia where you grew up. I booked a flight and here I am.' She grinned proudly, as if she'd pulled off a marvellous feat, and he should be pleased.

Martin groaned. Back when he and Sofia had been an item, she was the one who'd persuaded him to get an agent, introduced him to Ed, and promoted the idea of the coffee table books. At the time he thought it was her way of keeping him close and was flattered. He was easily flattered in those days.

Undeterred by his silence, Sofia continued to speak. 'That skunk who stole your photos has been found out. He tried that copyright trick once too often. And Gareth was a big mistake. I realised right away it was you I loved, you I want to spend the rest of my life with. This exhibition is child's play. We can organise a much bigger one in New York. Ed will help. I've already spoken to him, and he's really keen on the idea. I called him as soon as I arrived here and saw you on television this morning. I couldn't believe it. My Martin a television star!'

'I'm not...' he began, paying no attention to her reference to Barry Young.

Sofia took his arm. 'Let us get out of here. I have a room at the hotel on the edge of town. I know how to make you feel good.' She smiled coquettishly, running her fingers up and down his arm in the way he used to find irresistible.

But her wiles. which had once beguiled Martin, now left him cold. He glanced around the room again to see Ailsa staring straight at him, a shocked expression on her face.

'No!' Martin removed her hand from his arm and disentangled

himself. 'I'm not your Martin. I'm not a television star. I have no intention of returning to New York or anywhere else in the States. I'm staying here in Bellbird Bay.' Until he said the words, Martin hadn't realised how much his old home had come to mean to him. After all those years away, this was where he belonged. It had taken the ruination of his career to bring him back, but now he was here, he knew it was home.

'Please, Martin, let me show you...' Sofia pulled on his arm.

'Leave me alone.' Martin looked across to where Ailsa was standing, only to see her turn away, then walk towards the door. He pulled out of Sofia's grasp to follow her. He had to explain, to tell her...

'Martin, I want you to meet Oscar Redmond. He owns a gallery in Sydney and is keen to offer you an exhibition there.' John Baldwin grasped Martin's elbow, preventing him from moving.

Martin's heart plummeted as he watched Alisa leave the gallery. Maybe he could catch her. But John was steering him in the direction of a stout grey-haired man who was the centre of a group Martin recognised as the television crew from the morning's interview. He sighed and followed John's lead. There would be time enough later to talk to Ailsa. Surely she'd understand?

Forty

Tears filled Ailsa's eyes as she pushed her way through the crowd and out into the fresh air where she stopped for a moment to draw breath. She should have known. Bev had warned her, and Martin had told her himself about his history with women. He'd said it was all in the past, claiming to have changed.

But the sultry beauty hanging on his arm didn't look like his past. She was very much in the present. Ailsa was glad she'd discovered her before her relationship with Martin went any further, before they moved on from kisses on the beach to anything more intimate. She was too old to be willing to share a man with a… She shuddered as she pictured the image of the stunning young woman with Martin.

Once back at Bev's, Ailsa sat in the empty house gazing into space for what seemed like for ever. Her head was spinning but whether from champagne or the sight of Martin with the woman, she wasn't sure. One thing she *was* sure of, first thing in the morning, she'd pack her bag and go back to Canberra. It was what she should have done long before now, but she'd promised Bev to stay till Martin's exhibition. And, if she was honest with herself, she hadn't wanted to leave while she and Martin were getting along so well. What a fool she'd been.

She roused herself, going to the kitchen to drink two glasses of water before going to bed. She didn't want to face Bev or Martin, though she didn't expect Martin would return that evening. Even from a distance Ailsa had recognised the lust in the eyes of the dark-haired woman.

Ailsa lay in the darkness, hearing first Bev then to her surprise, Martin, return. Then there was silence, but still she couldn't fall asleep, images of Bob, then Martin, flitting behind her closed eyelids. Finally, as dawn broke, she fell into a restless slumber, only waking again to a tap on her bedroom door.

'Are you awake?' Bev peered round the door, a cup of tea in her hand.

'Almost.' Ailsa pushed herself up in bed, blinking at the sun now streaming through the window. She'd forgotten to pull the blinds.

'What happened to you last night? I turned around and you were gone. Martin was looking for you.'

'I suddenly felt tired and didn't want to spoil your evening.'

'It didn't have anything to do with the woman who commandeered Martin's attention, did it? He explained...'

'I don't need to hear his explanation, Bev. I promised to stay till the exhibition, and I did. I'm heading back to Canberra this morning. I'll catch up with Nate at the beach on the way, to let him know.'

'But what about Martin? I thought you and him...'

So did I. 'No, not really.' She bit the inside of her cheek. 'Is Martin...?'

'He's gone for his swim. He'll be back for breakfast. You should speak with him before you go.'

Ailsa frowned, suddenly wide awake. She didn't want to face Martin this morning but knew she must. 'I will.' She'd listen to what he had to say, but wasn't going to change her mind.

'Are you sure you have to leave? I've so enjoyed having you here.'

'I've enjoyed it, too, Bev, especially our long chats on the deck over a glass of wine. But my life's in Canberra. Last night convinced me of that.'

'Okay.' Bev sighed. 'I'll leave you to drink your tea and get dressed.'

Showered and dressed in a casual pair of jeans and loose tee-shirt which would be comfortable for travelling, Ailsa quickly packed her bag before going to the kitchen where she could hear Bev and Martin chatting.

'You're leaving?' Martin's words sounded like an accusation. His forehead was creased, his eyes bloodshot.

How much had he had to drink last night?

'I'm going home. Congratulations on a successful exhibition. I'm sure it'll reinstate your reputation. John Baldwin did a good job.' Even to Ailsa, her voice sounded cold.

'I'll leave you two to it,' Bev said, rising. 'I should get to the garden centre. Take care, Ailsa. Drive carefully. And remember, you're welcome here anytime.' She gave Ailsa a warm hug and kiss on the cheek and, with a glare in Martin's direction, hurried off.

Left alone, Martin and Ailsa looked at each other.

'Coffee?' Martin asked, as Ailsa took a seat at the table and helped herself to muesli and yoghurt.

She nodded. Despite preferring herbal tea in the morning, she needed a caffeine hit if she was to make it through breakfast with Martin.

'I need to explain,' Martin said, once the coffee was poured.

Ailsa steeled herself for his explanation. She pushed her bowl away, her appetite suddenly gone.

'Last night,' he said. 'It wasn't what it seemed.'

'Was she or was she not the woman you told me about, the one you were involved with, the one who left you for a movie star?'

'Yes, it was Sofia, but...'

Sofia. So that was the hussy's name?

'Then I don't know why you're surprised to hear I'm leaving. I thought... I thought we...' Ailsa fought back the tears.

'Ailsa. I didn't know she'd be here. I never expected... I have no...'

Ailsa's phone rang. Annoyed with the disruption, she checked the caller, then pressed to accept the call, keeping her eyes fixed on Martin. Why was Bev calling? She'd only just left. She hadn't had time to reach the garden centre.

'Bev?'

'Ailsa, it's Nate.'

A curl of fear tightened in the pit of Ailsa's stomach. She felt sick. 'What's happened?'

'He came off his bike. I was behind him. He was going pretty fast, misjudged the left turn into Gray Street, swerved and hit the kerb. He's conscious, but injured and disorientated. I've called an ambulance. Will you...?'

'I'll meet you at the hospital.' Ailsa sat looking at her phone, unable to move.

'Who's injured? Is it Bev?' Martin had risen and was at her side, his hand a comforting weight on her shoulder.

'It's Nate. He's come off his bike. Bev was there. I don't know...'

'I'll drive you.'

'No, I can...'

'You're in no state to drive yourself.'

Ailsa looked at her hand which was still clutching her phone. It was shaking. Maybe Martin was right. They still hadn't finished what they had to say to each other, but perhaps it was just as well. What more could he add? It was more important she get to the hospital, find out about Nate. She couldn't bear it if... All thought of driving to Canberra forgotten, Ailsa allowed herself to be helped into Martin's little yellow car and driven to the hospital.

Forty-one

Martin ensured Ailsa's seatbelt was securely fastened before firing up the engine and driving as fast as was legal and safe to the local hospital. Every few seconds he risked a glance at the woman sitting beside him. Ailsa's face was as white as a sheet. Her jaw was tight, as if she was trying to stop herself from crying, and her hands were tightly clenched in her lap. The poor woman was traumatised.

But even in this state she looked beautiful to Martin. Seeing Sofia last night had opened his eyes to what he really wanted. While, till now, he'd been sure he had feelings for Ailsa, strong feelings he wanted to act on, it wasn't till he told Sofia he planned to remain in Bellbird Bay, that he knew exactly what he wanted.

It wasn't just Bellbird Bay, it was Ailsa McNeil. He wanted to spend the rest of his life with her. And, thanks to Sofia turning up when she did, he might have lost any chance of it happening.

'We're here.' Martin glanced at Ailsa again as he drew into the hospital car park. She hadn't moved since they left Bev's. 'Are you all right?' he asked.

'What? Yes. I need to see Nate.' She tried to step out of the car, forgetting about the seatbelt. 'Damn!' A tear trickled down her cheek. 'Sorry.'

'Stay there.' Martin hopped out of the car and dashed around to her side. He unfastened the seatbelt she was struggling with, her hands shaking too much to be of any use. 'Done.' He took her hand and helped her out of the car.

Martin wanted to hug her, to assure her Nate would be fine, but he didn't know how badly injured the boy was. He settled for taking her by the arm and leading the distraught Ailsa into the Emergency reception area. This felt all too familiar, reminding him of coming to see Bev only a few weeks earlier. At least now he knew the ropes. 'We've come to see Nate McNeil,' he said. 'This is his mother.'

*

Ailsa felt as if she was in a bad dream. She'd been listening to Martin trying to explain himself, to make excuses for his conduct the previous night, when, with one phone call, her world had collapsed. Thank goodness Bev had been on the scene and been able to call an ambulance right away. She barely remembered Martin driving her to the hospital, but he must have because here she was in the Emergency department and Martin was by her side.

She looked up at the man who had caused her so much grief, finding his presence comforting.

'Nate's with the doctor now,' the bright young nurse said with a smile. 'You can go through and wait till he's seen him.' She pointed to the door Ailsa recalled from her previous visit.

They didn't have long to wait before a doctor who looked even younger than Nate pushed a curtain aside.

'Mrs McNeil?'

'Yes. Is Nate...?' Ailsa's voice quivered.

'Your son was lucky. He was wearing a helmet so there's no concussion, though he's suffering from shock and is somewhat disoriented. He's sustained a dislocated shoulder and a broken arm and has severe road rash on both arms and legs from skidding across the surface of the road.'

Lucky? It sounded serious enough to Ailsa. 'What...?'

'We'll have to immobilise the shoulder and arm, wait till the swelling goes down before we apply a cast to the arm. It'll take around five to seven days. Meantime, we'll put on a splint. There's nothing to worry about. A fit young man like Nate will be right in no time. He'll just need to take things easy for the next three weeks or so.'

Three weeks! So much for her plans to return to Canberra. And how would Nate manage at the backpackers with his arm immobilised?

'You can see him now.'

Ailsa realised the doctor was speaking to her. 'Thanks,' she said, as Martin propelled her through the curtain into the cubicle where Nate was lying propped up against a pillow. His face had lost the healthy colour he'd managed to acquire and her normally ebullient son appeared subdued.

'Nate! I'm so glad to see you.' Ailsa rushed to his bedside and, taking care not to touch his wounded shoulder and arm, placed a kiss on his forehead and swept back a lock of hair from his brow.

'Mum, I'm sorry.'

'So you should be. Bev said you were going too fast,' she said, relief turning to anger that he'd brought this on himself.

'I was running late for Will. Heck, has anyone told him?' his eyes went to Martin standing behind her.

'I'll call him.' Martin took his phone from his pocket and walked out of the cubicle.

'Sorry, Mum,' Nate repeated. 'But it could have been worse. Do you know what happened to my bike?' He tried to push himself upright.

His damned bike was the least of her worries. If it hadn't been for that... But, 'I'm sure it's fine,' she said. 'I'll check with Bev, see if she knows anything.'

'Thanks.' Nate relaxed back against the pillow. 'What did the doc say?'

'Looks like your arm will be immobilised for three weeks.' Ailsa bit her lip. 'You can't stay at the backpackers. I'll talk with Bev, see what we can organise. I'm sure...' But what could they do? There wasn't a spare room at Bev's. Maybe she could sleep on the sofa. Her mind was going round in circles when Martin returned.

'Fixed it with Will,' he said. 'He says to make sure you rest up. He doesn't want to see you till you have the okay from the doc. I contacted the club, too. They'll keep the job open for you till you're well again.'

'Thanks, Martin, You're a good man.' Nate managed a weak grin.

'And I spoke to Bev,' Martin went on. 'Your bike doesn't have too much damage. I've arranged to have Glen from the local motorcycle place pick it up and repair it.'

'Thanks.'

'And...' he glanced at Ailsa, '...I've arranged to stay at Will's for a bit, so you can have my room at Bev's. I know your mum would like to be able to take care of you.'

'Thanks,' Ailsa said, both grateful at Martin's thoughtfulness and annoyed she was forced to be grateful to him again. Despite his helpfulness today she hadn't forgiven him for last night, and it irked her to be forced into his debt.

'Dad?' Nate asked, turning to Ailsa. 'Does he have to know?'

Till now, Ailsa hadn't given a thought to Bob, but of course she'd have to contact him. Nate was his son and he deserved to be informed. He'd be as upset as she was. He might even decide to come here. Her stomach turned over at the notion of her husband coming to Bellbird Bay. 'Yes, he does,' she said, more firmly than she felt. 'I'll ring him when I get back to Bev's.'

'Thanks for all your help,' Ailsa said, as she and Martin left the hospital together. 'You didn't need to...'

'Yes, I did. You know how I feel about you, and I was trying to explain what happened last night when...' Martin pushed a hand through his hair. 'As the doc said, Nate's a strong guy, he'll be fine.'

Surprised at the sudden change of topic, Ailsa was lost for words. By this time, they'd reached the car and she climbed in, this time able to fasten her seatbelt without his assistance.

They drove in silence for a few minutes then Martin said, 'She's gone, you know. And I had no idea she was going to be here. It seems she winkled information about my whereabouts from the guy who calls himself my agent. She always was good at that.' His last words were muttered and barely audible.

Ailsa glanced across at Martin, seeing his clenched jaw, the way his hands tightened on the steering wheel. Perhaps he was speaking the truth and she'd been too quick to condemn him. If the woman she'd seen him with last night had been a surprise to him too, then maybe she'd misjudged him. Maybe she should have accepted his explanation, trusted him, acknowledged he had really changed, was no longer the womaniser of the past and had turned over a new leaf.

By the time they reached Bev's house, she had decided to give Martin the benefit of the doubt.

Forty-two

After dinner, Martin packed up and headed off to Will's, but not before extracting a promise from Ailsa to meet on the beach below the boardwalk after dark.

Ailsa shivered as she climbed down to the beach on her own, her footsteps lit by the small torch Bev insisted on lending her.

'You don't think I've been blind to you and Martin sneaking off once I'd gone to bed,' she'd said to an embarrassed Ailsa.

Martin was waiting for her at the foot of the steps. He greeted her with a smile and a brief kiss before drawing her towards him, wrapping his arms around her and burying his face in her hair

'How are you holding up?' he asked, when they separated to walk along the hard-packed sand at the edge of the water.

'I'm okay. Thanks again for being so understanding. I can't imagine what I'd be like if Nate...' She shivered again at the thought of how much worse the accident could have been. 'I knew he'd come to no good on that bike, I wish...' She wished the damned bike had been more seriously damaged, too damaged to ever be used again.

'Boys and their bikes. I had one for a while, too, before...'

'Don't tell me you had an accident, too.'

'Okay, I won't,' Martin chuckled. He threw an arm around Ailsa's shoulders, pulling her close. 'But there's a silver lining. It's brought us together again, hasn't it?'

Ailsa turned her face up to see Martin grinning, his eyes twinkling in the moonlight. She supposed he was right. If it hadn't been for

Nate, she'd be on her way to Canberra right now, determined to put Martin Cooper out of her mind.

Thinking of Canberra and Bob reminded her of the call she'd made to him when she returned from the hospital. He'd answered immediately. It was almost as if he knew something was wrong. He was flying up next day and planning to stay till Nate was discharged from hospital.

It would be odd to have him here. Bellbird Bay had become *her* place. Bob, belonged in Canberra, not in this coastal town. Ailsa trembled, prompting Martin to pull her even closer. She relished the feel of his warm skin against hers, the sound of his heart beating, the...

Martin's head bent. Ailsa felt his breath on her cheek, then... his lips met hers in a searing kiss.

Ailsa sank into Martin's embrace, her body melting at his touch, her whole being aflame with desire. For what seemed like for ever, time stood still. When they drew apart, even the stars seemed brighter.

'Oh, Ailsa! What are we going to do? I can't believe you were planning to go back to Canberra. I can't let you. I love you. I want to...'

Ailsa put a finger on his lips. She wanted to stop him saying anything he might regret later. They were both overwrought tonight, and caught up in the magic of the moment. Nate's accident may have been the catalyst which brought them back together, and she might now believe the Sofia woman meant nothing to him, but nothing else had really changed.

*

Martin sensed Ailsa's withdrawal. It seemed to happen each time they became close, each time he thought they might... But, he reasoned, his timing was not the best. Ailsa had had a traumatic day, her son had been in an accident, her plans to go back to Canberra had been overturned. Instead, her husband was coming here to Bellbird Bay. Martin wished things were different. But at least Ailsa was here with him, willing to be in his arms. He would have to be satisfied with that for the time being.

But not for ever.

Martin was a red-blooded man and wanted more from Ailsa than a few kisses in the moonlight, regardless how pleasurable they might be. He wanted her to be his woman, to spend the rest of his life with her. But, for now, he'd be patient and hope she would come to the same conclusion as him, in her own good time.

He cursed himself for leaving her all those years ago in Canberra. What a life they could have had, travelling the world together. For a few moments he let his imagination run wild as he visualised what it could have been like. Then he came down to earth, remembering the callous youth he'd been back then, how innocent and unsophisticated Ailsa had been. It would never have worked. They'd have driven each other mad in no time and been divorced long ago.

'We're back.'

Martin looked up in surprise to the realisation they'd walked the length of the beach and back again and had reached the steps up to Bev's house. He'd been so engrossed in his thoughts and the headiness of being so close to Ailsa, he hadn't been paying attention to his surroundings.

'Thanks for tonight,' she said awkwardly. 'Bob arrives tomorrow, so I don't know when we can do this again.'

'I still want to see you. Will your husband's arrival make such a difference?' Even as he spoke, Martin knew it was a foregone conclusion Ailsa's family would come first.

'Don't forget me, don't forget what I said.' He pulled her to him again. This time his kiss was gentler. He held Ailsa tightly, not wanting to let her go. What if she and her husband decided to stay together? What if she didn't feel the same way? What if...?

Ailsa smiled. 'Goodnight, Martin. I won't forget.' She turned and left him standing on the sand at the foot of the steps.

Martin watched Ailsa climb up and disappear into the darkness, wishing things could be different.

Forty-three

Ailsa spent most of the next day at the hospital. Nate now had a splint on his arm, and both it and his shoulder had been immobilised, the arm strapped to his body. Luckily it was his left one and Nate was right-handed. He was looking more like himself and eager to leave the hospital. They spent the day chatting, watching television and doing the crossword in the weekend paper. It was something Ailsa used to enjoy doing with Nate and Pat when they lived at home and would compete to see who could solve the clues first.

It was almost lunchtime when a doctor appeared with the news Nate could be discharged next day.

Nate beamed. 'That is good news. I can't stand lying in bed any longer. At least if I'm at Aunt Bev's I can move around. I can check up on my bike, too. Hopefully, there's not too much damage. And I can contact Will and the club. I know what Martin said, but I want to check with them for myself. It was good of Martin to move out and let me have a room at Aunt Bev's, wasn't it, Mum?'

'Yes, he's a good man,' Ailsa agreed. She was still trying to come to terms with her feelings for Martin. When she was with him, everything was wonderful and she couldn't imagine life without him, but once she was alone again, the doubts trickled in. Could she really uproot herself from her life in Canberra and move to Bellbird Bay to be with Martin, or would she be happier trying to make a new life without Bob in the city that was her home? What if Martin resurrected his career and went off on his travels again? He said he loved her, but did he mean it? And was what she felt for him love or merely a physical attraction, a reaction to Bob's rejection?

At heart she knew she did love Martin, but her feelings scared her. After living with one man for so many years, thinking she knew him inside out, then to discover she didn't know him at all, Ailsa didn't know if she could trust her feelings anymore. What if what she felt for Martin was merely a reaction to the end of her marriage to Bob? It was a common thing, being on the rebound they called it. What if she gave up the life she knew only to discover what she thought was love was a mirage? How could she ever be sure again?

'When do Dad and Pat get here?' Nate asked, interrupting her thoughts.

'In a couple of hours.' Pat had been with Bob when she called and he insisted he accompany his dad to Bellbird Bay. Ailsa was pleased. She wasn't looking forward to seeing Bob here and hoped Pat's presence might help.

The arrival of Nate's lunch prompted Ailsa to rise. 'I'll go and get myself something to eat in the café while you have your lunch,' she said. 'Dad said he and Pat will come straight here from the airport, so they'll be here before long.'

In the café, Ailsa ordered a chicken and salad wrap and a cappuccino and carried it to a seat in the outside courtyard. Once there, she marvelled at how this sliver of open space managed to give the impression of being in a garden and took away the hospital atmosphere pervading the rest of the building. Hospitals weren't her favourite places. She supposed everyone felt that way about them. They would always remind her of visiting her father in hospital when he had a hip replacement, then there was Bev, and now Nate.

But it was peaceful, sitting here with only a couple of others who were seated some distance away. From the blue garments they were wearing, Ailsa knew they were members of staff. If she closed her eyes, she could hear the raucous sound of birds and pretend she was somewhere else entirely.

When Ailsa returned to Nate's room, he wasn't alone.

'Martin.' Ailsa hadn't expected to see him today. After last night, she hadn't anticipated meeting him again until Nate was home from hospital, maybe not even then, since Bob and Pat would be in town. She'd be surrounded by her family.

And now Martin was staying with Will, there would be no cosy chats over breakfast, no walks on the beach after dark, no stolen kisses and no opportunity to move their relationship forward. Well, it was a good thing, wasn't it? It helped solve one of Ailsa's problems. But she was still left with what to do about Bob, and how the boys would react when they knew.

'Ailsa.' Martin's eyes twinkled but he made no move to touch her. 'Thought I'd pop in to see how this reprobate is doing. I have to say, he looks better than I expected.'

'Going home tomorrow,' Nate said, 'Well, to Aunt Bev's. Thanks again for letting me have your room. Mum, my stuff's all still at the backpackers. Can you...?'

'I can pick it up for you,' Martin offered.

'I can...' Ailsa began, only to be silenced by Martin holding up a hand.

'You should stay here with Nate. It's no trouble.'

Ailsa was about to argue that Martin had already done enough for them, when there was the sound of voices, and the door opened to reveal a slightly older version of Nate and an older man with greying hair.

'Dad!' Nate grinned with delight. 'And Pat!'

Ailsa's heart leapt into her mouth as she stared at her husband and older son, then across to where Martin was standing.

'Who's this?' Bob asked, his tone more curious than anything else.

'Martin Cooper.' Martin stretched out his hand. 'I'm...'

'...Bev's brother,' Ailsa finished for him, flustered at the sight of the two men standing together.

Bob took his hand. 'I'm Nate's dad.'

There was an awkward silence, broken only by Pat saying with a chuckle, 'Hey, bro. You really did it this time. Dad's even taking time off to come up here to see you.'

'I'll be off,' Martin said, giving Ailsa an odd look. 'I'll drop your things into Bev's, Nate, and catch up with you another time. Take care and rest your arm. Your bike's in good hands.' He nodded to Nate and Ailsa and was gone before anyone could speak.

'Seems like a nice guy,' Bob said, as the door closed behind Martin. 'Bev's twin brother, I think you said.'

Had she? Ailsa couldn't remember mentioning Martin to Bob, but she supposed she must have – or Nate had, or Liz.

'He's great,' Nate said. 'He's moved out to let me have his room, he's arranged to get my bike fixed and he's going to pick up my stuff from the backpackers. He...'

'That's enough, Nate. Dad and Pat don't want to hear about Martin.' Ailsa tried to stem Nate's litany of praise.

'You're looking well, son.' Bob moved closer to the bed on which Pat had already taken a seat. He ruffled Nate's hair. 'Your mum and I were worried about you.'

'Mum?' Nate gave her a puzzled glance.

Ailsa shook her head. There would be time enough to talk about Bob and her later. At least, with Bob and both boys here in Bellbird Bay, there should be an opportunity for him to talk to them, for her and Bob to talk, to get some matters resolved. She should be happy to have her family around her, but she couldn't help wishing Martin hadn't left so abruptly.

'Good to see you, Pat.' Ailsa gave him a hug. 'You, too, Bob.'

Bob put an arm around Ailsa's shoulder and gave her a peck on the cheek. It felt odd, more like an old friend who she hadn't seen for a while, than her husband and lover of so many years.

'How's Vee?' she asked Pat, in an attempt to break the awkwardness she was experiencing.

'Great. In fact, she's moving in with me next weekend.' He grinned.

'Wowee! Far out!' Nate said.

'Bob?' Ailsa looked at her husband.

'Pat told me on the way here. It's no surprise.'

'No. I'm pleased for you both, Pat. As long as...' Ailsa checked herself. Who was she to offer advice on relationships? 'I'm pleased,' she repeated.

After chatting about how Nate's bike had gone off the road, and what the doctor had said, and Nate having to suffer the usual teasing from Pat, Bob stretched his arms above his head. 'It's been a long day – and a worrying one – wonderful to see you in such good spirits, Nate. Pat and I...'

'Where are you staying?' Ailsa asked, feeling remiss not to have considered it sooner. 'Bev doesn't have another spare room.' And Bob couldn't expect to share hers, could he?

'I didn't expect to stay at Bev's. I've booked Pat and me into a motel. I was hoping the three of us could have dinner together.' Bob raised an eyebrow and smiled.

Suddenly all the awkwardness disappeared. It was the old Bob smiling at her, the man she'd fallen in love with at nineteen, the father of their two boys, the man she'd envisioned spending the rest of her life with. 'What a good idea. I'd like that,' she said, smiling back at him.

Forty-four

Martin couldn't get out of the hospital fast enough. So that was Bob, Ailsa's husband. He wasn't at all what he'd expected, though what had he expected? Bob McNeil was an older version of Nate, not quite as tall as his son, his hair beginning to turn grey, but still a handsome man. He could see why Ailsa had fallen for him, why she might still love him.

He got into the Moke and drove back into town, heading for the backpackers, glad he'd promised to pick up Nate's belongings. He had nothing else to do. The future which had seemed so bright, so filled with opportunities only the previous night, now stretched out ahead in a sea of loneliness.

When Martin arrived at his destination, he found the building a hive of activity with young people dashing back and forth, yelling and shouting to each other and the sound of music coming from a large room to one side of the front door. He found a door marked *Office* and knocked, hoping it was manned on a Sunday. Before long, a short, bearded youth wearing a tee-shirt which proclaimed him to be a Friend of the Earth, opened the door.

'How can I help you? Wow, you're Martin Cooper.' The youth's eyes widened.

Martin squirmed. He was recognised even here.

'I'm Grant. I look after things here.'

'Hi, Grant. I've come to collect Nate McNeil's belongings. He...'

'Yeah, heard about the accident. Guessed he wouldn't be back. Is he badly hurt?'

'Not too bad, but he's going to need lots of rest and care. He'll be moving in with my sister and his mother when he gets out of hospital.'

'Right. Well, I guess I can let you into his room. Follow me.' Grant led Martin along a narrow corridor where several young people were sitting on the floor or leaning against the walls chatting, till they came to a shabby, white door which looked exactly like all the others they had passed.

'This is it,' he said, unlocking the door and pushing it open. 'I guess I can leave you to it.'

'Thanks.' Martin walked into a tiny room clearly designed for two occupants. A pair of bunk beds sat against one wall while the other held a shabby chest of drawers and a small desk and chair. From the collection of clothes on the top bunk, it appeared Nate had used that as his wardrobe and slept on the lower one. A rucksack lay on the floor with several items of clothing sticking out of it. A half-empty bottle of water and a book were lying on the desk along with a laptop.

Right, this shouldn't take long. Martin started to fold Nate's clothes and pack them into the rucksack. He was interrupted several times by passing residents asking what had happened to Nate, how he was and when he was coming back. Martin answered as best he could, glad when he'd finally packed everything. He gave one last glance around the room to check he hadn't missed anything, then swung the bag onto his back.

'Thanks a lot, Grant,' he said, as he passed the office. 'Does Nate owe you anything?'

'No, all accommodation is paid for in advance. Nate has paid up to the end of the month and I'm afraid there's no refund.'

'No worries.' Martin hoisted the bag higher on his back and went out to the car where he dropped it into the back seat before heading to Bev's.

As he expected, the house was empty. Martin stashed the rucksack in the room he'd been occupying, then went to the kitchen where he brewed himself a coffee which he took out to the deck. It was a lazy Sunday afternoon, the sort of day he'd loved as a child and teenager when their parents would often organise a beach picnic, and he and Bev would spend their time swimming or surfing.

A lot had happened since then, not all of it good. But till now, Martin had never felt the urge to return to Bellbird Bay. Now he wondered if he'd ever leave again. His thoughts travelled back to the scene he'd left in the hospital, Ailsa surrounded by her family, her husband and two sons. He had no place there. What would she do next? Would she return to Canberra when Nate was well again?

Martin looked back into the house. It was tempting to wait, to be here when Ailsa returned, but what if her husband and son were with her? Sighing, he fetched his surfboard from the garage where he'd left it, packed it into the back of the car and headed to the surf beach on the other side of the headland. Once he was out on the water, he'd be able to forget Ailsa McNeil, forget what was happening in that hospital room, and concentrate on catching the next wave and the one after that.

Forty-five

Dinner the previous night had been good, Bob almost his usual self, albeit a tad more subdued. But it had been like old times, only Nate was missing. This morning they were to meet again at the hospital to bring Nate back to Bev's. Even though Ailsa had vowed she could manage, Bob had insisted he and Pat would be there, too. 'In case you need any help.'

Ailsa stifled the burst of anger threatening to erupt at Bob's sudden flood of concern. Where had that been for the past year when he'd shut himself away in his study, and chosen to sleep in the spare room? He did seem more content, she reflected. Perhaps confiding in her had helped the depression or whatever it was causing his antisocial behaviour. It was a pleasant change. Bob was almost the man he had been before he'd become so distant and uncommunicative.

They met in the hospital car park, Ailsa hugging Pat, and Bob giving her an impersonal peck on the cheek. But it didn't feel as odd as the day before.

'Let's get the show on the road,' Pat said, leading them into the hospital and to the room where Nate was still lying in bed.

'Still milking the patient thing,' Pat said to his brother with a grin. 'Are they really going to let you out today?'

'The doc's been round and said they just need to finalise some paperwork. They took away my clothes when they brought me in, so…'

'I brought you a pair of shorts and a shirt,' Ailsa said. 'Martin left them in what will be your room.' He had been and gone by the time she got home, and she was sorry to have missed him, having harboured the small hope he'd want to see her and wait till she returned.

'Good stuff.' Nate swung his legs out of the bed, wobbling a little, the arm tightly bound to his chest sending him off balance.

A staff member arrived, just as Ailsa was helping drape the shirt around Nate's shoulder. 'You're right to go now,' she said, handing him a sheaf of papers. 'These detail what you need to do to ensure you don't damage yourself any further. You must have plenty of rest. You'll receive notification when to return to have the plaster put on your arm. It should take around a week for the swelling to go down. It'll be easier for you to manage then. I understand your mother will be looking after you?'

'Yes, I will.' Ailsa smiled, seeing Nate roll his eyes. 'I'll make sure he behaves.'

'I'm not a kid, Mum. I can take care of myself.'

'So you say, but look where taking care of yourself has got you.'

'Listen to your mum,' Bob said. 'She loves you. We both do.'

Pat chuckled. 'If we're done here, let's go. How about we go out to lunch? Where's a good place, Nate?'

'Can't beat the surf club,' Nate said with a grin. 'And I can check with Dan about my job.'

It was Ailsa's turn to roll her eyes. She could see that ensuring Nate rested was going to take all her time and energy.

'I don't think...' she began

'Don't be silly, Mum.'

Ailsa looked to Bob for support, but he was smiling at Nate.

'Great,' Pat said. 'The surf club it is.'

Realising she was beaten, Ailsa nodded. 'I'll meet you there.'

The surf club was fairly quiet with only a few locals and visitors from the city making the most of the good weather to have one more long weekend by the beach. Nate was greeted with sympathy and questions from both staff and customers. In the short time he'd been here, it seemed he'd become popular.

'Far out, mate,' Pat said, as one more young woman approached Nate to say how good it was to see him and to ask how he was faring.

Nate grinned.

'Let's find somewhere to sit,' Ailsa said, scanning the room before leading the others out to the deck. She'd been hoping to see Martin there, but there was no sign of him, though there was no reason why there should be. He'd be busy doing whatever it was that kept him busy these days. Ailsa realised she had no idea what he was doing to occupy himself now the exhibition was over. Maybe he was even planning another trip. Why did the thought make her heart plummet?

'Beer?' Pat asked, when they were seated.

'Not for me,' Nate said glumly. 'I have to steer clear of alcohol for a bit. I'll have a Coke.'

'Mum? Dad?'

'Beer for me,' Bob said.

'I'll have a glass of wine, chardonnay,' Ailsa said.

'What do you recommend for lunch?' Bob asked Nate.

'The hamburgers here are to die for,' Nate said. 'But you might prefer a salad, Mum.'

Ailsa agreed, choosing a Caesar salad with Bob and Pat opting for the hamburgers Nate recommended.

During lunch, the conversation revolved around what Nate had been doing since he arrived in Bellbird Bay, making Pat envious with his stories of swimming, surfing and his work with Will and here at the club. But towards the end of their meal, Ailsa could see Nate was becoming tired.

'Why don't we go back to Bev's for coffee?' she suggested. 'Then Nate can lie down if he wants to.'

'I'm fine, Mum,' Nate protested.

But Bob could evidently see him flagging, too. 'Good idea,' he said. 'We'll follow your car.'

Back at Bev's, Bob was interested to see through the house, commenting on how cosy it was. 'Bev's made a few changes since we stayed here when you two were only nippers,' he said to Pat and Nate. 'Do you remember our holiday here?'

Both Pat and Nate nodded.

'Why did we never come back?' Nate asked, repeating the question he'd asked Ailsa when he first arrived.

'I don't know.' Bob scratched his head. 'It never seemed to be the right time, I guess. Then you became too old to want to go on holiday with us oldies.'

'If you all go onto the deck, I'll bring out the coffee,' Ailsa said, 'And I think there's some of the orange and almond cake Bev brought back from the café.'

'How is Bev?' Bob asked, when they had all been served coffee and cake and Pat and Bob had admired the view. 'Has she quite recovered from her accident?' He gave Ailsa an odd look, as if to remind her of the reason she'd given him and her parents for her extended stay in Bellbird Bay.

'She's fully recovered now,' Ailsa said. 'Martin, who you met, had an exhibition of his photographs on Friday, I promised to stay till then. I had intended to come back to Canberra on Saturday, then Nate...' She nodded at her son who was looking shamefaced.

'I hadn't realised,' Bob said, reddening.

There was a moment's silence, during which Ailsa glanced meaningfully at Bob. Now they were all together it would be a good time for him to tell the boys.

Bob cleared his throat. He looked at Ailsa, then at his sons. 'I need to tell you something. Your mum and I...' He glanced at Ailsa who nodded for him to continue. 'We've decided to live separately.'

'Mum?' Nate looked at Ailsa. 'You already...'

Ailsa shook her head, to indicate to Nate he should listen to what his father had to say.

'Dad? Mum?' Pat turned from one to the other, his eyes wide with disbelief. 'What...?'

'It's like this, son.' Bob hesitated then appeared to gain confidence. 'I told your mum some time back, before she came up here to Bellbird Bay. I'm gay. I've always known, but I met your mum. I love her. I love both of you. But I can't live a lie any longer. You're both grown now. You have your own lives. I don't need to hide who I am.'

There was silence on the deck, broken only by the raucous cry of a flock of seabirds choosing that moment to fly overhead.

'Pat? Nate?' Bob stammered.

Ailsa looked at her sons, at their shocked expressions.

Pat was the first to recover. He cleared his throat. 'It's your life, Dad. I'm sorry you and Mum are splitting up. I guess that's why you were packing things up at home. What will you do?'

'I'm renting a unit close to the school in the short term. When the house sells, I'll be able to buy something small. Your mum will too.'

'Mum?'

'What your dad says, Pat,' Ailsa said, relieved her older son appeared to have accepted his dad's explanation without any fuss.

'Will you come back to Canberra?'

It was Ailsa's turn to hesitate. 'Possibly. Initially, anyway. There's a lot to sort out about the house. And there's you and my job.' She suddenly realised Nate hadn't spoken. 'Nate?'

Nate had turned his face away.

'Nate?' she repeated.

He turned to face her. 'I can't get my head around this. I can't… Sorry, I need time to think. I…' He stood up.

'Nate…' Bob began. But Nate put up a hand to silence him.

'Not now, Dad. I'm going to lie down.' He walked into the house, and they heard a door open and close.

'I'll…' Pat began, rising.

'No, leave him, Pat,' Ailsa said. 'He needs to work through this in his own time. Maybe later, when he's had time to digest what your dad said, when…'

'I might go for a walk then,' Pat said, stepping down from the deck and onto the boardwalk.

'I may have chosen the wrong time,' Bob said ruefully when Ailsa and he were left alone.

'No, there probably was no good time for our news, your news.' She sighed. 'Thanks for finally telling them, Bob. I know it wasn't easy for you. Nate's always been the more sensitive of the two. He puts on a good show of being full of confidence and able to handle anything life throws at him, but underneath he's still a vulnerable little boy.'

'He's still our little boy. We tend to forget as they grow older the old insecurities of childhood are still there lurking below the surface ready to…' He drew a hand through his still thick curly hair. 'I have to admit I was worried how they'd react. I suppose it's why I put off telling them. Now…' He sighed.

Ailsa reached across to squeeze Bob's hand. 'They'll be fine, both of them. Nate just needs time, and Pat… I bet when he comes back from his walk, he'll have lots of questions for us both.'

'Nate seemed…'

'He knew we were planning to separate. He managed to wheedle it out of me, but not the reason. It was a shock to him, but he'll get over it.'

'I hope you're right.'

They sat in silence for a few minutes, still holding hands, then Ailsa withdrew hers. 'I think we both need a drink. Brandy? Bev keeps a bottle for medicinal purposes and emergencies. This could probably count as both.'

'Good idea. I can always get Pat to drive us back to the motel.'

After a glass of brandy from Bev's secret hoard, Ailsa felt better.

'How long do you intend to stay in Bellbird Bay?' she asked.

'Not long. I have to get back to school. The boss was good letting me take off in term time, but it's not fair on Brad who has to take my classes.' He stared into space. 'I could probably stay till next weekend. I want to be sure Nate understands, accepts it's who I am.'

Looking across at her husband, his forehead creased with concern, Ailsa remembered why she loved Bob. She still did, but, since his disclosure, her love had changed, morphed into something more like friendship. He was such a caring, empathetic man, or had been until lately, and could be again. He'd been so different from all the other men she'd met at uni, most of whom were intent on proving their manhood by acting like fools. He was different from Martin, too.

But Martin had changed. He was no longer the arrogant, selfish man she'd first encountered all those years ago, the man who'd sent her nineteen-year-old heart aflutter but who had seemed too worldly and experienced for her. Now he was as sensitive as Bob in a different way. She stifled the urge to see him, to feel his arms around her, guilty to be having such thoughts while she was with Bob, and their sons were coming to terms with their dad's disclosure.

'Ready to go, Dad?' Pat appeared at the top of the steps, looking windblown but otherwise as normal.

Bob rose. 'Good idea. We'll see you tomorrow, Ailsa. Maybe by then, Nate…'

'I'm sure he will.' Ailsa hugged Pat goodbye then after a brief pause hugged Bob, too. 'Take care and don't worry.'

Ailsa waved them off at the door then went back inside. She walked along the hallway and stopped outside Nate's bedroom door, lifting her hand to knock, before letting it drop to her side again. She'd take her own advice and leave him alone. It would all look better in the morning.

Forty-six

The afternoon in the surf provided Martin with some relief, and the evening spent with Will and Owen at the surf club helped take his mind off the sight of Ailsa surrounded by her family. While he wanted to contact her, he knew he needed to allow her time with them, time to reconnect and perhaps work out how to end her marriage.

When he awoke on Tuesday morning, he remembered he'd promised John Baldwin to meet him in the gallery. It was closed to the public Mondays to Wednesdays to enable John to catch up on paperwork, and John had suggested Martin drop by today around ten for coffee and a review of the exhibition.

After breakfast which he ate alone – both Will and Owen having risen earlier and set off for the beach – Martin went for a swim. Then, showered and dressed in jeans and a loose shirt, he drove into town.

'Welcome. Good to see you,' John said, as he ushered Martin into the gallery and through to the office which was filled with the aroma of coffee.

'Thanks again for Friday,' Martin said, when he was seated and had taken a first sip of coffee. 'It seemed to go well. I hadn't expected there would be such a crowd.'

'I think we can say it was a great success,' John said with a satisfied smile. 'Exactly what I expected. Editions of all of the photographs were sold, and there are only a few remaining. I'm confident they'll be picked up by the end of the week. You really should consider offering limited editions of more of your work. I'd be happy to...'

'No.' Martin held up a hand to stop John saying any more. 'I'm not ready for that yet. I may never be. It's not really what I'm about.'

John looked disappointed. 'Well, if you ever change your mind… But what we need to do now, is arrange for the copies which have been purchased to be organised. I presume you have secure records of each set of editions?'

'I have.' Martin remembered how enjoyable it had been to work with Ailsa on this, how it had brought them closer together.

'And we could perhaps raise the price of those pieces which remain to be sold. It's customary to do so as the value of unsold items in limited editions tends to increase.'

'Oh, I don't think so.' Martin felt awkward enough at the high prices John had already placed on his work, work for which, apart from his more recent shots, he'd already been handsomely compensated by the travel magazines.

'It's your choice, but you shouldn't sell yourself short. You've developed quite a following and you won't be able to trek around the world for ever, you know.'

This was too close to Martin's own recent thinking for comfort, but he hadn't considered what he might do instead, except improve his proficiency in the surfing field. 'There's plenty to keep me occupied here in Queensland,' he said.

'True, but now we have an army of collectors of your work, it would be foolish to ignore them. There are others who have been able to capitalise on a success such as you had on Friday. With the television and other media, you could make a killing. And there's the offer of another exhibition in Sydney to consider.'

Martin shifted uncomfortably in his seat, part of him wishing he'd never agreed to the exhibition in the first place. It was the same old story – the one Sofia had told him, and Ed had pursued with him, was still pursuing. But would it really be so bad if it enabled him to spend time here in Bellbird Bay, to make a life with Ailsa? 'Let me think about it,' he said to buy time, time to see Ailsa again, to find out how she felt about him, to make sure he wasn't tilting at windmills to imagine she'd want a future with him.

*

After catching an early lunch in *The Greedy Gecko*, next door to the gallery, Martin decided to drop in on Ailsa and Nate. It made sense for him to enquire how the boy was doing, and he wanted to find out what was happening with Ailsa and her husband. It made him feel sick to think of them bonding again over their son's accident.

'Anyone home?' Martin called, sliding open the door from the deck. He'd parked at the surf club and walked up the boardwalk, reasoning the exercise would do him good. It felt odd to be a visitor in the house where he'd been living for the past few weeks, but it was Bev's house, and he had every right to be there.

'Oh!' Ailsa was in the kitchen fixing a salad. 'I didn't expect to see you today.' She appeared flustered.

'I popped round to see how Nate is doing.'

'Hey, Martin. Good to see you.' Nate appeared in the doorway. There were bags under his eyes. He looked as if he hadn't slept. But otherwise, he appeared well. 'What's up?'

'Good to see you too, Nate. You're looking better.'

'Apart from this.' Nate nodded to where his left arm was fastened to his body by a sling. 'But I should be getting a cast on it next week, though I might still need to have a brace on the shoulder. I checked on my bike this morning and it should be good to go by the time I get use in my shoulder and arm again.'

Martin saw Ailsa's lips tighten but she didn't speak.

'I know what you're thinking, Mum,' Nate said, 'but it's my only form of transport and I love riding it.'

'Hmm.' Ailsa turned to Martin. 'It's good of you to drop round. Thanks for your help with Nate. I... I didn't know when we'd see you again.' She blushed.

Martin took the reddening of her cheeks as a good sign and since Nate had strolled out to the deck, decided to press his advantage. 'I wondered if you were still open to an evening walk along the beach, or will you be too tied up with your family? I realise with Nate needing care, and your husband and other son here, you may find your time...' His voice trailed off as he wasn't sure exactly what he wanted to say. He didn't want to scare Ailsa off, but hoped, by issuing the invitation, to let her know his feelings.

'I'd like to, but I don't know. I can't make plans till I know what Bob and Pat intend. They're only here for a week.' She gave a quick glance out to where Nate was leaning against the railing, gazing out to sea. In a low voice she said, 'Bob told the boys yesterday… about us…about why our marriage is ending. Nate didn't take it well. But he seems a little better today. Bob and Pat should be arriving for lunch shortly. I hope…' She bit her lip.

Martin glanced around quickly. He didn't want to be here when they arrived. This had been a bad idea, but he'd been desperate to see Ailsa, to find out what was happening. 'I'll be on the beach at nine,' he said. 'It'd be great if you can make it. No worries if you can't. I'll wait at the foot of the steps.'

Ailsa looked so vulnerable, he wanted to take her in his arms and give her a big hug. But he was conscious of her husband's imminent arrival and, even if the marriage was all but over, he was still her husband, while Martin was… what?

There was the sound of a car stopping outside, followed by footsteps and a loud knock on the front door.

'I'd better be off.' Martin touched Ailsa gently on the shoulder to be rewarded by a warm look and a smile. Then he headed out onto the deck where he said goodbye to Nate, and ran down the steps, cursing himself for being all sorts of a fool to have become involved with a woman who was still tied up in a marriage, even if it was on the skids. He hadn't learned anything in his fifty-two years. He still picked the wrong women.

Forty-seven

Ailsa was sitting on the deck drinking a cup of lemon and ginger tea and thinking dreamily about her meeting with Martin the previous evening, when Nate appeared. Bev had already left for work.

Nate's eyes were bleary from lack of sleep, and his hair was tousled, making her want to push her fingers through the curls like she did when he was much younger.

'How are you this morning? Sleep well?' she asked.

'Not really.' Nate pushed his hair out of his eyes and slumped into a chair.

'Coffee?'

'Please.'

Ailsa put her cup down and went inside where she brewed coffee and popped a couple of slices of bread into the toaster. While waiting for the coffee and toast to be ready, her thoughts went to Martin again. How she wanted to believe him, to give in to her feelings for him, but there was always something holding her back. When she was with him, in his arms, his lips on hers, his arms round her she wanted to stay there forever. But once back home, the misgivings always appeared again, and she doubted her judgment.

'Here you go,' she said, handing Nate the mug of coffee and plate of toast and vegemite – his favourite food when he was feeling out-of-sorts.

'Thanks, Mum.' Nate took a gulp of coffee.

Ailsa waited till he was almost finished then spoke again. 'About Monday... your dad...'

Nate looked down at his bare feet on the wooden deck. 'Yeah.'

'He'd like it if you could try to be more understanding.'

'Yeah.'

'Nate!'

'What do you want me to say, Mum? I've just discovered my dad's gay, my parents are getting a divorce, and you want me to be happy about it?'

'Your dad hasn't changed. He's still the same loving dad he's always been, the same person he was last week and the week before and…'

'I know that!' Nate's voice rose an octave.

'I know it's been a shock. It was to me, too.' Ailsa remembered her own feelings of shock, anger, and grief, realising they had now mellowed into an acceptance of the *status quo*. 'But it's who your dad is. It's really pretty brave of him to open up to us like he has.'

'Brave?' Nate scowled.

But Ailsa could see Nate was beginning to give the matter more thought.

After a few minutes, he asked, 'Dad… will he… does he…'

'He's not with anyone else, but who knows what might happen in the future.' It was something she'd considered herself and knew she'd manage to cope with the situation if and when it arose.

Nate fell silent again.

'Just think about it, Nate. Try to think how your dad must feel.' Ailsa rose and patted Nate on the shoulder before going inside to shower and dress. She'd promised Bev to drop into the garden centre and wanted to check with the gallery first to see how the sales of Martin's work had gone.

To Ailsa's disappointment, the gallery was closed. As she moved away from the building, she found herself face-to-face with the woman she hadn't seen since Australia Day.

'Hello, dear,' Ruby Sullivan said with a smile. 'The gallery is always closed at the beginning of the week. Did you want to make a purchase, or perhaps check out the current exhibition?'

'No, I…' What was it about this woman that got under Ailsa's skin? It was as if she could read her mind.

'I believe it's Martin Cooper's photographs which are on display. But, of course, you'd know all about that, wouldn't you?'

About to give a rude retort, Ailsa realised Ruby's eyes held a kind expression. 'Yes,' she said weakly.

'He's done well for himself, for a boy who grew up in Bellbird Bay and spent his teenage years surfing. But life hasn't always been kind to him.' She nodded to herself. 'His star is about to rise again. You'll see. And...' she peered into Ailsa's eyes, '...you need to take care. The road ahead might not seem clear to you at the moment, but there's happiness ahead for you if you choose the right path. Don't be fooled by appearances. Things aren't always what they seem.'

What was the woman talking about? Ailsa smiled warily and pushed past, sensing the old woman's eyes on her as she hurried to where she'd parked her car.

But Ruby's words stuck in Ailsa's mind and were still there when she reached the garden centre.

'What's up? Something's bothering you,' Bev said, when they were enjoying a cup of tea and sharing one of Ruby's mouth-watering chocolate brownies.

'That woman,' Ailsa fumed. 'Her cakes might be delicious, but... she pokes her nose in where it's not wanted, and she speaks in riddles.'

'What's Ruby been up to now?' Bev chuckled. 'Did you meet her again?'

'I went to the gallery on my way here. It was closed, and Ruby saw me and stopped to talk. She...' Ailsa took a deep breath. 'It's nothing really, but she implied Martin... Heck, I'm not really sure what she implied. I don't know why I'm so upset.' Ailsa exhaled.

'Ruby's a strange woman. She can have that effect on people. She sees things. Some people call her a witch, but I think it's just that she watches people and is very perceptive. She's lived here a long time, seen a lot and...'

'And that gives her the right to poke her nose into people's business?'

'I'm sure she doesn't see it like that. She probably thinks she's helping, offering advice. What did she say this time?'

'She...' But when Ailsa tried to recall the actual words Ruby had spoken, she couldn't. 'She talked about Martin, something about roads and paths. Made me think about that quote about the road less-travelled.' Ailsa had no idea what brought that to mind. She was sure it wasn't what Ruby had said. But what did she say, and why had it annoyed her so much? 'Oh, ignore me. I'm probably being overly sensitive.'

'It must be difficult, having Bob here.'

'It is. He told the boys on Monday.' Ailsa picked up her cup and put it down again, placing and replacing the teaspoon.

'How did they take it?'

'Pat seemed to accept it okay, but Nate is having trouble. I talked with him again this morning.' She sighed. 'He's finding it hard to acknowledge that although his dad may have been living a lie all those years, he's still the same person he always was, and he loves him.'

'Give him time. It must have been a shock.'

'Yes, you're right. It's difficult for Bob, too.'

'Mmm. And what about you... and Martin?'

'Don't go there, Bev. I have no idea.' Ailsa clasped her cup in both hands. 'Your brother is a lovely man. I like him a lot, but...'

'But?'

'I was so wrong about Bob. I can't trust my judgment about men, or even my own feelings. I don't know if I can ever trust myself with a man again.'

'I know I may be biased because he's my brother, but I do think Martin's turned over a new leaf. And he likes you – a lot. I've never seen him so... enamoured is the word my mother would have used.'

'You haven't seen him for years.'

'True, but...'

Ailsa could see Bev was floundering. 'Look, I know you'd like to see us together. At times, it's what I think I'd like, too. Then...' Ailsa shook her head. 'I don't know, Bev. But I can't make any decisions while Bob and Pat are here, or till Nate's better. Maybe by then...'

'I guess I'll have to be satisfied with that.'

'Thanks.' Ailsa smiled, but she knew she had a decision to make. She just wished it was easier to know what she wanted – and if she did decide to throw in her lot with Martin, if it was what he really wanted, too.

*

Ailsa's head was still whirling when she arrived back at Bev's to discover Bob and Pat were already there.

'We brought some lunch, Mum,' Pat said, pointing to the collection of packages on the kitchen table which Bob was unwrapping. 'There's bread, meat, cheese and pickles. A veritable feast.'

Nate was nowhere to be seen.

'Where's Nate?' she asked.

'Don't know. We came in via the deck. The door was open. He's not with you?'

'Obviously not.' Ailsa went through to Nate's room to find the door open, the room empty and his belongings strewn across the bed. This was nothing new. Nate had never been the tidiest of people and with one arm immobilised, it wouldn't be easy for him to dress. Ailsa frowned. She should have stayed home to help him. Now, she'd worry till he appeared.

'Speak of the devil,' Pat was saying, when she returned to the kitchen to see Nate walk in, his unbuttoned shirt slung over his left shoulder and arm.

'Where have you been?' Ailsa had trouble keeping the worry out of her voice.

'Keep your hair on, Mum. I didn't say anything about staying in. I met up with Owen and we took a turn along the beach. I needed to talk to someone, clear my head.'

'And?'

'All right, son?'

Ailsa and Bob spoke at the same time.

'I will be.' He kicked at the baseboard of the kitchen bench. 'Owen reminded me I should be grateful I still have two parents.' He raised his eyes to where Ailsa and Bob were standing together. 'I'm sorry, Dad, Mum. I was only thinking of myself. I should have been more... empathetic.'

'Wow. Swallowed a dictionary?' Pat grinned.

Ailsa's tension eased. Trust young Owen to set Nate straight. Why hadn't she thought of that? It had taken someone of his own generation to help Nate come to terms with what had been for him a lifechanging discovery.

Lunch was a light-hearted affair, though Ailsa could see Nate still felt a little uncomfortable with his dad. But he was moving in the right direction, and she hoped by the time Bob and Pat left at the end of the week, everything would be back to normal, or as normal as it could be, given the circumstances.

*

It was almost a relief to Ailsa when the end of the week arrived. While it had been lovely to have Pat here, things had been a bit strained with Bob, and Nate hadn't yet fully accepted his dad's revelation, though he was trying to act as naturally as possible with him.

Bob and Pat were due to fly out next day and they had planned a farewell meal together for Saturday night. Bev had suggested that, instead of the surf club, they splash out and book a table at *The Beach House*, a restaurant made of glass and timber built on an outcrop of rock and seeming to stand on top of the sea.

Bob and Pat had arrived at Bev's to pick up Ailsa and Nate and they were about to walk out the door when Ailsa's phone rang.

'Leave it, Mum,' Nate said.

But thinking it might be Martin, and unwilling to miss his call, Ailsa took the phone out of her pocket and glanced at it, frowning when she saw her sister's face on the screen. 'It's your Aunt Liz. You go on. I'll catch up,' she said, a curl of fear in the pit of her stomach. Her dad had been sick. It had only been a chill and last she heard he was recovering. But it was unlike Liz to call at this time on a Saturday evening. She knew Bob and Pat were there.

'Liz? What's wrong? Is it Dad?'

'Glad I caught you, Ailsa. I know you said you were all going out to dinner. Dad's taken a turn for the worse. The doctor says it's pneumonia. It's not good. He's been admitted to hospital. I'm driving there now. You should…'

'If I can get a seat, I'll fly down tomorrow with Bob and Pat.'

'Something the matter?' Bob popped his head around the door.

'It's Dad.' Ailsa's eyes filled with tears. 'He's in hospital. Pneumonia. I need to…'

But Bob had already opened his phone and was dialling the airline.

By the time Ailsa had wiped away her tears, he had booked her on the same flight to Canberra next day as Pat and him.

The news about Ailsa's dad and the boys' beloved grandfather, put a dampener on what was to have been a celebratory meal.

'Are you sure you don't want to come, too?' Pat asked Nate, when they all decided to forego dessert and finish the evening early.

'Wish I could, but I have the follow up for my arm tomorrow. They're putting the cast on.'

'Will you be all right to get to the hospital?' Ailsa asked.

'Sure. Martin or Will can drive me. You'll let me know how Gramps is?'

'Of course. Thanks for arranging my flight so quickly, Bob.' Ailsa put a hand on Bob's arm. It was almost like old times, except…

'You'll let Martin know?' Ailsa asked Bev and Nate next morning when Bob came to pick her up for the airport. She'd foolishly left her phone in her bag, and it had run out of charge. She'd call him from Canberra and let him know what had happened, but perhaps it was for the best. This way, the decision had been taken for her. She was going back to Canberra.

Forty-eight

Martin's phone wakened him at some ungodly hour, forcing him to screw up his eyes to check the time. Four a.m. Who could be calling him at this time in the morning?

'Hello?' he said, his voice thick with sleep. He'd spent the previous day helping Will out. Ailsa hadn't answered her phone, so he and Will had downed more than a few beers together, reminiscing about the good old days. It had been late when he'd finally fallen into bed.

'Martin!' Ed Holstein's voice boomed in his ear, causing him to hold the phone away from it.

'Just a minute, Ed.' Didn't the man know it was still the middle of the night here, even though it must be early afternoon in New York. Martin sat up and switched on the bedside lamp. 'What do you want?'

'Congratulations! I hear you had an extremely successful exhibition in that little town where you've been hibernating, and there are noises of another one in the city of Sydney. And Young has been persuaded to back off.'

Martin smiled to himself. His legal guru had already confirmed Sofia's claim. 'You're very well informed.' How had the news of the exhibition travelled to Ed in New York? Martin could guess. He'd bet Sofia had hightailed it back there to cry on Ed's shoulder.

'Well, when one of my favourite clients starts selling limited editions of his photographs, it behoves me to wonder why he hasn't contacted me.'

So that was it. Ed wanted his cut.

But Ed hadn't finished. 'It seems this might be an opportune time to capitalise on your recent success and talk about those books we discussed.'

Martin drew a hand across the top of his head. He should have seen this coming. 'I don't think so, Ed. You already know my opinion on that.'

'Don't be so hasty, Marty.'

Martin flinched. He hated to be called that.

'I hear the news has reached Jackson, too – about your recent work. Surfing shots, isn't it? A new avenue for you.'

How did...?

'The answer's still *no*. But thanks for the call.' Martin hung up. He turned out the light but couldn't get back to sleep. The sun would be up in a couple of hours. He rose, dressed, and grabbed a bite to eat and a cup of instant coffee. Then he stacked his surfboard into the back of the Moke and headed for the beach.

*

'You were out early,' Will greeted Martin when he returned, having worked off his annoyance with Ed, while wondering how to respond to the news about Jackson, if it was even true. He wouldn't put it past Ed Holstein to be bluffing in the hope of enticing him back to New York.

'Yeah, got an early call from the States, from the guy who wants to be my agent.'

'Interesting?'

'Not really.' Martin helped himself to a mug of the coffee Will had already brewed.

'Oh, Nate McNeil called.'

Martin paused, the mug part-way to his mouth. Had something happened to Ailsa?

'Not bad news,' Will said, seeing Martin's expression. 'He wanted to know if one of us could drive him to the hospital this morning. I have to be at the school, so I volunteered your services. That okay?'

'Sure.' Martin took a seat and a gulp of coffee. Nate would be due to have his cast put on today. But why couldn't Ailsa drive him? No doubt he'd find out.

*

Nate was waiting at the door for Martin when he drove up. There was no sign of Ailsa. On the way to hospital, Nate was full of news about a group of locals who were banding together to do planting on the sand dunes on the edge of town. He enthused about their efforts for most of the trip, preventing Martin from asking about Ailsa.

It was only when they finally arrived at the hospital that Martin was able to get a word in. 'Your mum couldn't drive you today?' he asked.

'She's not here. She flew back to Canberra with Dad and Pat yesterday.'

Martin felt suddenly sick. He was about to ask more questions when a nurse arrived to escort Nate into another room, so he was left without any further explanation. Knowing the procedure would take around twenty minutes, he decided to pick up a coffee while he was waiting and try to digest the news he'd just heard about Ailsa.

Taking his coffee out into the hospital courtyard, Martin paced up and down, unable to contain his anger and disappointment. How could Ailsa have gone off with Bob without letting him know? Did their relationship mean so little to her? He'd thought they had some sort of understanding. Seemed he was wrong.

He gulped down the coffee, burning his tongue in the process, crushed the cardboard cup and tossed it into a nearby bin.

Alerted by the ping of a notification, Martin slid his phone out of his pocket. He read the message with amazement.

Young has backed off. Heard about your new work. We're planning to feature surfing destinations in the next edition of Destination. *Interested to see what you have to offer. Call me. J Green*

Without thinking, Martin keyed in Jackson Green's number and, after a brief conversation, made another call, this time to Qantas. He could be on a plane that night. He'd go to New York, talk with Green, show him his latest work. With Ailsa gone there was nothing to keep him here.

Forty-nine

It was only a few weeks since Ailsa had returned to Canberra, but so much had happened. The day after she got back, her dad had taken a turn for the worse and had quietly passed away, Ailsa, Liz and their mother by his side. Ailsa still couldn't believe he was gone. She missed him so much. Doug had always been there to intervene between her and her mother, now there was no one to soften Sheila Browne's acerbic comments. And now Martin was gone, too. A text from Nate when she arrived in Canberra telling her Martin was in New York, but little more, had sent her heart plummeting. She hadn't enquired further and hadn't called him, waiting for him to contact her. He hadn't.

Surprisingly, Ailsa's mother had coped with her husband's death without the expected outpouring of grief, turning to her church and strong faith to support her rather than her daughters. Now, only a few weeks later, she had thrown herself into a whirlwind of activity – arranging flowers for the church, joining a choir and various women's groups. It was her way of dealing with the void in her life.

Nate had flown down for the funeral and back again immediately afterwards. He hadn't said anything about Martin, and she hadn't asked. She'd been too proud to ask Bev about Martin, too, when her friend rang with her condolences. When there was still no word from Martin himself, Ailsa took the lack of contact as a sign she had made the right decision to move on with her life, her pride continuing to prevent her from contacting him.

But it wasn't easy. Memories kept popping up at the most unexpected moments. She sometimes felt as if she was caught up in a whirlpool and didn't know which side was up. It was all she could do to keep going. She knew she must, and it would get easier. But the loss of her father combined with Martin's defection was a double blow from which she'd take time to recover.

When she'd arrived in Canberra, Ailsa had gone straight to the hospital, intending to call Martin as soon as her phone was charged. But Doug had been sicker than she'd anticipated, and she had been fully occupied sitting at his bedside and trying to comfort her mother and sister while coping with her own anguish. There had been no time to call Martin and, while she'd wondered why he hadn't contacted her, she'd thrust the thought aside, planning to deal with it later.

Nate's news of Martin's departure to New York had just been one more thing to add to her grief, something to try to put behind her.

Ailsa peered at herself in the mirror realising how quickly she'd lost the healthy colour acquired in her time on the coast. The maximum temperature here in Canberra in April was not unlike the minimum in Bellbird Bay. But while Ailsa missed the sun and warmth of the small town on the Sunshine Coast, the present weather suited her mood. She sighed, dragged a comb through her unruly hair and renewed her lipstick.

Bob was coming around to discuss their next step, a process delayed by her father's death and subsequent funeral. But now it was over, they couldn't put it off any longer.

The doorbell rang before Ailsa was mentally or emotionally ready to face her husband. They'd flown back together, and Bob had been a tower of strength when Ailsa's dad died, making all the necessary arrangements Ailsa and her mum were too upset to take care of. But they hadn't met since the funeral, only communicating by phone and email.

'Hi, honey.' Bob drew Ailsa into a warm hug and gave her a peck on the cheek. 'How are you holding up?'

'I'm fine,' she said, feeling herself stiffen in his embrace. 'I thought we could sit in the snug. It's the warmest room in the house. I've been practically living there.' It was her favourite room, the one in which they'd spent so many evenings together, reading, watching television, or chatting about their day over a glass of wine. Now it, too, was filled with memories of happier times.

'Okay by me.'

'Would you like tea, coffee, or something stronger?' Ailsa was beginning to feel edgy. This was a big deal. She and Bob were about to discuss how to end their marriage, a marriage lasting almost twenty-five years – they would have been due to celebrate their silver wedding anniversary later that year. Now they were to decide how to unpick the years of living together as if they were only a collection of items which were no longer required.

'I think a glass of scotch might help things along. You sit down. I'll get them.'

Ailsa perched on the edge of the two-seater sofa while Bob fetched the drinks, just as he had always done. Ailsa sniffed back a tear. Bob belonged here, in this house, with her, not in some impersonal apartment in the neighbouring suburb. But this wasn't his home any longer, and soon it wouldn't be hers either.

'You look as if you need this, and I know I certainly do.' Bob handed Ailsa a glass and took a seat opposite.

She took a gulp of the fiery liquid, flinching as it made its way down her throat. Bob was right. It did make her feel better.

'I'm sorry it's come to this,' Bob said, swirling the whisky in his glass before taking a sip.

'I'm sorry, too.' For a moment, Ailsa thought he was going to tell her it had all been a mistake, he didn't want a divorce and was going to move back in. She wasn't sure how she'd feel about that.

'We have some decisions to make,' Bob said instead. 'I consulted a lawyer – a new one. I thought you'd prefer to deal with Geoff Richards.'

Ailsa nodded. Geoff Richards had been her family's lawyer for as long as she could remember. She'd last seen him at the reading of her dad's will only a few days earlier. 'Okay, let's do this.'

By the time Bob left, they'd made decisions about the divorce, and had plans to put the house on the market. To Ailsa's surprise, she was feeling calmer than she had since returning to Canberra. She was almost looking forward to the future.

Fifty

It was a shock being back in the hustle and bustle of New York after the peace of Bellbird Bay. Martin pushed through the throng of travellers, walked out of the station at Union Square and stared up at the skyscrapers, feeling claustrophobic at the way they hid the sky. The feeling was nothing new. He experienced it every time he returned from location. But this time, it hit him more forcibly than usual. This time he felt like a foreigner. He didn't belong here.

It had been late when he arrived at JFK, New York's international airport, the previous night and all he wanted was to find somewhere to lay his head. He took the shuttle to the Radisson and was asleep almost before his head hit the pillow. This morning he'd called Jackson Green to let him know he'd arrived, then Tony Bianchi, a photojournalist he knew from way back. Tony was always good for a spare room when Martin was in town. Today was no exception.

'Drop by when you've done your business with your editor,' he said. 'You can fill me in on what you've been up to. Heard a few rumours, but I don't put much faith in what I hear. We can have a good Italian meal together and sink a few brews.'

It was good to hear Tony's voice again, to remember some of the scrapes they'd got into together. Then Tony had decided to go legit. He now worked for one of the networks and was on a regular salary. Martin was looking forward to catching up with him.

Now, Martin swung his bag over his shoulder and gripped his camera bag tightly, before making his way to the familiar skyscraper which housed the offices of *Destination*. He'd been here many times before, Jackson Green being one of the old school editors who preferred to talk face-to-face.

'Can I help you, sir?' The young girl on the reception desk wasn't someone Martin recognised, and she clearly didn't have a clue who he was. He guessed he should have smartened up for this interview – the jeans, chambray shirt and leather jacket in which he'd travelled from Queensland to New York were hardly suitable attire for the interview he was about to have, but Jackson had seen him in worse. He recalled one occasion when he'd come here straight from an earthquake zone where he'd been lucky to escape with his life, his cameras and the clothes he was wearing.

'I have an appointment with Mr Green. Martin Cooper.'

'You're Martin Cooper? *The* Martin Cooper?' Her eyes widened with surprise and something that looked like admiration. 'He said to show you right in when you arrived.' She pointed to the door which Martin knew led directly into Jackson Green's office.

'Thanks.' He pushed open the door to see Jackson seated in his usual position at a large oak desk, the skyline of New York visible through the full-length glass window behind him. He had a cigarette in one hand, there was an overflowing ashtray on the desk, and the room reeked of cigarette smoke.

'Martin, my boy. Welcome back. It's been too long.' He stood up and walked around the desk to clap Martin on the shoulder.

Martin smiled inwardly. So, there was to be no mention of the issue which almost cost him his career. They were to pretend it had never happened.

The young girl, whose name turned out to be Yvonne, was summoned to bring coffee and Jackson proceeded to tell Martin how a good friend – unnamed – had told him about the exhibition Martin had in *a tiny town in the back of beyond at the other end of the world*. 'I was intrigued,' Jackson said, 'Intrigued enough to do some research, and there you were on the website of this gallery in a town by the name of Bellbird Bay. It sounds like a bad movie from the sixties or seventies. But…' he said, waving his cigarette in the air, '…it's good stuff. Oh, I know I've seen some of them before. But the surf shots. You've really caught it – the movement, the light, the feeling of freedom. I'm willing to publish them in our new feature. Same terms as usual. And I'd like more. We can have a regular section. You can travel to surfing beaches all over the world and...' Jackson continued in this vein for several minutes, waxing lyrical about what Martin could offer, and what *Destination* would do.

By the time Martin left, Jackson had purchased several of his shots from Bellbird Bay for the magazine and he had the promise of commissions for others to be shot in various locations around the world. He was back in business.

*

'If you're back on the trail again, why aren't you more cheerful?' Tony asked, when they'd polished off a traditional Italian feast and a couple of bottles of wine in a little restaurant close to where he lived in Greenwich Village.

'I don't know. I should be over the moon, but...'

'It must be a woman. It's always a woman,' Tony said, tapping the side of his nose with one finger. 'From one who knows. What happened to the one you were with last time – the South American beauty?'

'Long gone.'

'So, not her.' Tony thought for a few moments. 'There must be someone in Australia, then. A woman who's been carrying a torch for you since you were both teenagers and who...' He mimed playing a violin.

Martin reddened. It was too close to the truth. But Ailsa was lost to him. It appeared her husband had had a change of heart, or some such, and she'd decided to stay with him. He remembered the chill running down his spine, the sudden heaviness in his stomach when Nate told him she'd flown to Canberra. There had been no point in trying to contact her. He'd been there before. He should have learnt from his experience with Sofia, but he'd thought Ailsa was different. He'd never be able to understand women.

But it wasn't only the memory of Ailsa making him hesitate. He'd enjoyed being back in Australia, back in Bellbird Bay, having somewhere to call home instead of living out of a suitcase or, more often, a backpack.

'I don't know, Tony. Maybe I'm getting too old to be traipsing around the world with a camera. I've agreed to do an event in Santa Cruz featuring old longboards, but after that...' Martin shook his head.

'Never thought I'd hear Martin Cooper say he was getting old,' Tony chuckled. 'Seems you're human after all.'

'Ha ha.' But it was true. Martin's time back home in Bellbird Bay had got him thinking about his future, about growing older. He'd seen his old mate, Will, content with his life, his sister happy with her garden centre, and... Who was he kidding? He'd met Ailsa again and realised there was more to life than the nomadic one he'd been leading. He was ready to settle down.

*

The vintage board riding event in California was a blast. Martin enjoyed being in the sun and surf again. But, as he set about shooting the guys and girls on their longboards, he couldn't help remembering how it had been in his old stamping ground, when he'd been riding the waves on the far side of the headland in Bellbird Bay.

Martin was feeling pretty disheartened when he returned to New York. Once again, he was staying at Tony's bachelor pad, but he knew it could only be a temporary arrangement, sure he was cramping Tony's style by camping out on the sofa in his minuscule apartment.

Bev's call came when he was relaxing after a successful meeting with Jackson Green, who was delighted with the shots he brought back from California, and eager for Martin to produce more similar work. But at this stage, he'd given the editor no firm commitment, undecided as to what he wanted to do next. He'd taken a similar line with Ed Holstein, who'd tried to persuade him coffee table books of his collections would sell like hot cakes. Tony had gone out to dinner with one of his lady friends, and Martin was lying on the sofa drinking beer and feeling sorry for himself.

'Hey, bro. What are you up to? You left pretty abruptly and haven't been in touch.'

'Sorry, Bev. Been busy. Just back from California.'

'So, back to your old ways. I'd hoped... You heard about Ailsa?'

Martin's heart lurched at the sound of Ailsa's name. He could see her face, feel her lips on his, smell the unique scent she carried with her. 'Nate said she's gone back to Canberra, back to her husband, I always knew it was on the cards.'

'She's gone back to Canberra, but not to her husband. Didn't Nate tell you her dad was sick? That's why she left so suddenly. I thought you knew.'

'No.' Martin sat upright. Ailsa hadn't gone back to her husband? Then why hadn't she contacted him?

'Didn't you call her?'

'No,' Martin said again, cursing his stupidity. He'd made assumptions, acted on impulse and now... what must Ailsa think of him?

'Is she still there? How is her dad?'

'He passed away and, yes, Ailsa is still in Canberra. I guess she had a lot to take care of. There's her widowed mother, her divorce and...'

'Did you say divorce?'

'She and Bob are getting a divorce. I thought you knew that, too.'

'Has she asked about me?'

'No, but I wouldn't have expected her to. The pair of you always tried to hide your relationship from me, but I could see the chemistry between you.'

'Hell, Bev, I've been a fool.' He dragged a hand through his hair. 'What can I do?'

'You're asking *me* for advice on your love life?'

'I guess I am.' Martin sighed. This was a first.

'Well...' Bev paused, '...seems like there may have been a few misunderstandings – at least one. You need to contact her, but...' she paused again, '...I'd strongly suggest you do it in person. You need to see her face when you explain – and she needs to see yours. How committed are you in New York? Can you get away easily?'

No sooner had Martin ended the call, than he made another, this time to the airline. Two hours later he was packed and heading to the airport to catch a flight to Canberra.

Fifty-one

Ailsa had spent the day packing boxes and tagging the furniture to indicate which pieces were to be auctioned with the house, which pieces Bob wanted, and which were to go into storage until she found somewhere new to live.

Divorce proceedings had been set in motion and should be finalised in three months. Thank goodness for no fault divorce which made the process so straightforward as they'd been able to demonstrate she and Bob had been living separate lives for some time, albeit under the same roof. They'd always maintained separate bank accounts and Bob had been meticulous about keeping records of separate expenses. It seemed very cold and clinical but now she was glad of it.

Ailsa still hadn't found anywhere to live. She hadn't expected it to be so difficult, but it seemed there was a shortage of houses which suited both her requirements and her budget and were located in the areas of the city where she wanted to live.

Bev had suggested she move up to Bellbird Bay, but though tempted, Ailsa couldn't bear the thought of the memories such a move would provoke – and what if Martin returned? Her sister, Liz, had also offered her refuge, reiterating how Granite Springs had provided her with healing when she needed it. But having made such a mess of her own love life, Ailsa couldn't bear the thought of facing her sister's newfound happiness every day. No, it was better to stay here in Canberra, in the place with which she was familiar, even if it meant accepting her mother's offer.

Sheila Browne had been scathing when she heard Ailsa and Bob were divorcing, even though Ailsa had managed to keep the reason why from her. Both Ailsa and Bob came in for criticism as Sheila seethed about what 'those poor boys' would do with the loss of their home, regardless of the fact Ailsa reminded her both Pat and Nate were grown men with lives of their own and hadn't lived at home for some time. Her annoyance with Ailsa seemed to have superseded her sorrow at the loss of her husband of over fifty years.

Ailsa wiped a bead of perspiration from her forehead and pushed back a lock of hair, promising herself a visit to the hairdresser when this was done. She'd need something to cheer her up, to stop the memories of Martin which flooded in when she least expected them. Checking the time, she realised it was mid-afternoon and she still hadn't had any lunch.

She was making a cheese sandwich when the doorbell rang. Hoping it was the realtor who'd promised to drop by with information about the forthcoming auction, Ailsa put down her knife and went to answer the door, grimacing at the reflection of her grime-streaked face and wild hair in the hall mirror as she passed. She really needed that hair appointment, and maybe a facial, too.

When she opened the door, Ailsa stood still, frozen with shock at the sight of the man who stood there, the man the memory of whom she'd been trying unsuccessfully to dismiss from her thoughts and dreams.

'Martin!' she gasped, her hand automatically going to her hair in a fruitless attempt to tidy it.

'Ailsa... I... Can I come in?'

She swallowed. 'Of course.' She opened the door wider to allow him to enter, leading him through to the kitchen.

'Coffee?' she asked, madly trying to calm her heart which was beating madly. Martin looked even better than she remembered. But, she reminded herself, he'd been quick to return to the States after she left for Canberra and he hadn't tried to contact her. What was he doing here?

'Please. I was sorry to hear about your dad.'

'Thanks.' Ailsa busied herself with the coffee machine, her back to Martin, reluctant to meet his eyes.

'I didn't know. No one told me he was sick, that it was why you came back to Canberra. I thought...'

Ailsa turned in surprise. 'But Bev, Nate...'

'Nate told me you'd flown back with Bob and Pat. I thought you'd gone back to your husband.' He dragged a hand through his hair and her heart ached for him.

'Oh!' Ailsa turned back to her task, unsure what to think, her mind in a whirl.

'I came as soon as I heard. Bev...'

Ailsa heard the pleading note in his voice and all the memories came back in a rush.

'Bev told me about your dad. I'm sorry,' he said again. 'When Nate told me you'd flown back here with Bob, I... Shit, Ailsa, what was I supposed to think? One minute you were there, then you were gone.'

'It wasn't my fault.' Here was Martin, standing in her kitchen, and all they could do was argue?

The coffee machine started to gurgle and hiss, making conversation impossible. Ailsa filled two mugs and handed one to Martin. 'Perhaps we should both calm down. I've been living in the snug while I'm packing up. Come through.'

She led Martin through to the room in which she and Bob had finalised the decisions about their future, this time choosing to sit on the old armchair and curling her legs under her, clasping the mug in both hands.

'Why don't you tell me your side of it?' she asked.

Martin sat down on the sofa and took a gulp of his coffee. He gazed into space and began to speak. 'That day... Will asked me to take Nate to the hospital. I didn't know why you couldn't do it, but I agreed. When Nate told me you'd flown to Canberra with Bob, I thought... Hell, what else could I think? Earlier that morning, I'd received a call from my agent in New York, then I got a message from Jackson Green, the editor of *Destination*, the magazine I was working with before everything went pear-shaped. The bastard who claimed my photos had backed down. You had gone. There was nothing to keep me here. I took the first plane to New York.'

Ailsa flinched. If only she'd called Martin herself instead of relying on Nate. But hadn't it been Bev she asked to tell Martin? Clearly somewhere they got their wires crossed.

'Green had heard about the exhibition. He was interested in my surfing photos. I've been in California covering a vintage board carnival.'

So, Martin had returned to his old life? Then why was he here? Ailsa's expression must have shown her confusion.

'It didn't feel right,' Martin continued. 'It was as if being back in Bellbird Bay, meeting you again, had taken me in a new direction. I don't want my old life any longer. I want Bellbird Bay. I want you.' Martin put down his mug and clasped his hands letting them drop between his knees. 'I'm not putting this very well, am I?' he asked ruefully. 'I thought you were lost to me, Ailsa, and the idea of Bellbird Bay without you… I'd have been overwhelmed by memories of us there together. It wasn't till I spoke with Bev, and I learned why you came back, about your dad, that I realised how wrong I'd been. Can you ever forgive me?'

The hard shell which Ailsa had built around her heart began to crack. She'd never seen Martin like this. She longed to reach out to hug him, but something still held her back.

'Can you forgive me, Ailsa?' he asked again. 'I love you. I want to spend the rest of my life with you. In Bellbird Bay or here in Canberra. I don't care, as long as we can be together. I won't be going away again. I can take photographs here in Australia. Green will publish them. I can even go along with Baldwin and Holstein and their commercial nonsense. All I want is to be with you, to know you care for me even a little. I can…'

Ailsa didn't allow him to finish. 'I do care,' she said in a quiet voice. 'I've tried so hard to forget you, to tell myself I didn't care, that I could make a future for myself here in Canberra. But I knew, deep down I was fooling myself. I knew I couldn't forget you. Not this time.'

'You mean…?' Martin's eyes brightened.

'I mean, I love you, too, Martin Cooper. I've never been able to forget you since that night in Canberra when we were only nineteen. I never thought we'd get a second chance. I still can't believe you're sitting here, telling me…'

Before Ailsa had finished speaking, Martin was on his feet. He picked her up and pulled her into an embrace.

As Ailsa felt Martins arms around her, his lips on hers again, the astonishing feeling of freedom washed through her, of tension releasing as they removed each other's clothes, as they kissed and they fell to the sofa, as they coupled together in the warmest embrace, as they made love so perfectly, and the only thought intruding into Ailsa's consciousness was how glad she was she'd decided to spend summer in Bellbird Bay.

THE END

If you've enjoyed Ailsa's story, I'd really appreciate it if you could leave a review. A few words will suffice, no need for a lengthy review. It will mean a lot to me and help other readers find my books.

If you enjoyed this book, you'll also enjoy the next book in the series, *Coming Home to Bellbird Bay*. It features a new character who has moved to Bellbird Bay from Granite Springs, and you'll meet many of the characters from *Summer in Bellbird Bay* again.

When widow *Grace Winter* makes the decision to sell the family property in Granite Springs and move to the small coastal town of Bellbird Bay, her children are horrified. Doing her best to ignore their protests, Grace settles into the small-town community and starts creating a new life for herself. However, the surprise arrival of her demanding daughter throws all that she's established into disarray.

Retired solicitor *Ted Crawford* has the ideal life. He surfs, takes care of local turtle hatching and is becoming well known locally as a landscape artist. But his calm existence is upended by the sudden appearance of his son whose professional life is in jeopardy.

Happy in their single lives, neither Grace nor Ted is looking for love, but when their paths keep crossing, it looks as if fate has other ideas. However, as their friendship evolves into something more, family issues threaten to derail any hope of a new relationship. Is a second chance at love going to be torn from their grasp?

A heart-warming story of families, friends, the importance of living for the present, and how a second chance at love can happen when you least expect it.

You can order it here mybook.to/CominghometoBellbird

From the Author

Dear Reader,

If you'd like to stay up to date with my new releases and special offers you can sign up to my reader's group.

You can sign up here

https://mailchi.mp/f5cbde96a5e6/maggiechristensensreadersgroup

I'll never share your email address, and you can unsubscribe at any time. You can also contact me via Facebook, Twitter or by email. I love hearing from my readers and will always reply.

Thanks again.

Acknowledgements

As always, this book could not have been written without the help and advice of a number of people.

Firstly, my husband Jim for listening to my plotlines without complaint, for his patience and insights as I discuss my characters and storyline with him, for his patience and help with difficult passages and advice on my male dialogue, and for being there when I need him.

John Hudspith, editor extraordinaire for his ideas, suggestions, encouragement and attention to detail.

Jane Dixon-Smith for her patience and for working her magic on my beautiful cover and interior.

My thanks also to early readers of this book —Helen, Maggie, Louise and Lorraine, for their helpful comments and advice, plus a special thanks to Pete for making sure I got Bob right. Also, to Annie of *Annie's books at Peregian* and Graeme of *The Bookshop at Caloundra* for their ongoing support.

And to all of my readers. Your support and comments make it all worthwhile.

About the Author

After a career in education, Maggie Christensen began writing contemporary women's fiction portraying mature women facing life-changing situations, and historical fiction set in her native Scotland. Her travels inspire her writing, be it her trips to visit family in Scotland, in Oregon, USA or her home on Queensland's beautiful Sunshine Coast. Maggie writes of mature heroines coming to terms with changes in their lives and the heroes worthy of them. Her writing has been described by one reviewer as *like a nice warm cup of tea. It is warm, nourishing, comforting and embracing.*

From the small town in Scotland where she grew up Scotland, Maggie was lured to Australia by the call 'Come and teach in the sun'. Once there, she worked as a primary school teacher, university lecturer and in educational management. Now living with her husband of over thirty years on Queensland's Sunshine Coast, she loves walking on the deserted beach in the early mornings and having coffee by the river on weekends. Her days are spent surrounded by books, either reading or writing them – her idea of heaven!

Maggie can be found on Facebook, Twitter, Goodreads, Instagram, Bookbub or on her website.
https://www.facebook.com/maggiechristensenauthor
https://twitter.com/MaggieChriste33
https://www.goodreads.com/author/show/8120020.Maggie_Christensen
https://www.instagram.com/maggiechriste33/
https://www.bookbub.com/profile/maggie-christensen
https://maggiechristensenauthor.com/

Printed in Great Britain
by Amazon

78379842R00144